SAFE & SOUND

A novel

SAFE & SOUND

A novel

T.S. KRUPA

Advantage®

Published by Advantage, Charleston, South Carolina.
Member of Advantage Media Group.

ADVANTAGE is a registered trademark and the Advantage colophon is a trademark of Advantage Media Group, Inc.

Printed in the United States of America.

ISBN: 978-1-59932-465-4
LCCN: 2013956889

The characters in this book are fictitious. Any similarity to real persons, living or dead, is coincidental and not intended by the author.

Credit for poem on page 64:
From the book *Chicken Soup for the Teenage Soul on Tough Stuff* by Jack Canfield, Mark Victor Hansen, and Kimberly Kirberger. Copyright 2012 by Chicken Soup for the Soul Publishing, LLC. Published by Backlist, LLC, a unit of Chicken Soup for the Soul Publishing, LLC. Chicken Soup for the Soul is a registered trademark of Chicken Soup for the Soul Publishing, LLC.
Reprinted by permission. All rights reserved.

 Advantage Media Group is proud to be a part of the Tree Neutral® program. Tree Neutral offsets the number of trees consumed in the production and printing of this book by taking proactive steps such as planting trees in direct proportion to the number of trees used to print books. To learn more about Tree Neutral, please visit www.treeneutral.com. To learn more about Advantage's commitment to being a responsible steward of the environment, please visit www.advantagefamily.com/green

Advantage Media Group is a publisher of business, self-improvement, and professional development books and online learning. We help entrepreneurs, business leaders, and professionals share their Stories, Passion, and Knowledge to help others Learn & Grow. Do you have a manuscript or book idea that you would like us to consider for publishing? Please visit advantagefamily.com or call 1.866.775.1696.

To B.A.—You believed in me before I did.

CHAPTER 1

....

I could hear him rustling in the bedroom. A hint of sunlight was streaming through the windows. The air was still damp and cool, telling me it was early, too early for a Sunday. I slowly stirred in bed, stretching my legs, trying to ease from my body the soreness of yesterday's long run.

"No. You sleep," he whispered as he leaned down, moving my long chestnut-colored hair out of the way and kissing my forehead. "I'm just going to run the short course today and I'll be back soon."

"Sounds good. Love you," I mumbled, rolling over in bed.

"Love you too," he said as he closed the door to the bedroom.

....

I could hear my phone ringing in the distance as I tried to bring myself out of a deep sleep. I wondered what time it was. The bedroom was now bright as the sun shone directly in through the windows, but I could feel the chill in the air. I squinted at the clock that sat on the nightstand. It was already past 10 in the morning. I must not have heard Jay come back from his run. Maybe he was letting me sleep in. I sighed and pushed myself up and out of bed. I found an old pair of sweatpants on the floor and pulled them up on my slender frame. Then I pulled a tank top out of the dresser and grabbed my robe from the end of the bed, wrapping it tightly around me. I made my way downstairs and as I entered the kitchen, I heard the loud chime from my iPhone, indicating someone had left a message.

"Jay?" I called out throughout the house. No answer. The smell of freshly brewed coffee hit me as I walked into the kitchen. I drew a deep breath in and instantly made my way over to the coffee pot. I drew my favorite oversized green mug out of the cupboard and poured myself a cup. I then fished through the drawer for a spoon and came up empty. I pulled the dishwasher open and grabbed a spoon and examined it closely, determining that it was clean enough for me. After I added two large spoonfuls of sugar to my morning coffee, it was finally ready for consumption. I took a sip and leaned against the counter, examining the kitchen and looking for Jay's running shoes.

Just then, my phone started to ring again. Sighing, I leaned over and grabbed it off the counter. An unknown number registered across the screen. I instantly hit *Ignore* and made my way to the living room, sinking into our oversized sofa with my coffee in one hand and my phone in the other. Turning the TV on, I found it was already on ESPN. Jay must have turned it on earlier to catch the baseball scores from the night before. Letting ESPN continue, I leaned back on the sofa, taking a big sip from my coffee and felt content in the moment. My phone chimed again as another voicemail recorded. Taking another long sip of my coffee, I wondered who was so persistent this morning. I made a mental list of who could possibly be calling. None of them really made any sense, so I quickly gave up. I shrugged my shoulders at my mystery caller and reached over and picked my phone back up. Only then did I notice that there were four missed calls and two voice messages. A knot started to form in my stomach as I punched the voicemail button to listen to the messages.

"This is Officer Patrick Thomas with the Greensboro Police Department. I'm looking for Jill Greenfield. Please call me at the following number as soon as possible."

Stunned, I felt cemented to my place on the sofa, coffee in one trembling hand and phone in the other. The next message started to play.

"Jill, it's Harry. Pat said that there was an accident this morning involving Jay and they were having trouble getting a hold of you. Listen. I'm going to send someone to your house. Call me back."

Involuntarily, I was on my feet. A low moan escaped from my lips. The coffee mug fell from my hands and shattered on the floor, sending hot coffee and shards of ceramic all over my feet. I turned and dashed into the kitchen, ignoring the sharp pain that I now felt on my legs. I grabbed my running shoes by the back door and jammed my feet into them. I grabbed my bag, which hung on the back of one of the kitchen chairs and checked to see if my car keys were still inside. I raced to the front door, pulled it open, and tried to bolt down the sidewalk to my car, only to find myself running into a policewoman.

"Jill Greenfield?" the female police officer asked.

"Yes," I stammered.

"My name is Officer Sarah Steely. Officer Henry Conner sent me to—"

"What the hell is going on?"

"Yes, ma'am, I understand you are upset. Please, Officer Conner sent me to bring you to the hospital as soon as possible. There has been an accident involving your husband."

Not able to muster any more words, I just nodded.

"Do you have everything you need?"

Again I nodded, not allowing my mind to drift to the endless possibilities of what could have happened to Jay that had resulted in my getting a police escort to the hospital.

"Are you sure? Perhaps you'd like to get dressed?" She gave me a quizzical look as I stood in a bathrobe and tennis shoes in the doorway of my home.

"Um …" I stammered, not knowing what I should do but ultimately decided that the officer's suggestion was reasonable. "Alright, give me five minutes," I said, holding up my hand.

She nodded and I dashed back into the house and up the stairs to the bedroom, leaving her in the doorway. I kicked off my running shoes and threw my bathrobe on the bed. I pulled off my sweatpants and put on a pair of blue jeans and a cream knit sweater. I tied my long hair up in a loose ponytail and slid on my beige boat shoes after cleaning up the blood and coffee that had been drying on my leg. Finally ready, I hurried down the stairs to where the officer was waiting.

"Ma'am, do you want to close up the house?" she shouted after me as I walked past her on my way out the front door. I stopped and turned around to face her. I was sure the look of desperation on my face convinced her that I was ready to leave. She closed the door wordlessly and came down the driveway. By the time she arrived, I had taken a seat on the passenger side of the patrol car. I wasn't sure if I was allowed to sit up front, but I wasn't about to sit in the back.

"Do you know what happened to Jay? Is he alright?" I asked as soon as she was seated in the car with me.

"I'm sorry. I don't know very much. I owed Officer Conner a favor and I was on this side of town, so I told him I would swing by and bring you to the hospital." She threw a sideways look in my direction as if unsure of what to say next. "I know that the accident involved your husband and another driver just after seven thirty this morning on Horse Creek Road." Horse Creek Road was a dangerously windy road that Jay insisted on including on some of our running routes. It had always made me super nervous because of the speed of the cars and the lack of shoulder space.

I corrected her. "My husband wasn't driving. He was off on a morning run." She looked startled and unsettled by this additional information. Her slipup let me know that she truly did not know what was going on, nor was she going to give me any more details. I sighed and settled into the seat, staring out the window, trying not to let my mind wander to all the possibilities that awaited me at the hospital. Involuntarily tears formed and started to slowly stream down my cheeks. I was gripped by fear. My instincts indicated I should prepare myself for the worst.

....

When Officer Steely pulled up to the emergency entrance of the hospital, I was out of the patrol car before it came to a complete stop. I jogged in and located the check-in desk where the receptionist told me to speak with someone at the nurse's station. She pointed me down the hallway to my left. When I arrived at the nurse's station, there was no one around to direct me further. I waited impatiently for a nurse to return, drumming my fingers on the counter and frantically looking around for anyone who could direct me to where Jay was.

"Jill." I heard my name called from farther down the hallway. I turned around and saw Harry Conner walking my way. He was dressed in his police uniform, his black hair slicked back. I noticed that his normally tan complexion was pale under the fluorescent glow of the hospital lights.

Harry and Jay had been childhood friends and had done everything together since the age of five. Harry was the best man at our wedding and often a semipermanent guest in our spare bedroom, especially when Jay was out of town, traveling. When Jay and Harry graduated from Boston College, they vowed to move around the country together, enjoying bachelorhood and the open road. Plans changed when Jay's mom was involved in a plane crash and passed away. She was traveling from Boston to the Cape with friends in a privately owned jet when it went down. Jay suddenly felt a sense of responsibility to follow in his parents' footsteps. So he applied to various law schools and eventually chose to attend Wake Forest University. Harry followed him to North Carolina and decided to join the Greensboro police force.

"Harry!" I turned and ran straight toward him, embracing him in a giant hug. "What's going on? Where is Jay? Is he alright?"

"Whoa! Slow down. I just got here myself. I was waiting to speak with the officer from the scene or the doctor on duty. From what I gather, Jay was hit by a car this morning on his morning run on Horse Creek Road ... Damn him!" Harry said, referring to Jay. "I told him repeatedly that road was dangerous, but he can be so stubborn." Harry ran his hands thru his jet-black hair in frustration.

"This can't be happening," I whispered, letting go of Harry and wrapping my arms around myself. He led me down another hall, and we made our way to a smaller waiting room where several doctors and officers had congregated. As we drew closer, I could see several people shifting their eyes in my direction. An officer pointed at me as I approached.

"Jill Greenfield?" asked a middle-aged man with salt and pepper hair and wearing scrubs as Harry and I approached.

"Yes. That's me," I replied.

"Dr. Shippling." He extended his hand to shake mine. I quickly made introductions between Dr. Shippling and Harry.

"Dr. Shippling, can you please tell me what is going on?" I could hear the panic and desperation in my voice.

"Why don't we sit down?" He motioned toward a set of pale-green chairs by the window.

"No. I would prefer you just tell me whatever is going on," I said, raising my voice. I could feel the frustration radiate through me as my question seemed to be left unanswered.

"Mr. Greenfield was involved in a serious collision this morning. We have determined that he was struck from behind while he was—"

"He was running," I added. The doctor nodded that he understood and continued.

"The driver of the vehicle was under the influence of alcohol and was not able to react in time." He described the scene of the accident, but I felt the room spin around me and my knees start to buckle.

"Maybe we should sit down," Harry suggested as he held me up and led me over to the chairs.

"Where is he now?" I asked Dr. Shippling.

"He is in surgery. Mrs. Greenfield, try and understand that Mr. Greenfield was in a very serious accident. We suspect possible complications occurring from the accident. It will be several more hours before we know the extent of Mr. Greenfield's injuries."

"He's going to make it, right?" I asked.

"At this point ..." He paused, looking me straight in the eyes, "praying wouldn't hurt. I'll have more to report when Mr. Greenfield is out of surgery." He frowned and excused himself. I could feel the tears streaming down my cheeks in desperation. My stomach was in knots and a wave of nausea swept over me.

"This can't be happening," I whispered to myself, folding my knees up to my chest and wrapping my arms around myself. Finally, after several minutes, Harry spoke up.

"We need to call Jay's dad ... and maybe you should call Stella and Lanie."

I must have looked like a deer in headlights at his suggestion.

"I'll call Peter," Harry said and I nodded in agreement.

"Will you stay with me while I call Stella and Lanie?" I asked, my voice trembling.

"Of course," he said, giving my shoulder a squeeze.

....

"Stella," I whimpered into the phone.

"Jill, what's wrong?"

"It's Jay … He's been in an accident," and with that statement I was unable to continue. As had been the case with the phone call I had tried to make to Lanie, Harry reached over and took the phone from me and relayed the rest of the conversation I had had with Dr. Shippling and what the officers had determined from their assessment of the accident. This time I stood up and wandered to the window, looking out into the hustle and bustle of everyone moving around down below. The day was beautiful, not a cloud in the sky. The air was cool and crisp, a perfect October day for North Carolina. People were smiling, hugging, rushing about, completely unaware of the agony and grief that now engulfed my life, creating my own personal hell. The sensation was maddening. I felt a hand on my shoulder and turned around. It was Harry.

"Stella and Lanie are both making arrangements to be here as soon as possible," he said quietly. Stella Conner (no relation to Harry) and Lanie Alexander had been my best friends since before kindergarten. We had all grown up on the same block, brought together by our own respective torments of growing up in broken homes. The three of us became our own little family and had been there for each other ever since.

"And Peter?" I asked. Jay and his dad, Peter, had not been very close since his mother had passed away several years earlier, but I knew that Jay would want his dad there, given the circumstances.

"Peter is going to try and catch a flight in the morning," Harry said.

"He could stay—" I started to say.

"He will stay with me." Harry finished my sentence and gave my shoulder another squeeze as I nodded. He walked over to greet several other officers who had just trickled into the room. After making the rounds and speaking to everyone, he returned to my side at the window.

"Before you leave the hospital today, you will need to give a statement," he said.

"What?" I asked. "I wasn't in the accident. Why do they need to speak with me?"

"It's just procedure. They need to get as much background information about Jay as they can," he replied, unfazed by the increased anxiety he had just caused in me.

The next hour dragged on and so did the hour after that. Finally, the doors opened and Dr. Shippling and another middle-aged doctor emerged, both dressed in mint-green scrubs this time.

"Mrs. Greenfield, this is Dr. Matthews. He performed Mr. Greenfield's surgery," Dr. Shippling said.

"Mrs. Greenfield." Dr. Matthews extended his hand.

"Jill, please."

"Jill, your husband suffered a very severe traumatic accident and you need to know the surgical staff tried everything, but we have determined that Mr. Greenfield is brain dead," Dr. Matthews paused to let the finality of his words sink in. I felt Harry stiffen next to me and in that moment my world crashed down around me.

"That's not possible," I whispered, staring in disbelief at the doctors.

"We would like to discuss with you whether Mr. Greenfield was an organ donor or if that is something you would be willing to consider," Dr. Matthews continued.

"You just informed me that my husband is brain dead and now you want to know about cutting him up and giving away his organs?" My temper flared at the doctors' audacity.

"Doc, why don't we wait on that?" Harry whispered, wrapping his arm around me.

"Can I see him?" I asked, still glaring at the doctors.

"Yes. They are just finishing up after the surgery. I must warn you, Mrs. Greenfield, that Mr. Greenfield will be hooked up to ventilators and other machines that will make him look very much alive. But he has no brain function, so as soon as those machines are removed, his body will not be able to keep its systems going and he will flat-line," Dr. Shippling said flatly.

"Is there any chance?" I asked again, looking at both doctors.

"I'm sorry. This is an irreversible injury," Dr. Shippling said. Both doctors turned and spoke to Harry for several more minutes before leaving. All I could do was continue to stand where I was. I felt rooted to the floor, unable to speak, unable to breath as tears streaked down my face. This wasn't supposed to happen to us. We were still so young, just beginning our lives together. We were supposed to have our whole life ahead of us.

Harry had suggested we go out and grab something to eat and then come back. But I refused to leave until I could see Jay. Not long after, a nurse came into the lobby and informed us that Jay had been brought down to his room and I was now able to see him. Harry motioned for me to go on ahead without him. I walked down the long corridor behind the nurse until we reached room 2357.

"You can go on ahead in," she said to me when we reached the door. I slowly pushed the door open and walked into the small, bleak, dimly lit room that smelled of antiseptic. I could hear the respirator slowly moving up and down and the low hum of what I assumed to be a heart monitor. As I rounded the corner, Jay's bed came into full view and my hand involuntarily rose to my mouth.

"Oh Jay," I whispered as I walked closer. He had bandages wrapped around most of his head and several scratches and stitches that covered his once flawless face. I could tell his right leg was wrapped in some type of bandage and perhaps his ribs were also wrapped. I pulled up the hospital chair next to his bed and reached for his hand, careful not to disturb all the tubes and wires he was connected to. I let out a small gasp as our hands touched. His hand was so warm.

"Jay can you hear me?" I whispered. I don't know what I expected, but part of me thought he would open his eyes and answer me. I remembered once hearing it was good to speak with patients who were in a coma. I wondered if the same principal applied to brain-trauma victims. Probably not, but that wasn't going to stop me from trying to get through to him. He looked so calm and peaceful, just as if he were sleeping. I don't know why a particular thought popped into my mind, but it did and I started talking.

"Jay, remember that time on our honeymoon? You had wanted everything to be so perfect. You planned out every last painstaking detail, down to what food we were gonna eat. It had taken you months to get it all down, but instead we both ended up with the flu. We spent the entire two weeks holed up in our beach rental, eating chicken soup and watching reruns of *Friends*. It wasn't the honeymoon you planned, but it was the most magical trip I had ever been on. You know why? I was with you. I need you to know that." I squeezed his hand. "My life means so much more because you came into it," I whispered.

I rested my head on my arms, which were perched on the edge of the bed. Tears started to fall more heavily down my cheek. My chest started to heave and I could no longer contain the sadness that had been building up. It poured out of me and I sobbed into the bed. I don't know how long I sat there, but I didn't hear anyone come in until I felt a hand touch my shoulder.

"Jill, it's time to go," Lanie's soft voice whispered, "Say good-bye …"

"How do I say good-bye?" I sobbed and looked up at her.

"Say good-bye for today. We will be back in the morning. I promise."

She waited for me to stand. I gave Jay's hand one more squeeze and turned to follow her out. We walked back down the hallway, silently. When we reached the lobby, I could see Stella talking to Harry. I knew that Lanie had had a short drive from Raleigh and would have arrived pretty quickly after my phone call. Stella's appearance surprised me as she had farther to travel from Manhattan. But in that moment it didn't matter. The instant that Stella saw us leave Jay's room, she bounded toward us.

"Jill, I am so sorry," she mumbled through tears of her own. I felt another embrace and felt Lanie hugging us both. There were no more words. There didn't need to be. We just stood there, holding on tightly to each other.

....

As promised, before leaving the hospital, I spoke with one of the officer's working Jay's case. It took almost 30 minutes for me to collect myself before I was able to speak. Lanie and Stella both stood over me, questioning the officer about the appropriateness of these questions so soon after the accident. Harry, who stood off to the side, assured them it was just a routine procedure. It took another 30 minutes to answer the officer's questions before we were free to go.

Harry drove me home in silence as Lanie and Stella followed behind in Lanie's car. When we pulled up to the house, Harry got out of the car to give me one more hug. It was only then that I noticed his eyes were red and swollen. He must have been crying at some point. He said he would get Jay's dad from the airport in the morning and they would head to the hospital when visiting hours began. I asked if someone had informed him of Jay's condition and he let me know that he had called and updated him while I was in with Jay. I nodded and headed back up toward the house. Stella and Lanie stayed behind to talk with Harry about further details.

As I entered the house, it felt different, deflated. It no longer felt like home but an empty structure. What once used to hold all my hopes and dreams now just held the physical reminders of my short life with Jay. In reality, we had only been together about five years. We had celebrated our two-year wedding anniversary several months previously, in June. I wandered in and out of the rooms, staring idly at the pictures we had displayed throughout the house until I ended up in our bedroom. The bed was still unmade from that morning. Jay's clothes were laid out on the chair next to his side of the bed, waiting for him to come home. But he wasn't coming back. Having no more tears left to cry, I kicked off my shoes and crawled into bed, drifting into a dreamless sleep.

In the morning I stretched out, looking at the clock. It was past seven. I jumped up with a start. I was going to be late for work. I quickly stood and realized I was still dressed in the clothes I had worn the day before. Then, all the events of the previous 24 hours came crashing back and I sat down on the bed.

"I thought you might be up," Lanie said from the doorway. She came across the room and sat down next to me, placing her hand on my knee. "How are you doing?"

"How am I supposed to be doing?" I asked. Lanie had always been the most compassionate and sensitive of our group. So it was no surprise to any of us that she became a licensed child psychologist. She was already running a very successful practice of her own in Raleigh before the age of 30.

"Jill, it's not a question I can answer for you," Lanie replied, pushing her short blonde hair from her eyes.

"Don't psychobabble me, Lanie."

"I'm not. I am simply trying to see where you are at."

"Where I'm at? Let's see. My husband of a little over two years was hit by a drunk driver yesterday and the doctor informed me that he was brain dead." I paused to take a breath. "I'm not really sure what brain dead means, but I know he's not coming back, even though it just looks like he's lying there, sleeping." I stood up as the anger began to build. "How the hell am I expected to make all these decisions? Do you know they asked me yesterday whether I wanted to donate his organs? I mean he wasn't even out of surgery and they were already asking me these questions, and of course I have no idea how to answer them. Jay and I hadn't talked about stuff like that. We kept telling ourselves we had time, there was no need to rush. Now what do I do?" I said, facing Lanie and waving my hands in the air.

"Way to go, Lanie. Get her all worked up," Stella commented from the doorway. "I thought you were supposed to be the professional amongst us," she added dryly.

"This is normal. This is healthy," Lanie said, looking at Stella.

"Healthy? I'm standing right here, you know. I just lost my husband, remember? ... I'm not some patient you can just evaluate." I paused and stared at the two of them. "I need a shower," I finally said and stormed off toward the bathroom.

....

I stood in the shower, letting the hot water cascade over me until I had used it all up. I got out of the shower, dressed, and made my way downstairs. Lanie and Stella were both sitting at the kitchen table, hunched over, whispering to each other.

"You shouldn't whisper. It's not polite," I commented as I moved past them and poured myself a cup of coffee that someone had brewed that morning.

"We were just discussing what we should do today," Stella said defensively.

"What do you mean, 'what we should do'? We are going to see Jay."

"And then what?" Lanie asked.

"What do you mean, 'then what?'" I was confused. This wasn't some vacation. We didn't need an itinerary.

"We need to discuss your plans, Jill. What about funeral arrangements? Do you want to have a service? People need to be contacted," Stella added softly.

"He's lying in the hospital, hooked up to all those tubes. He's still breathing you know! And you two are ready to throw him in a pine box and put him in the ground." I was angry again, shouting at both Stella and Lanie.

"He's gone, Jill," Lanie said very firmly. "Those tubes and machines—they can't bring him back. They are just trying to keep his organs going until you decide what's next."

"How can I decide what's next when I don't know myself. I've never done this before and I thought it would be another 50 or 60 years before I would have to." I shouted less forcefully as the tears from the previous day started all over again. "We are … were … young … we didn't talk about this stuff. I don't know if we even completed our wills," I said through my tears.

"Don't know?" Stella asked.

"We started them a couple weeks ago. Jay was updating several policies and doing his investment stuff when he brought it up. I think we filled out some stuff, but I don't know if he ever sent them out." I paused. Talking about mundane things seemed to be more calming.

"Jill, come sit down. Let's figure this out as we always do, together," Lanie said and moved the kitchen chair out so I could sit down.

Just then, my phone rang. Stella grabbed it from the table and handed it to me.

"Shit," I said as I read the caller ID.

"What?" Stella and Lanie asked.

"It's my principal."

They both had alarmed faces as I answered the call.

"Jill? It's Jennifer Bentley."

"Hi Jennifer."

"I was just concerned because you didn't show up for school this morning, which is very unlike you. I have gotten someone to cover your class for the rest of the day, but I wanted to call and see if our communication lines got crossed." In reality this was her passive-aggressive manner of asking if I were playing hooky. I could tell she was agitated. She did not like it when teachers missed school and she had to find subs at the last minute.

"Jennifer, listen. Jay was in a terrible accident yesterday and I forgot to call," I stammered.

"Oh my! Is he okay?" She didn't wait for a reply and started to give me her customary "Let us know if we can do anything to help you" speech when I interrupted.

"Jennifer, Jay is dead." Renewed tears brimmed and threatened to begin flowing again. And just as she had at the hospital, Stella relieved me from phone duty and finished explaining the rest of the situation to my principal.

"She's kind of a really big bitch, but you are on indefinite leave from school," Stella said as she put down the phone. I didn't have any energy to question the decision. At that moment I couldn't even think about standing in front of a class with 20 five- and six-year-olds staring back at me. We sat in silence around the kitchen table for several moments before my phone started to light up with text messages and calls from different teachers and parents throughout the school system. Apparently, news of my tragedy was now spreading and everyone was probably gossiping about how "tragic" the whole thing was and how "young" we both were, all the while being glad they could still go home and hug their loved ones.

I knew that Stella and Lanie were right: I needed to make some decisions. The logical part of myself told me Jay was gone and I needed to start making the proper arrangements. The other part told me to hold on and fight for him, that somehow, by some miracle, he was going to recover. He would be the exception. I stood up from the table and looked at my friends.

"What time are we allowed back at the hospital?" I asked.

"After 11," Stella answered.

"What about Jay's dad?" I asked.

"Harry called earlier and said that he got in alright and that he was going to take him over right at 11 like you discussed yesterday. Harry mentioned that Jay's dad wasn't dealing with the news very well," Lanie said, adding, "Jay's dad—"

"Peter. That's his name," I said.

"Peter said he would support whatever decisions you decided on."

I knew that I should give Peter some time alone with Jay so there was no need to rush over to the hospital.

"Okay. I need a couple hours … alone. I need to look through some things in the office and figure out what Jay's wishes were and medically what my options are," I said.

"Do you want to call Dr. Matthews or Dr. Shippling?" Lanie asked.

"No. I need to do this on my own. In the meantime, I need you to manage my phone," I said, pointing to my iPhone on the kitchen table. "I can't deal with all the calls and the pity. I don't care what you tell them but I don't … I can't handle it right now."

I turned and headed to the small office we had made at the back of the house. It was probably the place Jay spent the most amount of time. Technically, he was employed by a large law firm back in Massachusetts, but since he spent most of his time on the road, traveling, making deals and negotiating mergers, they didn't care where he lived, so we ended up staying in Greensboro. I had grown up in the area and Jay fell in love with the area during his time at Wake Forest, so we decided to stay. Jay once told me he felt guilty after Harry followed him down there. Because of the pact they had made about traveling and being bachelors, he just couldn't get up and move away after Harry had established himself on the police force. Moreover, Jay had no interest in going home after his mother died.

I now sat in his big leather chair behind his oak desk. His papers were still all spread around the desk from whatever he had been working on that Friday. We were going to dinner with friends and Jay had worked until the time we needed to leave. I had been rushing him so that we wouldn't be late. I turned the computer on and as I waited for it to load up, I started shifting through various items, looking for the draft will we had discussed. I remembered we had just completed a rough outline and had to go back and make some major decisions. Not having any kids or large amounts of property or investments, it seemed to be a simple process. Jay was worried about some of his investments and said he wanted to discuss them further with me. But we hadn't had the time with all his business travel and my school year starting back up.

I finally located a copy of the document and noticed it had already been faxed to a lawyer's office. The name scribbled on the sheet read "Paul Wellon." When the computer finally loaded, I pulled up Google search and typed in the keywords that the doctors had used the previous night. I pored through various articles about brain trauma and vegetative states. Feeling deflated and more depressed then when I started, I changed my search to organ donation. The more I read, the more overwhelmed I became by all the wonderful stories from both the survivors and those who had lost loved ones. I glanced down at the clock and saw that it was after 12. I turned off the monitor and searched for a few more important numbers before heading back into the kitchen.

Stella and Lanie still sat at the kitchen table, both in deep conversations on their phones. It gave me a moment to observe my friends. Lanie still wore her sweats from the morning and an oversized Chapel Hill sweatshirt. Her short blonde hair was tucked behind her ears and she absent-mindedly picked at her cuticles. Stella on the other hand was dressed in designer jeans with a dark burgundy silk blouse. She looked as if she were ready to negotiate a deal anywhere on the planet. Her brown locks were styled in a trendy bob and her make-up was flawlessly applied. I smiled slightly to myself as I observed that she and Lanie had the same vice: Stella was also picking away at the paint on her manicured fingers. On the kitchen counter sat several sandwiches and snacks, none of which had been in the house earlier. Someone must have gone out, I thought.

"Hungry?" I whispered, motioning to the food.

"Your neighbors brought those by," Lanie said as she got off the phone. My neighbors? How did they know? I hadn't even heard the doorbell.

"News travels fast," I said with disdain.

"So what did you find out?" Stella asked as she hung up her phone and wandered over to the counter to fix herself a plate.

"I still need a little more information. First, I will need to talk to Dr. Shippling and Dr. Matthews. Second …"—I turned and faced Stella—"can you do me a favor? Actually two?"

"Sure," she replied.

"I need you to call Paul Wellon. He's the lawyer Jay was dealing with about getting our affairs in order. I need to know if we had any paperwork that might have indicated Jay's wishes. Then I need you to call Jay's office and let them know about the accident. They will probably want his files or computer or something crazy." I paused. I was already feeling drained and we hadn't even gone back to the hospital. "You're a lawyer. They are lawyers. It just makes sense." Lanie nodded in agreement.

"No problem," Stella said as I handed her the papers I had found and the numbers I had written down.

"Now, I'm ready to go back to the hospital."

"No. First you eat and then you can go to the hospital," Lanie instructed. I didn't know how to tell her that I had no appetite and food was the last thing on my mind. But in order to expedite our departure, I quickly ate a turkey sandwich and washed it down with a bottle of water.

CHAPTER 4

....

When we arrived at the hospital, Harry and Peter were leaving Jay's room. Both men were visibly exhausted. I hadn't seen Peter in almost a year and he had aged significantly since then. His hair was mostly white and now he leaned on a cane when he moved around.

"He loved you so much, Jill. After his mom died, you came into his life and gave it new meaning," he whispered in my ear as we embraced. I didn't know how to reply so I just nodded, trying to keep my tears in check.

"It's such a tragic end for both of their legacies," he mumbled, referring to Jay and his mother.

"Do you know what his wishes might have been?" I asked in a quiet voice. I was his wife but I had no idea.

"No. He never spoke to me about those things."

He grabbed my shoulder and looked me right in the eye. "But you could do no wrong by him, Jill. He was crazy about you."

Harry cleared his throat, suggesting they go grab a late lunch and try to rest. Neither wanted to return that day but said they would come back the next day unless something had been decided otherwise. It was as if an invisible weight had been placed on my shoulders. Their days—their grief—was now on my schedule, on

29

when I decided that I was able to let go. I watched them shuffle down the hallway and I turned to Stella and Lanie. Both were again on the phone and motioned for me to go ahead into Jay's room.

Nothing had changed from the night before. Jay was still lying in bed with multiple tubes running from various spots on his body. The soft hum of machines continued to be the only noise in the room. I took my seat next to his bed and reached for his hand.

"Hey Jay, it's me," I whispered. What should I say? There were things I thought I would have a lifetime to tell him. I sighed. Might as well start at the beginning.

"Remember the first night we met? You were in your last year of law school and Stella was in her first year of law school at Wake Forest. She had invited me along to a mixer off-campus that I really didn't want to attend. I had told her no, but you know Stella. She doesn't take the word *no* as a reasonable answer." I chuckled to myself. To Stella the word *no* meant that she would nag you to death until she got her way. It was a character flaw, for sure, but it was also endearing at the same time. Both Jay and I knew it. We had discussed it endlessly and mostly in disbelief as we watched Stella get her way.

"I thought all lawyers were pretentious, nerdy and no fun." I smiled as I thought back to that moment.

"I resent that!" Stella exclaimed as she entered the room, followed by Lanie. They arranged themselves in the various hospital chairs that cluttered the other side of the room.

"If I remember correctly, I invited both of you." Stella looked at Lanie.

"You know I couldn't make it. I was in the middle of exams at UNC," Lanie said.

It was true. Lanie had graduated, as Stella and I had, from Wake Forest and been accepted on a full scholarship into an accelerated doctoral program at UNC and she was buried with finals and papers that week.

"I remember you talking about it the next day," Lanie added. "You were so bubbly over this handsome guy that you had met at the party. But you were so sure he was never going to call you."

"That's right. Didn't you spill your drink all over him?" Stella laughed, pointing to Jay.

"Yea, I did. I got so nervous. Here was this tall, fit lawyer with dark brown hair and baby blue eyes, with the most classic features I have ever seen in my whole life, and he spent nearly the whole party talking to me, mostly about baseball. Then, at the very end, I was leaning forward to hear something he said and I spilled my whole drink on him," I said, squeezing Jay's hand. The three of us burst into giggles.

"Remember what we did the next day?" Stella asked mischievously.

"No. I don't think I ever told Jay that," I said, looking at Jay and back at them.

"What?" Lanie asked.

"Well, Miss Jill here was determined not to let her Prince Charming escape. She remembered he had mentioned that a group of them had a standing Sunday brunch at this small restaurant downtown. So, Jill got us out of bed that morning at nine!" Stella was still agitated about that incident, all these years later. "Mind you I was hung over and all I wanted to do was spend the day in bed, but instead we sat in that restaurant until one in the afternoon," Stella exclaimed.

"I had never drunk so much coffee in my life," I interjected.

"Oh, that's right. Jill felt bad we were occupying a prime table in this waitress's area all morning, just ordering coffee, so she left, like, a fifty dollar tip," Stella added.

"You did not!" Lanie laughed. "I don't think you ever told me."

"Well, we finally left and I was sure I was never going to hear from him. I mean I didn't just spill my drink. I dumped the whole thing all over him. He had this huge red stain right in the middle of his shirt for the rest of the evening. Anyway, by the time Stella and I got back to our apartment, I was sure that was it. He was going to graduate in a couple weeks and I would never see him again." I said.

"But ..." Lanie added, motioning for me to continue. She must have heard this story a thousand times, but she loved it for whatever reason.

"But when we got back to our apartment, there was a single yellow rose and a card waiting for me." I smiled sweetly.

"What did the card say?" she asked.

"Like you don't already know," Stella said, mocking her.

"I don't care. Tell me anyway." Lanie motioned again.

"The card said to meet him at seven o'clock that night outside this real trendy restaurant. But when we both got there, we realized it wasn't our thing, so we ended up getting a pizza and sitting out on the patio of this random bar, talking and drinking beer," I said.

"He brought her home at 11 o'clock and I swear that was the last night she spent alone ... They were inseparable after that," Stella said.

"Until now," I whispered, instantly changing the mood in the room.

"Until now," Lanie repeated, her face scrunched up and showing the sorrow she felt but wouldn't express around me.

"It's still an epic story," Stella added, "that just doesn't happen to anyone anymore."

"How did he know where you lived?" Lanie asked.

"Haven't I told you?"

"I don't remember."

"While I was trying to stalk him at the brunch place, he had Harry, who was already established on the force by that time, run Stella's information."

"Which he got from a law school friend of his, whom I had dated earlier that year," Stella said, finishing the sentence.

"Sneaky," Lanie said.

"Yea. He has always been good at getting exactly what he wanted from whomever he wanted. I remember that first night he was so charismatic and charming. I remember thinking he could have sold ice cubes to a polar bear," I said.

"Seriously … you are so corny," Stella said.

"I think it's sweet," Lanie said.

"You would." Stella laughed and stuck out her tongue at Lanie.

"Very mature," Lanie said. There were times when Stella and Lanie would struggle over who got the last word in a conversation and I sensed this was going to be one of those. Just as I was about to try and break up their conversation, Dr. Matthews entered the room.

"Jill," he said, shaking my hand.

"Ladies." He addressed both Stella and Lanie and I quickly made further introductions.

"Any change overnight?" I asked. I was still hopeful, even if everything I had read told me otherwise.

"No, Jill. I told you yesterday—" he started.

"I know, I know, but a girl has to cling to hope, doesn't she?" I held up my hands in defeat.

"Fair point," he said.

"I do have some questions for you," I added.

"Really?"

This seemed to surprise the doctor and I suggested that perhaps we could talk privately in the hallway. As much as I loved my friends,

I needed the doctor to answer my questions without the quips and opinions they often freely unloaded on me. We excused ourselves and left Stella and Lanie in the room with Jay.

Dr. Matthews was patient as he answered all my questions about Jay's current condition and other possible treatment plans or methods that might have been in the clinical stages. With every option I offered, he crafted a logical and easily explainable reason why that option wouldn't work or didn't pertain to Jay's condition. Seeing I was out of options, I finally took a big breath and asked, "Doc, what can you tell me about organ donation?"

This launched Dr. Matthews into a 10-minute explanation of the impact that organ donation would have on other families. When he was done, he looked at me as if to gauge what my reaction and decision would be.

"If I agree to this, how soon would it be?" I asked.

"After you have completed all the paperwork and release forms, it will be about finding the correct matches, but it all happens really fast." I mulled this information over in my head. Jay was really gone. The body that lay in that room was a shell of the man I loved. Rationally, I understood that. I sighed and Dr. Matthews must have mistaken my sigh for defiance rather than resignation.

"Jill, I strongly insist you think about this—"

I held up my hand for him to stop. "I'll do it. I'll sign your paperwork, but can I ask you not to process it until the morning? I need a little more time." It was my compromise. Give me one more night and then I would share him with others that needed him. That was all I could control at this moment.

Dr. Matthews nodded, commenting that they would begin to draw up the forms. He then shook my hand and went to speak with a nurse, leaving me alone in the hallway. When I went back into Jay's room, Stella and Lanie were talking to Jay about the surprise birthday he had thrown for me several years earlier.

"From what I remember, that was one of the best parties I have ever had," I said.

"I'm surprised you remember that much," Stella quipped back.

It was true that most of the night was a blur. I had spent a great deal of it getting sick in our hotel bathroom. I sat down next to Jay and told them all about my discussion with Dr. Matthews.

"Are you okay with this?" Lanie asked.

"Not really, but I don't have a choice. It's selfish to keep him here hooked up. He needs to be at peace and, just because I can't cope with it doesn't mean I should leave him in limbo."

"And the organ donation?" Lanie asked.

"He made me so happy. He gave me so much. The least I can do is share him in some form or fashion with everyone else." The more I said it aloud, the more convinced I was that this was the right thing to do.

We talked quietly for a couple more minutes, deciding that Stella and Lanie would say their good-byes that night before we left. Neither friend wanted to come back in the morning, opting, instead, to allow me to say my good-byes in private. I stood and kissed Jay on the cheek and walked out into the hallway.

Dr. Matthews returned with all the paperwork that needed to be completed. I sat down on a bench and started to complete the endless forms, outlining Jay's medical history as best as I could. I became frustrated and called Harry. After relaying to him what I had decided about Jay's status, I asked to speak with Peter. When Peter got on the phone, I told him about my plans and he gave me his blessing. I asked him about some of the information about Jay I was not able to complete myself. Almost 30 minutes later, as I was finishing the forms, Stella and Lanie emerged from Jay's room. Both had tear-stained faces and Lanie was sniffling, wiping her nose with a tissue. I got up and embraced them in a long hug. It was my turn to let them lean on me after they had said good-bye.

We left the hospital shortly after six in the evening. We had given all the completed forms to the nurse, who had paged Dr. Matthews. He came down and discussed some of the forms with me in greater detail. He informed me that once the paperwork was filed, he had no control over the timeline at that point, reminding me that it would probably happen quickly. I nodded that I understood. They had made special arrangements for me to come back early the next morning to sit with Jay until that time arrived. I thanked the doctors and nurses and walked out of the hospital with Lanie on one side and Stella on the other. We didn't speak. We were all lost in our own thoughts.

CHAPTER 5

....

My nightmare startled me awake. I reached for Jay's side of the bed and came up empty. Again the realization of everything around me settled in. Looking at the clock, I saw it was just after midnight. I flopped back down onto my pillow. In a couple of hours I would go to the hospital to say good-bye to Jay. My stomach tensed in knots and I felt anxious. There were a million places I would have rather been than there in bed, alone. Slowly forming a plan that bordered on insanity, I got up and dressed. As I wove my way through the house, I grabbed a couple of photos and put them in my purse. After leaving a note on the table for Stella and Lanie, I headed for the hospital.

As I entered the hospital, I saw an elderly man sitting at the check-in desk. He seemed to be reading something and as I approached, I saw a Bible in his hands.

"Can I help you?'

"I need to see my husband," I said confidently.

"Visiting hours are at 11. You're a little early." He tried to joke with me.

"Is there any way I can get in right now?"

"No, ma'am."

"Please, sir, I'll do anything," I begged.

"Are you trying to bribe me?"

"Possibly. Would it work if I did?"

"Ma'am, I'm going to have to call security," he said after a long pause.

"Sir, are you married?" I asked in one last-ditch effort before I lost my nerve.

"Why yes. Thirty-five years," he said very proudly. I smiled politely at his enthusiasm.

"Sir, my husband of two years is lying in a hospital bed, brain dead. In a couple hours they are going to take him off the machines and cut him up in small pieces." The tears streamed down my face, blurring my vision as I continued. "I know I'm not supposed to be here. But I woke up a little while ago from a nightmare and I needed him. This is the last chance I'm going to get for him to be there for me." I was sobbing. My shoulders were heaving as I reached for a tissue on the counter. The old man stood and looked at me for a minute. He set down his Bible and came around the desk with his arms outstretched. This was not how I pictured this encounter going, but I fell into his embrace until the tears slowly stopped.

"Two years would never have been enough with my Doris," he stated. He let me go and wandered off down the hallway. I looked around and saw he had left the door open. I quickly followed behind him and ducked down the hallway that led to Jay's room. When I entered the room, I saw that everything was as I had left it. I approached Jay's side and took his hand.

"I made it," I whispered. I kicked off my shoes, curled myself around Jay and the tubes and told him about my nightmare until I fell asleep.

"Excuse me. You cannot be in here."

I was startled awake by a burly nurse standing by Jay's bed shaking her finger at me.

"But I'm his wife," I said defensively.

"I don't care if you are the pope. You can't be here."

"You can call Dr. Matthews. He approved it," I lied.

"I seriously doubt that. I'm not waking the good doctor at three in the morning to tell him about some lunatic breaking in after hours."

"Listen, lady. I know you have a job to do and I respect that. But at this moment in time, I'm not going anywhere. This is my last night with my husband and I don't care if you give a damn about that or not, but I do. We made vows 'until death do us part' and I plan on upholding those vows tonight." I sat up and stared at the nurse as the frustration and anger started to build up.

"Honey, you cannot be in here," she fired back, motioning for me to leave.

"Maybe you didn't hear me. I'm not going anywhere," I shot back. "Don't you care about this man lying here and his family? Are you blinded by the rules and regulations that you can't see they don't make any sense? I'm not hurting anyone and I'm not bothering anyone. Can't you just move on and forget you ever saw me?" I was pushing it and I didn't care.

"You leave me no choice. I'm calling security," and with that she turned and walked from the room. For the second time that night somebody had threatened to call security on me. Sighing, I lay back down next to Jay and waited.

....

Soon I could hear voices in the hallway and then the nurse returned with security. They both stared at me in my pathetic state curled up next to my husband.

"She can't be here." The nurse pointed in my direction.

"Ma'am, I have to ask you to leave," the security guard said. He started to move toward me and I burst into tears, unleashing the whole story going back to Sunday and Jay's accident. When I was done, both the nurse and security guard looked at each other.

"Who can I call to vouch for this story?" he finally asked.

Apparently, someone in the room had a heart.

"Really?" I couldn't make this up. "Officer Henry Connor."

"Harry?"

"Ya. You know him?" I asked.

"Yes. I used to work with him until I retired. I took this gig part-time to keep me busy," he said.

"That is all very touching, but she still can't be here," the nurse interjected.

"Harry and Jay are best friends." I threw that in for good measure as he took out his phone.

He stepped out of the room while the nurse continued to glare in my direction. Apparently, dying husbands and true love was not her weak spot. A few minutes later the security guard reentered the room and handed me the phone.

"What the fuck is going on, Jill?" Harry yelled into the phone. "They should be dragging you out of that bed, handcuffing your ass and throwing you in jail!"

"I had to. It's our last night together," I whispered.

"I have convinced Jack to forget this whole thing ever happened, but he said there was a nurse who did not look like she was going to drop it," he said in a calmer tone.

"You got that right," I said.

"Well, you'll have to work your magic on her." He paused. "But seriously, Jill, what you did tonight was boarding on insane … but knowing Jay, he would have loved it. It's probably what he would have done, but he would have gotten arrested, and I would be bailing his ass out of jail. You stay put until the morning. Peter and I will be by to say our good-byes."

"Thank you, Harry." I meant it more than he would know. I could see Jack leaning over and whispering something to the nurse.

"You're welcome," and with that he ended the conversation. I handed the phone back to Jack and he looked at the nurse. She looked from him to me and finally threw her hands up.

"I'm off in an hour. What do I care? That's what I get for covering for Frannie tonight," she muttered to herself and stormed out of the room.

Jack gave me one more look and tipped his hat and followed her out.

"That was close," I whispered to Jay as I lay back down.

....

I lay there for a couple more hours before I heard more noises out in the hallway as the hospital came to life. At a little past seven in the morning, I got up and went to use the restroom and freshen up.

"Mrs. Greenfield, you here?" I heard a muffled voice call my name.

"I'm here," I said as I left the bathroom and came face to face with a dark-haired petite nurse who was giving me a wide grin.

"Do I know you?" I asked, and I couldn't help but grin back at her.

"Oh, I don't think so. But I heard all about your story. It's all over the hospital—sweet-talking Mr. Davis at the front desk and then taking on Mrs. Betty and several security guards," she rambled, checking Jay's chart and vitals.

"It was just one security guard." I made my way over to Jay's side.

She threw her hands up in a no-nonsense move. "It's the most romantic story this hospital has had in such a long time. It's just so sweet, you going to all these lengths." She sighed.

"A real Romeo and Juliet," I muttered.

She made a face and fussed over us for a couple more minutes before disappearing down the hallway.

"Looks like even at the end we are going down in infamy, Jay!" I paused. "That reminds me. I brought you some things." I reached into my purse and pulled out several photos.

"Remember this one?" I asked him. It was a photo of our first time out to Oak Island. Oak Island was a small beach down on the far southern coast of North Carolina, easily a three-hour drive from Greensboro. The photo had been taken the weekend after Jay's graduation. In the picture, we were sitting on the beach. Our beach towels were stretched out underneath us and a row of summer houses stretched out behind us. We had these crazy, stupid, wide grins stretched across our faces. We had spent the night in our car in sleeping bags and had got up superearly to watch the sunrise. Jay then talked me into a nice long run on the beach, telling me how romantic it would be. I don't think we saw a soul that morning. It was heaven.

"Or this one?" I asked him. The next picture was from the first 5k road race we completed together. I had long been a runner and when we started dating, we found that we had that in common. Jay was a faster runner than I was, but whenever we ran together, he would slow down, making sure he never left me behind. He was a fierce competitor and loved racing, but I was too scared to enter a race. It took him a little over a year to convince me to enter one. We had decided to enter a short 5k race, a distance we had run numerous times together. He ran with me until the very end of the race. I kept waving him on and telling him to go ahead and finish strong. So at the end, with half a mile left to go, it didn't surprise me that he took off at full speed to finish the race. By the time I arrived at the finish line, he was there, holding up a "Will you marry me?" sign with a single yellow rose. After I was able to catch my breath, I accepted.

"I think this is my favorite," I said holding up another picture. It was from our wedding day, but it wasn't one of the many formal portraits we had taken. It was a picture that Stella had snapped when we both thought no one was looking. It was a close-up, but we were just standing off to the side by ourselves, holding hands, talking with our heads close together. I couldn't remember what we were talking about, but it was probably something very mundane. I loved the picture because it was just us in our little world and we were so happy. We had our whole life ahead of us in that moment and we were ready to tackle it together.

I had several other photos I showed Jay and when I was done, I sat next to him in silence for as long as time allowed us to, just holding his hand. I had been attracted to him from the first time I saw him. I never believed in love at first sight, but after meeting him, everything fit into place. I had come from a broken home and Jay had made me feel part of a family again. My mom had died from breast cancer when I was eight. She was always promising that she was going to be fine, but in the end she lost her four-year battle. It took me a very long time to understand her struggle. My dad was never the same after her death. He fell down a dark path of drugs and alcohol, eventually getting arrested for possession with intent to distribute to minors as well as endangering a minor. It was my seventeenth birthday, the night the police showed up at the house to arrest him.

Stella's parents divorced when she was young, so it was just her and her mom, and they were struggling to make ends meet, but her mom agreed to take me in until I turned 18. That fall Stella, Lanie and I all enrolled at Wake Forest University. To pay for tuition, I used whatever money was left over from my mom that my dad hadn't squandered away. Stella and Lanie both got huge scholarships based on their grades and SAT scores. Then, after we finished our freshman year, Stella, Lanie and I rented an apartment not far from campus. Stella and I continued to live together after graduation when Lanie moved to Raleigh. But I never felt that I belonged to a family until the day I met Jay. It wasn't about the fact that his family was more functional than mine, because it wasn't. While his mother was alive, Jay resisted his father, who was much older than his mother and had been grooming Jay to become a major player in the Massachusetts firm in which he was currently a partner. But eventually Jay went to law school and joined the firm right before his dad retired but not before causing irrefutable damage to their relationship.

Simply stated, when I was with Jay, I felt I was exactly where I was supposed to be.

"I'm afraid I'll be lost again," I whispered as I squeezed his hand.

"Knock, knock," I heard someone say from behind me. There in the doorway stood Harry, Peter, Stella and Lanie.

"Hi," I said meekly. "I thought you two weren't coming back."

"Well, we weren't planning on it until we saw your note this morning and were convinced we were going to be bailing you out of jail," Stella said, waving my note at me.

"Or at least reading about it on the front of the paper this morning," Lanie added.

"It would have never made the morning paper but maybe the evening news," Peter said as he winked in my direction.

"And Harry called and ripped into us about being the worst babysitters in the world," Lanie added. I mouthed the word *sorry* to her and she just shrugged.

"I think it took guts. You must have really talked yourself out of a sticky situation from what Harry told me ... I told you that you would have made a great lawyer," Peter said very seriously and everyone started to laugh. In truth, Peter had tried to convince me to go to law school every time I saw him after Jay and I started dating. I refused, saying I knew enough lawyers to last me a lifetime.

"I'm glad I could catch everyone," Dr. Matthews said as he entered the room. Immediately, the feeling in the room changed as if we were all holding our breath. "I heard it was an interesting night," he added, raising an eyebrow in my direction.

"Sorry about that," I said quietly, looking back at Jay.

"It's time." Dr. Matthews paused before saying, "We will need to prep Mr. Greenfield and get him ready for surgery in one hour." No one moved. No one expected it to happen so fast. Dr. Matthews gave us a couple more instructions and left us to say our final good-byes. We decided that we would each say our good-byes privately and that I would go last.

"Jill, have you contacted a funeral home?" Peter asked me as I stood in the hallway alongside him, Harry and Stella. Lanie was the first to say good-bye.

Stella jumped in. "I called one yesterday."

The home she mentioned was the same one that had arranged my mom's service many years ago.

"Are you doing a funeral or cremation?" Peter asked. He was a very direct man who showed little emotion. I often thought that though Jay looked like his dad, his personality must have been much more like his mom's, although I had never met her.

"I'm not sure. Stella did you hear back from the lawyer?" I asked.

"Yes. Paul Wellon sends his condolences and said he would fax me the documents this morning. He also said we will need to set up a meeting with him to settle Jay's estate in the next several weeks."

"What estate? We don't have anything," I said. She just shrugged.

"What are you unsure about?" Harry asked.

Just then, Lanie came out and tapped Stella on the shoulder, indicating it was her turn.

"Well . . ." I hesitated before I started in on the endless questions that had been racing through my mind. "If I bury Jay, where do I bury him? Back in Massachusetts? Here in North Carolina? But then I might not live in North Carolina forever, so then who would visit him? I can't just dig him up and take him with me every time I relocate. But then if I cremate him, do I keep him on my mantel?" I stopped to take a breath. The idea of Jay's ashes on the mantel of any house really bothered me. "If I scatter his ashes, where do I scatter them, and would he even be okay with that?" I looked around and no one had any answers for my questions. Stella came out wiping the tears from her eyes, and Harry turned to go in.

"I worry about Harry," Peter said when Harry left. The thought of Peter worrying about anyone surprised me. "Jay and Harry were best of friends since they were so young. Jay was his entire support system." I nodded in agreement. Harry came from a solid family

CHAPTER 5

back in Massachusetts but had created some waves when he married a pretty young girl soon after Jay had decided on going to law school. It had been a quick courtship and an even quicker marriage before it all fell apart. Since then Harry had distanced himself from his family and spent more and more time at the local dive bar.

"This might push him over the edge," Peter added.

"Jill." Stella leaned in and whispered, "We have an appointment at the funeral home this afternoon. They have some paperwork you need to complete as well as major decisions you need to make."

I nodded. I was afraid that if I started speaking, the tears would begin and I wouldn't be able to turn them off.

Harry emerged from Jay's room a couple of minutes later. His eyes were red and he was sniffling as he waved at us, indicating he needed a minute. He walked down the other hallway to be alone. Peter took his cue and went in to see Jay.

"What do you think he has to say to him?" Stella wondered.

"You are so nosy," Lanie said. "I would hope he says he loves him and was proud of him."

"Boring! I wonder if he will spill all his secrets," Stella whispered conspiratorially. Peter was the lawyer that many of Boston's worst criminals sought out to keep them out of jail in the late '60s through the mid-'80s when he retired from public service and went into the private sector. From what Jay had said, he never spoke of those cases or clients. That didn't stop Stella from asking. Having studied several historic cases while in law school, she was convinced there was more to every story.

"Why are you even thinking of that?" Lanie asked.

"What? It could happen … What I wouldn't give to be a fly on the wall right now," Stella said, defending herself.

47

"Tact, Stella. You need some serious tact," Lanie said, shaking her head. Just then, Peter emerged from Jay's room. He looked very solemn and stoic. The man was a rock. Nothing ever moved him.

"I never thought I would be the one to outlive them both," he said as he came and stood by me, giving my shoulder a tight squeeze.

"Jill, it's you," Lanie said quietly. I nodded and headed into Jay's room one last time.

....

I sat by Jay's bed and held his hand. I wasn't sure what I wanted to say. There was so much to say and nothing at all. I took a deep breath, trying to fight the tears that started to slide down my cheeks. Finally, I mustered the courage and I told Jay what our future together would have looked like.

"In a year or so, we would have our first baby, a baby boy. We would spend the summer at Oak Island and then you would finally be made partner. We would then have our second baby, a girl. I would quit teaching and stay at home with the kids. We would travel to Tahiti for our 10-year anniversary, leaving the kids with Harry or Stella," I giggled at the crazy thought of either of them with children. "We would then buy that house on the beach we have been talking about and maybe have our third kid, a boy," I winked at Jay. It had forever been a discussion of ours whether we would have two or three kids. I wanted three. He wanted two. So I thought we could compromise and have three. "We would then raise them and watch them grow up. They would have my great looks and your brains." I squeezed Jay's hand as I joked. "We would watch them play ball or go to ballet, make tons of mistakes, break hearts and have their hearts broken. We would watch them go off to college and we would be there at graduation, hand in hand, for each of them. We would let them pave their own way and when they finally fell in love, we would be able to share in those special moments. You would be able to give our little girl away at her wedding and I would dance with the boys at theirs. They would have kids and make us grandparents. Our house would grow in size and holidays would be loud and filled with lots of food and memories. We would make our own traditions, but we would be together as a family. Then you and I would grow old together and at the very end I would hope we would go in our sleep, together," I whispered.

I knew it was never to be, but it painted the life we wished for each other. The life we would never get to live out. I leaned over on Jay's bed and cried. I cried for all those memories I would never get to share but most of all for all the time Jay had been cheated out of. Me? I would get up tomorrow and I would see, hear, listen, and one day at a time, I would heal, but he would never get to do those things. How long would people remember Jay Greenfield before he slipped from their memory? How long would he stay in my memory before I had trouble recalling every detail of his face?

A hand touched my shoulder. Dr. Matthews and Dr. Shippling were there along with the bubbly petite nurse from earlier.

"It's time," Dr. Matthews said. I nodded and leaned over and kissed Jay on cheek. I squeezed his hand one more time and whispered, "I love you," into his ear. It was almost as if that phrase wasn't enough, but it was all I had. I stepped off to the side as the nurse moved in and starting removing the tubes and adjusting the monitors. As they moved Jay from the room, I couldn't handle him leaving. I rushed forward and grabbed his hand one more time.

"I don't know if I can do this," I said, looking wildly around me.

"Nurse?" the doctor called, directing her attention toward my erratic behavior.

"I got her," a voice from the hallway called. Harry walked in and wrapped his arms around me from behind. "Say good-bye," he said.

They again started to move Jay and my grip on his hand started to slip.

"No, Jay. Come back!" I yelled as I lost my grip on his hand. "I love you," I shouted after him. I started to sob and soon my knees grew weak and I couldn't hold myself up. "I love you," I sobbed as they continued to wheel him down the hallway until I could no longer see them. Harry set me down on a chair in the room and handed me a box of tissues.

"We all did," he commented as he watched me cry it out. Soon Stella and Lanie joined me in the room, each consoling me in different ways. Eventually the nurses came in and said we would need to either go to the lobby or move to another room. I gathered up my things and shuffled out of the room. In the hallway Harry and Peter decided to go back to Harry's apartment. Stella suggested we go home as well. On the ride home I went through the motions of trying to listen as Stella and Lanie laid out the details of what we needed to do next, but I wasn't listening. I was trying to figure out how to wake up from this nightmare I found myself in. I had been robbed of my past by my parents and now my future had just slipped through my fingertips.

CHAPTER 6

....

It wasn't even 10 in the morning when we got back to the house. Stella and Lanie insisted I go upstairs and lie down. Lanie even threaten to give me some form of sedative if I didn't go. Begrudgingly, I headed upstairs and soon drifted off to sleep.

"Jill, it's time to get up." Stella was by my side with a sandwich and cup of green tea.

"What time is it?" I mumbled. I felt as if I had been hit by a Mack truck. Again I sat up not realizing what had happened and then all the events came rushing back. I wondered how long that sensation would continue. Would I always wake up with a sense of ease only to be replaced by immediate dread?

"It's a little after one. I really hate to wake you, but we have to go meet the funeral director and you really need to be there. Those are not decisions Lanie and I can make on your behalf."

"Sure," I mumbled, sitting up.

She handed me the sandwich and I did my best to eat as much as I could, but I really didn't feel like eating. When I was done, Stella instructed me to take shower and meet them downstairs. As I entered the kitchen, I was overwhelmed with all the bouquets of flowers and baskets of food that had appeared.

"They started arriving right after you went to bed," Lanie explained.

"Who are they all from?" I wondered out loud.

"Friends from school, Jay's office, coworkers, friends, family and some others I don't recognize," Lanie answered.

"Here." Stella handed me some paperwork and settled me onto the sofa as if I were a child.

"What is this?"

"It's the paperwork from the lawyer's office. I figured you would want to read it before we went down to the funeral home."

She was right. I wanted to read it, but I wasn't in the right state of mind to do anything. I stared at her in disbelief.

"Now, Jill," she said, motioning me one more time to read it. I was startled a little bit by her tone but did as she asked. Over the next hour, while I poured through the paperwork, more floral arrangements arrived and several neighbors and friends stopped by to drop off food. Lanie, Stella and I then piled into the car and headed off to the funeral home.

....

Swanford and Sons had handled the funeral arrangements for my mother nearly 18 years earlier. I was so young when that happened. I had very fragmented memories of the funeral and the days surrounding it. I guess it didn't matter much as my mom had preplanned everything from the outfit she wore to the music that would be played and the types of flowers people should send. My dad only had to follow her instructions. We arrived outside the large white building with black lettering on the front. It had always looked more like a residence than a commercial business, I thought.

"Mrs. Greenfield?" A large, older man with white hair and a long white mustache greeted us at the door. I nodded and extended my hand.

"I'm Gary Swanford," he said.

"I'm Stella. We spoke on the phone earlier." Stella shook the man's hand as Lanie followed suit.

"Pleasure meeting everyone. Now, Mrs. Greenfield …"

"Jill, please."

"Very well, Jill. First I want to extend our sincerest condolences during this most difficult time." Mr. Swanford carried on about how tragic the accident was and showed us around the facility until we ended up in his large office at the back of the building.

"Now, I remember your mother's service," he said. This brought me out of my daze and I stared at the man. Was he really the same man from so many years earlier? Given the time that had passed, I thought he could probably pass for the energetic director with jet-black hair who kept sneaking me lollipops during the service.

"You were so young," he continued. "I never expected to see you back so soon."

I knew he meant well, but there was something creepy about a funeral director telling people when he expected to see them.

"Perhaps we should get on with the planning. Jill has had a very trying day," Lanie interjected when she could tell the conversation was going nowhere.

"Oh yes, please sit." Mr. Swanford gestured to the four chairs that sat around his large desk. "Have you decided on cremation or burial?" he asked.

"I still can't decide and Jay's last wishes didn't make any mention of funeral arrangements."

The paperwork from the lawyer's office dealt more with Jay's wishes about not being left hooked up to machines and how I would be given control over all medical decisions should he not be able to.

"Well, if you do a burial, have you thought where you would buy the plots? Locally or out-of-state? In addition, nowadays, most people go ahead and buy two plots, one for the deceased and one for themselves. Kind of a two-for-one deal," he said, taking a book out from the bookcase behind his desk and laying it out in front of me. "Of course you're so young, that complicates matters," he added.

"How so?" I replied.

"Well, what if you remarry in several years? Then, at the end of your life, you could change your mind and decide you want to be buried next to your new husband, but you already bought this plot. Then you have to consider the family of your new husband. Would they understand that you want to be buried next to some guy you married years prior for a couple years versus their dad whom you have known for 30+ years? Young love is simple but time complicates matters." He stopped talking to look at me.

"Remarry …?" I stammered. Jay wasn't even gone a full 12 hours and this guy was already talking about me getting hitched to another guy. I couldn't even process the statement.

"I know it's difficult, but these are situations we come across everyday and I just ask you consider them."

"I really don't know," I said, shaking my head.

"Jill, what would you want done if this was you?" Lanie quietly asked.

"I want to be cremated," Stella interjected.

"I want to be buried," Lanie said.

The entire idea of being in the cold ground alone was not appealing to me in any way.

"I think at this moment in time I would prefer cremation." Hearing Stella and Lanie talk about it helped me process the entire ordeal more abstractly.

"Cremation is an excellent choice." Mr. Swanford pulled another catalog from the bookcase and laid it out in front of me.

"Are you going to prefer cremation after or before the service?"

Gary Swanford was just full of questions, wasn't he?

"The idea of people coming to a service and not having him there, in one piece, just feels wrong," I said and both Stella and Lanie nodded their head.

"Then, are you going to need a coffin?" he said, pulling a third catalog from the shelf.

"I guess so," I said.

We progressed in this fashion for the next several hours going through every possible detail of the service and final cremation. I had wanted a small service at the church Jay and I had married in, which was downtown. After the service, there would be a reception, or "celebration of life," as Lanie called it, at Jay's favorite bar, also downtown, called The Draft. Stella had insisted on that.

"Finally, will anyone be speaking at the service?" he asked. I must have given him a confused look because we had already covered the music and what few words I wished the pastor to say.

"Usually, a family member or several family members like to get up and speak during the service to share stories or funny tidbits of the deceased."

All three of us paused and looked at him. Who would speak? Neither Peter nor Harry was good with words. I didn't think it was appropriate for anyone from work to say anything and Stella and Lanie were my friends. They hadn't known Jay on such an intimate level.

"No one needs to speak; it's not required," he quickly added when we didn't say anything.

"I'll say something," I finally said.

"What?" Stella and Lanie asked at the same time.

"No offense, Jill, but you're not really dealing with this whole thing very well. I don't think that is a good idea," Stella said.

"I agree," Lanie added.

"It's his funeral. How would you feel if no one got up and said anything about you? It's like the life you led seems less important if there is no one to vouch for you, to speak up in front of everyone, someone needs to say he mattered and he mattered to me," I said.

"You hate public speaking," muttered Stella.

"I know but I need to do this. I want to do this," I said, looking at the funeral director.

"Okay. That takes care of it all. How would you like to pay for it all?" he asked while he totaled up his services.

My mind was reeling. How would I pay for this? Could I pay for this? The bill was in the thousands. I knew we had savings, but would they be enough?

"Do you take Visa?" I asked, pulling out my credit card. I wasn't even sure my limit would cover the entire thing, but Gary took my card and went to run it at the desk.

"Don't worry. Once you file with Jay's life insurance and they send you the payout, it will cover these costs. Jay was a smart man. I'm sure he took out a good insurance policy," Stella said as if she were talking business with a client.

"Life insurance?" I asked.

"Jay had life insurance, right?" she asked, becoming alarmed.

"Yes. We both do," I assured her. It just startled me because it was nothing I ever thought we would use. In fact, I still remember sitting with Jay in the insurance agent's office going through the most boring presentation of my life. Both Jay and the insurance agent were having a lively discussion about extra benefits and add-ons while I counted the ceiling tiles over and over again. The only thing I took away from the conversation was the agent saying, "By signing this you are instantly covered. You could walk out the front door and get hit by a bus and you'll be covered." Ironically, it wasn't a bus. It was a car and it was Jay.

Gary walked back into the office and handed me my card. "You're all set. Just sign here." He produced a receipt and contract.

"Am I?" I asked no one in particular.

CHAPTER 7

....

I had left the funeral home, feeling completely drained. The memory of the hospital felt like a distant memory. When we arrived back home a little after seven, Stella and Lanie started tackling the endless things that needed to be done before the funeral service. They waved me away when I asked what I should be doing.

"Here," Stella said, handing me my phone. There were numerous texts and even more voicemails. I sighed, shuffled into the kitchen, and brewed three cups of tea. After setting down cups in front of Lanie and Stella, who were both on the phone again, I settled myself on the sofa and began to return the endless amounts of messages from friends and family members. I replied to each message with information about the service and assured callers that I didn't need anything at this time, but I would let them know if I did. It was well after 10 when I finally replied to the last message. I saw that Stella and Lanie were still busy in the kitchen and I motioned to them I was going to bed. Each one nodded and said goodnight. I made my way upstairs and quickly changed and practically fell into bed with exhaustion.

....

The next morning was much of the same. More phone calls, more text messages and more deliveries.

"I don't know where we are going to start putting some of these," Lanie mused as she signed for another flower arrangement. I shrugged and slumped down at the table as my phone started to ring again and I let out a groan.

"You don't have to answer it," Lanie suggested.

"If I don't, I will just need to return the call later."

I answered the call and spent the next five minutes listening to Aunt Judy on Jay's side of the family talk about how much she was going to miss Jay and that he was just so special to her. I finally was able to hang up just as Stella wandered in the kitchen.

"Who was that?" she inquired, making her way directly to the coffee pot.

"Does it matter? It was another person wanting to tell me how much they will miss Jay and how special he was to them. I'm starting to feel like a priest during confessional. They don't really want to send their condolences. It's almost as if they want me to validate their own grief." I sagged into my seat.

"Wow, now you sound like Lanie," Stella commented. Lanie stuck her tongue out at Stella.

"Really?" I said, letting out a slight laugh at the two of them.

We sat around the table and chatted some more about what was left to handle before the services the following day.

"Have you thought about what you wanted to say at the service?" Stella asked.

"No. I haven't had any time to just be," I said, looking at my friends.

They immediately took my cue and redivided the list among themselves and dismissed me from the kitchen. I wandered back up to the bedroom and showered and dressed in sweatpants and one of Jay's long, grey fleeces. The arms were too long, but I just rolled up the sleeves and headed down to the office. I pulled my journal from the bookcase behind his desk and sat down, skimming the pages.

Writing had always been my escape, ever since I was young. No matter what was going on in my life I could write about it. Now I sat there, staring at the blank pages. I didn't know what to say. I sighed and put the journal to the side and turned on the computer searching for the right inspiration. When nothing seemed to work, I found myself being distracted and landing on Jay's Facebook page. I did not have my own Facebook page. I had balked at the idea of creating one, finding it necessary to keep my private life separate from teachers and parents at school. Stella and Lanie said I was being paranoid. I just never felt the desire to share all my personal thoughts in such a public way. Now Jay, on the other hand felt very differently. He loved catching up with friends and knowing what was going on with everyone. He had written down his login and password information next to the computer so that I could use his account to catch up with the few people I did seek out through the social media world. I had to admit I enjoyed looking at all the crazy pictures that people posted.

But what I found there that day amazed me. Jay's page had been turned into a make-shift virtual memorial. People were posting pictures of Jay, resharing favorite memories and grieving. I felt overcome with grief but also with happiness that Jay had impacted so many people.

"Look at you, Facebook stalking," Harry said from the doorway. I swiveled in my chair to face him.

"Guilty as charged." I sniffled, tears still streaming down my face.

"Hope you don't mind me dropping by and all. Your babysitters let me in. The old man isn't much for company."

"Too sad?"

"No. I could take sad. He has been on the phone doing business most of the time," he replied.

"Don't tell Stella that. She will think he's reconnecting with the mob or something," I said, chuckling to myself. "How are you doing?"

"It's hard to tell. I kinda feel that Jay's just away on another business trip or something and he'll be back," Harry said, stuffing his hands in his jeans pockets.

"I know exactly what you mean. I go to bed at night and it doesn't bother me that he's not there, because I keep thinking he'll be back in a couple days."

Jay would often have to take off for several days or weeks or to fly back up to Massachusetts for business. It wasn't unusual for me to be at home alone several nights a week.

"Looks like it's gonna be just you and me kid," Harry said, and while his statement was probably meant to be comforting, a small knot began to form in my stomach. The thought made me uneasy. "Listen. You wanna get out of here and go grab a drink or something? Change of scenery would be good for you," he said.

"I really shouldn't. I'm trying to write a eulogy," I explained.

"I see. I'm not a detective or anything, but looked to me like you were playing on Facebook." He paused. "Should you really be doing that anyway … writing a eulogy?"

"I want to do this."

"You're better with words than I am. Jay will get a kick out of it. You up there in front of all those people saying something from that journal of yours ... the one you are always scribbling away in. Yea. That will make him happy."

"Why don't you see if Stella or Lanie want something? I'm sure one of my so-called babysitters needs to get out," I said quietly. I hadn't realized Harry knew about my journals.

"Yea. Sure. I'll go see." He paused as if he had something further to say but thought better of it.

....

I sat there in Jay's chair for hours, unsure of what to say. I started so many different versions of what I wanted to say, but none of the words I put down said exactly what I wanted to convey. How do you sum up a life in a couple moments? It was morbid, but I thought back to all the funerals or memorial services I had attended in my lifetime. The list was short. I had attended my mother's funeral when I was younger, the funeral of my grandmother on my father's side several years after that and Lanie's grandmother's funeral a couple years earlier. Nothing helped.

I spun around in the chair to look at the vast collection of books that sat on the large oak bookcases behind Jay's desk. Skimming over the titles, I found the book I was looking for. It was old and tattered and the pages had yellowed with age. Pulling it down, I gently flipped through its pages. This particular book had been mine by default. When I was younger, my mom had taken me to a pumpkin patch around Halloween. I was determined to pick the best pumpkin that year and I walked through that patch, picking up and inspecting each pumpkin. Under one particular pumpkin I found a book. My mom turned the book in to the older woman who was working the register. The woman said they would keep the book just in case someone returned to claim it, but if no one claimed it within the next two weeks, she would mail it to me. Sure enough, two weeks later, the book arrived in the mail with a short dedication to me, written on the inside cover. I was so excited I asked my mom to read to me from the book almost every night. The book was mostly poems and short stories and at that time I don't think I understood most of the tales. After she died, I put the book away for a long while. Now, I held the book in my hands, looking for guidance. As I flipped through its pages, a particular entry caught my eye, and as I read through it, I knew I had found what I was looking for: a way to say good-bye.

CHAPTER 8

....

"'When Tomorrow Starts Without Me' by David Romano," I started to say, my voice shaky as I opened the faded book to the page I had dog-eared the night before and set it on the podium. I could feel the tears stinging my eyes and I paused to take a ragged breath, trying to steady myself. I looked out into the sea of somber faces of friends and family. Taking one last, deep breath I started to read.

When tomorrow starts without me, and I'm not there to
    see;
If the sun should rise and find your eyes all filled with tears
    for me;
I wish so much you wouldn't cry the way you did today,
While thinking of the many things we didn't get to say.
I know how much you love me, as much as I love you,
And each time you think of me, I know you'll miss me, too;
But when tomorrow starts without me, please try to
    understand,
That an angel came and called my name and took me by
    the hand,
And said my place was ready in heaven far above,
And that I'd have to leave behind all those I dearly love.
But as I turned to walk away, a tear fell from my eye,

For all my life, I'd always thought I didn't want to die.

I had so much to live for and so much yet to do,

It seemed impossible that I was leaving you.

I thought of all the yesterdays, the good ones and the bad,

I thought of all the love we shared and all the fun we had.

If I could relive yesterday, I thought, just for a while,

I'd say good-bye and kiss you and maybe see your smile.

But then I fully realized that this could never be,

For emptiness and memories would take the place of me.

And when I thought of worldly things that I'd miss tomorrow,

I thought of you, and when I did, my heart was filled with sorrow.

But when I walked through heaven's gates, I felt so much at home.

When God looked down and smiled at me, from His great golden throne,

He said, "This is eternity and all I've promised you,

Today for life on Earth is past but here it starts anew.

I promise no tomorrow, but today will always last,

And since each day's the same day, there's no longing for the past.

But you have been faithful, so trusting and so true,

Though there were times you did some things you knew you shouldn't do.

But you have been forgiven and now at last you're free.

So won't you take my hand and share my life with me?"

So when tomorrow starts without me, don't think we're far apart,

For every time you think of me, I'm right here in your heart.

I closed the book and slowly walked back to my seat, passing by Jay's coffin and letting my hand trail along the outside edge of it. The church was silent except for the occasional sniffle or cough. I took my seat next to Stella, who reached over and grabbed my hand. I closed my eyes and let out a big sigh and started to cry.

....

CHAPTER 9

The only people left in the church were Harry, Stella, Lanie and I as Gary Swanford approached.

"Jill, we are going to move Jay back to the funeral home and prepare him for his final journey," he said. I nodded. I still hadn't left my seat in the front pew of the church.

"Do you need a minute?" he asked and I nodded again. Stella and Lanie both nudged me to move. I slowly got to my shaky feet and approached Jay's coffin one more time. A beautiful spray of yellow roses sat on the top of the coffin and the fragrance was overwhelming. I rested my hands on the coffin's shiny outer surface and leaned down and kissed it. I didn't have anything else left to say. I took a step back and nodded to Gary. He and several other men dressed in suits approached and rolled the coffin toward the side entrance. Stella and Lanie walked next to me as we passed through the front of the church with Harry in tow behind us.

The reception was only a few blocks from the church and we had decided to walk. The Draft was an old firehouse that had been converted into a bar and restaurant. It had become an establishment that Jay spent a lot of time in, especially during law school. We were the last to arrive and found that the restaurant was packed with our friends and family. In the entrance, Lanie and Stella had arranged a table full of pictures of Jay from his baby years to the present, along with a stack of cards on which people could leave their thoughts or favorite memories in lieu of a formal guestbook.

I sat at a table in the middle of the room with either Lanie or Stella by my side at all times. As I sat there, I observed all of our friends and family chatting, laughing and enjoying each other's company. Many snacked on the appetizers Lanie had preselected or drank Jay's favorite drink—Johnny Walker Red Label over a single large cube of ice with a lemon wedge—that Stella had arranged with the bartender to have in stock.

Slowly, the guests would all come by the table. They all wanted to talk about Jay and most shared their favorite memory or story. I just smiled and listened as Stella, Lanie or Harry continued to keep vigilance over me. People began to leave in specific groups. My coworkers were the first. The teachers and parents slowly gathered around and asked a couple questions before leaving.

"When do you think you will come back?" Jennifer Bentley, my principal, asked.

"I'm not sure now is the best time to discuss that," Lanie interjected.

"Of course. My apologies," Jennifer said before leaving.

Next was the handful of Jay's coworkers who had traveled down from Massachusetts. I had met them all once at a work function, but I couldn't remember their names. They seemed the most awkward and quickly gave their condolences. One guy, Denny, made arrangements with Stella to stop by the following day before his flight to collect Jay's work papers and laptop as they would need to be returned. Stella tried to confer with me, but I just shrugged my shoulders, indifferent to when they collected his belongings.

Peter and the few family members who attended left next. Most had traveled down together on a private chartered jet and would be leaving in the morning. All were very somber and quiet during the reception. Harry insisted on walking Peter out to his car so he could say some final words in private. Before he left, Peter gave me a big embrace and made me promise that we would see more of each other. When they walked out, I knew that would be the last time I saw Peter Greenfield.

Those left mingling in The Draft were the liveliest of all the guests, mostly because it consisted of Jay's law-school friends and Harry's police-force buddies. Both groups had a large overlap, given the type of work they each did, and many took the occasion to catch up with each other and share stories. Others let off steam from the job and some seemed to be drowning their sorrows. Harry spent a large portion of time mingling with everyone, thanking them for coming and sharing many shots in Jay's honor. Stella also did her fair share of mingling with the law-school buddies as she had shared classes with half of them and had probably dated the other half.

The bartender announced that the bar was getting ready to shut down and the rowdy bunch ordered one last round of shots.

"I really don't think she is in any state to be doing bar shots," Lanie said when a friend of Jay's offered me a shot.

"Lanie, you're never going to win against this group," Harry said, slurring his words.

"Yea, Lanie, you're not going to win," Stella chided.

Lanie shrugged her shoulders in a suit-yourself kind of way.

"In Jay's honor," I said. Shots were being handed out to everyone left in the bar. Even Lanie finally caved and took one. I was ushered into the center of this large group and with everyone holding up their shot, someone shouted "Speech."

"To a man of integrity," one person shouted from behind me.

"To a man of honor," added a lawyer named Nicky.

"To the best damn lawyer south of the Mississippi," another shouted and several chuckled.

"To a good friend," another added.

"Best of friends," Harry corrected.

"He was a stubborn SOB," an officer added.

"He was a fierce competitor. He hated losing," added another lawyer I didn't recognize. Again, this comment drew chuckles.

"He was the man we should all strive to be," added a lawyer named Billie.

"I'll drink to that," several shouted and we raised our drinks a little higher.

"To Jay," I said to several cheers and we emptied our glasses.

Everyone started to leave. Many waved in my direction or gave my shoulder a squeeze as they passed by the table I was sitting at. Lanie made sure that one of the officers gave Harry a ride home as he was in no shape to drive. Lanie shook hands with the final guest and started to clean up the pictures, while Stella squared the tab with the bartender. When we were finally ready to leave, Stella called the car service she had ordered and we piled inside.

"Jill?" Lanie asked when we were sitting in the car.

"Hm …"

"Jay was a great guy. I'm so sorry."

Her sudden expression of grief surprised me. I just nodded my head and squeezed her hand.

"He always treated you right and he treated us right, which made him alright with me," Stella said, slurring her words a little bit.

I reached over and grabbed her hand with my free hand. "Thank you both. I wouldn't have made it these five days without you. I love you both," I said.

We rode the rest of the way in silence.

CHAPTER 10

....

Saturday and Sunday went by in a daze. I moved from the bed, to the sofa and back again. The only exception was Saturday afternoon when Lanie insisted that it was unseasonably warm for October and suggested I sit outside to get some sun on my face. Harry stopped by at one point to see if there was anything we needed, but Stella and Lanie ushered him out, telling him that I needed my space. Stella and Lanie kept trying to get me to eat, but I refused and by Monday morning Lanie was looking at me as if I were a glass doll that would break at any moment. I could tell that Lanie and Stella were spending more time whispering about what was almost certainly my well-being, because they would stop abruptly when I entered the room, but I didn't care. Nothing seemed to matter anymore.

....

Tuesday morning was different. Stella marched into the bedroom at nine in the morning and threw the blankets back.

"Time to get up sleepy head," she declared.

"Are you insane?" I said, grabbing for the blankets.

"Nope, but if you don't shape up, your good friend Lanie is going to ship you off to some crazy hospital," Stella said.

"No, she's not, and you're going to leave me alone," I said.

"Lanie, will you help me?" Stella called down the hallway.

"Sure. What do you need?" Lanie said, coming into the room.

"Jill needs to shower and get dressed. I was hoping you could help me pick her up and put her in the shower."

"Fully clothed?"

"Fully clothed."

"You wouldn't dare," I mumbled back. I was fuming, why couldn't they just leave me alone. Lanie grabbed both my ankles and Stella grabbed my arms and together they dragged me into the bathroom, lifting me over the edge of the tub and placing me gently in the tub.

"If you wanted to lose some weight, I could think of better ways," Stella commented.

"Seriously, you can't do this. Let me go," I shouted as I tried to wiggle free but it was impossible.

"Seriously, we can do this and we will," Stella said as she turned on the shower. I started to scream as the cold water drenched my clothes. Each time I tried to stand, one of them pushed me back down. "Are you done feeling sorry for yourself?" Stella asked.

"Sorry for myself? Fuck you!" I screamed back. Who did they think they were? My husband had just died.

"Jill, this is for your own good," Lanie insisted.

I didn't comment as the cold water continued to cascade down over me. I was having trouble concentrating on anything other than my chattering teeth.

"Jill, we aren't going to let you become a zombie. You need to start moving forward," Stella said. I was about to protest when she added, "a little bit … every day."

"If I agree, can I get out of this shower?" I asked, my body shaking.

"I think you're agreeing too quickly and you don't mean it," Stella said.

"I agree," Lanie said.

"But we will let you shower," Stella added, turning the water off. They both gave me one final look and left the bathroom.

I slowly stood up and stripped off the cold wet clothes. This time I showered with hot water, dressed, and headed downstairs. Perhaps I could play pretend until they both left?

"There she is, all shiny and new," Stella said, teasingly.

Lanie laughed and I scowled.

"Now what?" I asked. I was acting like a sullen teenager, but I didn't care.

"Now you eat and then we go to Swanford and Sons," Lanie said.

"Why do we have to go to Swanford and Sons?" I whined.

"To pick up Jay," Stella said in a very matter-of-fact voice.

"Pick him up?"

"His ashes are ready," Lanie said.

"Oh."

It was after one in the afternoon by the time Stella and Lanie could convince me to head to the funeral home. When we arrived, there were several cars in the parking lot.

"I hope we're not interrupting," Lanie said.

"We did have an appointment earlier this morning, but Mrs. Greenfield here was too busy throwing a fit," Stella commented. I stuck my tongue out at her.

"Be nice," Lanie cautioned.

"This is me being nice," Stella said.

"Let's get this over with," I said and trudged up the steps.

Once inside, we could hear several voices off in the distance, so we decided to wait on one of the sofas in the lobby.

"Ladies." We heard Gary address us after several minutes.

"Sorry we are late. We had some ... trouble," Stella said after Lanie elbowed her.

"No problem. Just wait here a minute." He motioned he would be right back and left.

As he turned to leave, another man escorted a woman and her children into the lobby and told them that Gary would be right with them. I stared at them. The woman appeared to be in her mid-thirties. She wore jeans, a sweatshirt and running shoes as she carried two children's coats and a very large bag from which toys were sticking out. Her daughter appeared to be about 10 years old and wore a similar outfit to that of her mother. The little boy was wearing jeans and a T-shirt and was climbing over all the furniture. I could see myself in this woman. In another five or six years I wanted to be this woman. Jay and I had recently started talking about having a family. We had always wondered about the best time to start one. We would ask ourselves whether we had enough in savings, if our jobs were stable enough, how many children we would have. I sighed over the endless possibilities.

As my mind wandered over the idea of carrying Jay's child and how that could now never happen, I realized that I had missed my last period. Terror, panic and hope suddenly electrified me.

"We need to go home," I whispered to Stella. I could no longer sit still. There was a chance that I could be pregnant. I did the math in my head again, noting I was six days late.

"You can wait like five more minutes and then we will go." Stella rolled her eyes.

"You don't understand—" I started to say but was interrupted by Gary coming back down the hallway with a small, unassuming, gun-metal-gray canister and a small, brown paper bag in his hand.

"Mr. Greenfield," he said, handing the canister to me and turning to hand the bag to Stella. I didn't know what the right reaction should be after being handed my husband's ashes, so I decided to just nod.

"What's in the bag?" Lanie inquired.

"Mr. Greenfield's wedding band," Gary replied. I again just nodded in his direction. "Till death do us part" seemed to take on a new meaning.

"Is everything settled with the bill?" Stella inquired.

"Oh yes, everything has been cleared. It has been a pleasure," he said and then turned to help the woman and her children.

"Okay. Great. Let's go." Both Lanie and Stella shrugged and we headed toward the car.

As soon as Stella pulled up in front of the house, I raced out of the car and into the house and up the stairs. I slammed the bathroom door shut, locking it behind me. I could hear Lanie and Stella shouting after me, but I didn't care. I rummaged through the cabinet, looking for the pregnancy test I had gotten several weeks prior when we had started talking about having a baby. I ripped open the packaging, quickly skimming through the directions. After following the directions, I sat the stick down on the counter, waiting the obligatory three minutes for either a positive or negative sign. A pounding on the door startled me.

"What the hell is going on, Jill?" Stella demanded from the other side.

"Just a minute," I called back. I could hear her pause and mumble something to Lanie.

"Come on, Jill. Unlock the door," Lanie called through the door.

"Really. Just give me a minute," I called back. I must not have been very convincing, as I could again hear them whispering back and forth. I glanced down at the test again, thinking that three minutes must have passed. Slowly, the indicator on the stick started to light up. My heart sank and a low moan escaped my lips as I sank to the floor with the indicator stick in my hand.

"Jill, what's happening?" Lanie was now calling a little more frantically while banging on the door.

Hot tears streamed down my face and my shoulders heaved up and down.

"Jill," Stella yelled. I could hear them, but I couldn't reply as each sob ripped through my body, making me incapable of communication.

"Lanie, is there anything to open this door?" Stella shouted frantically.

I could hear them shuffling outside the door. It sounded as if someone were playing with the lock from the outside. Finally, the door burst open and Stella stood there with a butter knife in her hand. Horrified, she looked at me. "What the hell is going on?" she repeated.

"Jill?" Lanie rushed to my side and tried to check my vitals. Someone tried to pry the indicator stick from my hand, but I wouldn't let it go.

"What's in your hand?" Lanie asked.

"It's negative," I bellowed, burying my face in the bathmat.

"What's negative?" I could hear Stella whisper.

"This!" I finally said, shoving the stick in Lanie's face.

"A pregnancy test?" Lanie and Stella both said, shocked.

"Well, I didn't see that coming," Stella said, sitting down on the edge of the bathtub. Lanie started to rub my back until the heaving slowed down and my breathing half returned to normal.

"Jill, why don't you tell us what is going on," Lanie said quietly.

I nodded slowly, sniffling and wiping the tears from my face.

"When we were at the funeral home, I saw the lady and her two kids and I thought that would have been me sooner or later and then I realized that I was late with my period and that *really* could be me." I paused to sniffle again. "I had so much hope that maybe I was pregnant and then there would still be a piece of Jay left in this world."

"Oh Jill … it doesn't work that way," Lanie said.

"It could have," I said, waving the indicator stick in her face.

"Jay is gone and you can't bring him back," Lanie added.

"But a baby …" I started.

"Wouldn't solve anything," Stella said, finishing my sentence for me. I just nodded and adjusted my position on the floor so that my head now rested in Lanie's lap instead of on the floor.

"You gave us a really big scare," Stella said.

I crinkled up my forehead in confusion.

"Lanie thought you were racing in here to take a bunch of pills or something," Stella said.

"What?" I asked in disbelief.

"Well, in my defense, you have been supermoody and depressed … Rightfully so," Lanie added when I made a face at her. "But something changed at the funeral home, which I now know was false hope, but at the time I thought it was you reaching your breaking point over receiving Jay's ashes."

"Jay's ashes! Where are they?" I asked in a panic, trying to sit up. I had forgotten about the ashes in my rush to get upstairs.

"Calm down. They are safely on the kitchen table," Stella said as Lanie pushed me back down.

"When we got home, you raced out of the car like a bat out of hell and locked yourself in the bathroom," Stella continued.

"You didn't really give us anything to go on so we just had to assume the worst," Lanie said, finishing Stella's words. The three of us sat there for a while in silence while I thought through the events of the previous couple hours—and week.

"This has been the craziest week of my entire life," I finally said.

"Agreed," Lanie and Stella said at the same time.

We all stopped to look at each other and then we all burst out laughing. Nothing about the situation was funny, but something about it made laughter the only solution.

"Look, I know I have been sad and all those things you said about me are probably true, but I wasn't trying to kill myself. I really just let myself believe that maybe the family Jay and I dreamed about could still come true."

"It would never be the family you wanted. Jay wouldn't be there," Stella pointed out.

"You're right. I know you're right, but at the time it didn't seem to matter," I said trying to defend my crazy antics.

"Which is fine but you need to communicate that with us, Jill," Lanie said. "We don't know what is going on with you right now," she added.

"Fair enough," I said, yawning.

"Time for bed?" Stella asked and I nodded. Stella helped me stand up and took the pregnancy test that I was still clutching in my hand. She stood over the trash holding it out in one hand and looking at me for confirmation. I nodded that it was okay and she then unceremoniously threw it away.

"Jill, you don't really want a baby anyway," she said as we made our way to the bedroom.

"Why is that, Stella?"

"Well, it will ruin your figure and then for the next 18 years, it would whine and complain. Eventually it will learn to talk back and spend all your money ... Who wants that?"

"You're right ... Who wants that when I have all that already ... You are my friend after all," I said, grinning at her.

She considered my statement and shrugged. "I can't argue with you there." We all broke into laughter one more time and the tension of the evening seemed to dissipate. I quickly changed in my pj's and crawled into bed, motioning for Lanie and Stella to join me. They both sat on either side of me, quietly talking. I curled up in between the two of them and drifted off to sleep to the slow and constant hum of their voices, knowing that tomorrow was going to be a better day. Each day was going to get a little better.

CHAPTER 11

···

I t was around 10 in the morning when I finally stretched out, rolling to Jay's side of the bed. With all that had happened in the previous 10 days it was still hard to process that he wasn't coming back. Sighing, I got up, dressed and headed downstairs where I could hear Lanie and Stella moving about. As I passed by the front door, I saw two suitcases sitting there.

"Someone going somewhere?" I asked as I walked into the kitchen. To my surprise Harry was sitting at the table with a plate of eggs and toast in front of him.

"I have to head back to New York today," Stella said as she leaned against the counter, holding a cup of coffee.

"Jill, we all need to talk to you," Lanie said from her place by the stove where she was finishing up making what looked like a breakfast omelet.

"Alright," I said, cautiously sitting down at the table.

"We are really worried about you," Stella said and Harry nodded in agreement.

"What do you know?" I snapped at him.

"We told him … everything," Lanie said, sitting down at the table with her breakfast.

"What!" I couldn't believe what was going on. I started to stand. "Sit back down," Stella demanded and I instantly complied.

"We don't think you should be alone for awhile. The three of us have arranged it so that someone will always be with you. I am going to stay through the end of this week while Stella goes back to New York," Lanie said.

"My shift changes to day shift next week, so I'm gonna move into the guest room and stay for a couple weeks," Harry mumbled through a mouthful of eggs.

"Then, at Thanksgiving, we are going to see how things are going," Stella commented.

"This is really unnecessary," I said looking at each of them. In reality my mind was reeling. I didn't need babysitters. I needed time to be left alone.

"We all agree, that at least for now this is what is best for you," Lanie said and Stella nodded.

With that, my fate was decided. Lanie and Harry finished eating breakfast and Stella jabbered about a big case she was working on and how time consuming the trial was and now she was behind in work and needed to catch up.

"Sorry to disrupt your life," I commented at one point.

"Jill, I didn't mean it that way," she said defensively.

"It wasn't really a convenient time for Jay to die, was it? I'll try and remember that for next time," I said as I stood.

I headed back upstairs. I could hear Stella calling after me and someone telling her to forget it. Upstairs, I searched in the closet for one of Jay's T-shirts. I pulled it out and buried my nose in it, grateful that it still smelled like him. Shirt in hand, I crawled into bed and dozed off.

....

My life fell into a simple routine during the next week on what I dubbed "Lanie watch." During the day, I would sleep and ignore whatever Lanie had to say. At night after Lanie went to bed, I would get up and wander through the house, often sitting in Jay's office and staring into space. Then, as the sun would start to rise, I would bring myself back to bed. Some mornings I would be pulling the covers back over myself as Lanie's alarm clock in the other room would start to sound. After several days, Lanie came into my room and sat down on the bed.

"Jill, today's my last day," she said tentatively.

"What day is it?" I asked through the covers.

"Sunday."

"Jay's been gone two weeks," I commented and rolled away from Lanie.

"Jill, Harry will be here any minute. He is going to stay in the guest room." She paused. "Jill you need to think about Jay's ashes and his final resting place."

"Sure," I mumbled through the sheets.

She left the room. At some point later in the day I heard the doorbell ring and voices down the stairs. Changing of the guard. I rolled over and drifted back to sleep.

The next thing I knew, Harry was standing in my room with a towel wrapped around his waist. He was yelling at me.

"What the hell, Jill," he screamed. I sat up and looked at him in confusion. I glanced at the clock next to my bedside table and I saw that it was almost six in the morning.

"What?" I asked, my voice hoarse.

"There's no f-ing water. When was the last time you paid a bill around here?" He stopped and stared at me. "When was the last time you did anything around here? I'm going to be late for work now. You better fix this today. If not, I'm packing your skinny ass up and we are moving into my apartment," he said, storming out of my room. I continued to sit there and stare at the door as he fumbled around the house. Soon I heard the front door slam and I knew I was finally alone.

I crawled out of bed and made my way to the bathroom. I turned the water faucet on. A little bit of water trickled out and the pipes began to make clanging noises. Quickly, I turned off the water and made my way downstairs to the office. Jay had been in charge of paying all our bills. It was an arrangement we had had since the beginning of our marriage. We both had different views on how to pay bills and what would be a reasonable amount of spending money each month. So we decided, very early on, that we would put our monthly earnings in a joint account and Jay would pay the bills. Our other monthly expenditures would be paid for in cash.

Now I stood in the office, unsure of so many things. I wasn't even sure I knew of all the bills we had. I looked around for Jay's computer, hoping to log on to the Internet and find the name of our local water company. It was only after I stared at his empty desk that I realized his company had already come by to take the computer. I now vaguely recalled a conversation Stella had tried to have with me at Jay's funeral. Rummaging through the closet, I found an older laptop that I had used in college. As I set it up on the desk and let it charge up, I looked through the small filing cabinet Jay kept in his office. The words on many of the folder tabs didn't make any sense to me. They referred to investments and financial matters that Jay was always playing around with. I pulled out the files for the water, electricity, and cable services, insurance, mortgage, and so on. Soon I found myself sitting on the floor with a large stack of files next to me. I felt overwhelmed. I got up and went to the kitchen to make myself a cup of coffee.

Halfway to the kitchen I realized if there was no water, there was not going to be any coffee. My stomach rumbled slightly and I wondered if there was any food in the house. For the first time in weeks I was actually hungry. A quick scan of the fridge revealed that very few things were still edible. Locating my cell phone, I called the small bakery down the street to place an order of bagels and cream cheese and coffee. I figured that would be a good start. The woman at the bakery informed me that they were short-staffed that morning and couldn't deliver. I assured her it wouldn't be a problem and that I would be there in 10 to 15 minutes. I checked on the laptop and found it was still charging and rebooting. I went upstairs to change into cleaner clothes. I surveyed the bedroom. There were now piles of clothes covering every surface and in the corner still sat the clothes Jay had pulled out to wear several weeks earlier. I couldn't deal with it. I put on some jeans along with one of Jay's Wake Forest sweatshirts and looked at myself in the bathroom mirror for the first time in many weeks. I didn't recognize the woman staring back at me. My long chestnut-colored hair was matted and greasy in a sloppy bun. My skin was paler than normal and my eyes seemed too large. I had lost a considerable amount of weight from my already small frame. Not remembering when I had last brushed my teeth, I rinsed my mouth with mouthwash and applied a little bit of mascara to my lashes. Back in the bedroom, I found my Boston Red Sox cap and did my best to hide my untamed locks. The next 10 minutes I spent trying to locate simple things such as my sneakers, purse and house keys. After finding them scattered around the house, I headed down the street.

When I came back from the bakery, I devoured a bagel and a pastry. I felt exhausted and lay down on the sofa and drifted off to sleep. The sound of my phone awoke me from my slumber.

"Hello," I said without looking at the ID.

"Any luck with water?" Harry shouted.

"Working on it," I mumbled.

"Remember what I said: if there is no water, then we are packing up and moving to my apartment." Harry hung up the phone.

Harry's apartment was a loft-style apartment above a bar called Libby's in downtown Greensboro. He had a bed, sofa, TV and small table that sat two. He just wasn't one for furnishings or decorating. I shuddered at the thought of having to stay there. I got up from the sofa and headed back into the office. The laptop appeared to be fully charged, and I was able to connect to the Internet. At least that was still working. I pulled the file labeled "Water" and found a couple sheets of paper, but nothing gave me any information about our account. I was able to find a number and I called the company. After going through the automated menu several times, I was finally able to get a real person on the phone.

"Greensboro Water Company. This is Andrea. How can I help you?" a youngish woman said.

"Um, yes, my water was turned off this morning. I need to check on my account and possibly pay my bill," I stammered.

"Sure. I can help you with that. Account number please?" she said.

"I don't have an account number."

"Name on the account?"

"Jay Greenfield." I was guessing.

"For security purposes can you provide me with the address as well as last four of the Social Security number?" she asked. I was able to give her the address, but I didn't know the last four digits of Jay's Social Security number off the top of my head.

"Ma'am, I can't help you without that information," Andrea replied when I said I didn't have the last four numbers of the Social Security number.

"Is there anything else that I can provide you with?" I asked.

"No. Sorry. That is the policy. You can just have Mr. Greenfield call us himself and we can help him with this issue."

"I'm his wife. I live at this address. Why can't I just pay the bill?" I asked, getting frustrated with this line of questioning.

"It's the policy that only authorized people are able to make inquiries or make payments on an account," Andrea said.

"Andrea, Mr. Greenfield died in a tragic accident several weeks ago. I don't have the account number, and I'm just trying to piece things together. Is there any way you can help me?" I asked as the tension in my voice increased.

"Do you have any proof or documentation of his passing?" Andrea asked quietly.

"What?" I asked, slamming my hand on the desk. "Do you want me to bring you his ashes? They are sitting on my kitchen table, so that wouldn't be a problem. Maybe you would like to speak with the SOB that hit him with his car or maybe the doctor who operated on him to make sure he is dead," I said, raising my voice.

"I'm sorry, ma'am. It's our policy," Andrea said very quietly.

"Andrea, can I speak with your supervisor?" I asked, rubbing my temple with my free hand.

"Yes. Please hold." Andrea sounded grateful to hand me off to another individual. After I had listened to elevator music for several minutes, an older man spoke.

"Greensboro Water Company. This is Bruce. How can I help you?" he said.

"Bruce, my name is Jill Greenfield. My water was turned off this morning," I said.

"That shouldn't be a problem, ma'am," he said. He clearly had not received the whole story from Andrea.

"You would think. The account was in my husband's name, and I don't know the account number or any of the security passwords," I said.

"Well, you can just have Mr. Greenfield call us back and add you as a user so you don't run into this problem again," he said, seemingly pleased he had found a solution to my problem.

"Why didn't I think of that?" I said.

"Well, if there is anything else we can help you with?" Bruce asked, clearly in a hurry to get me off the phone.

"Yes, just one more thing," I said. "What if Mr. Greenfield is dead? How do you suggest I get him to call you back with that information?" I could hear the intake of breath on his end.

"Bruce, you still there?" I asked.

"Yes, ma'am. We will need official paperwork—" he started to say.

"Yes, Andrea and you keep telling me about this official paperwork. My husband is dead, not on vacation or in jail. What kind of paperwork do you need? I just need my water turned back on. I can give you a payment over the phone right now if you will just take it."

"Do you have a death certificate?" he asked.

Death certificate? I hadn't really paid attention to anything Stella or Lanie had said over the previous couple weeks and I wasn't sure if

I had one or not. Surely, someone would have mentioned it to me if I did?

"No. I don't have one of those. Do you know where I can get one?" I asked.

"Ma'am—"

"Bruce, is there anyone else I can speak to? I would rather resolve this over the phone. If I have to come down there, you aren't going to be happy about having a grieving widow in your lobby and your company refusing to turn her water on over paperwork. How will people react when they hear this story?" I asked with a slight smile. I knew that Jay would have been proud of my closing statement.

"Hold please," Bruce said very quickly, and I again waited listening to more elevator music.

"Greensboro Water Company. This is Beth," a third person now answered.

"Beth, this is Jill Greenfield—"

"Mrs. Greenfield, we are very sorry to hear about your husband. What can I do to help?" she asked.

Finally!

Relief set in. I quickly re-explained my situation to her. She confirmed my account and switched the information over, letting me know that when I received the death certificate, they would need a copy on file. With my bank card I then paid her the $24.87 that was due on the account, and she informed me that the water would be turned back on within the hour. I thanked her for her time and we ended the call.

Looking across the floor at the large stack of files of all the other companies I needed to call, I foresaw similar conversations with each of them. I picked the phone back up and called Stella.

"Hey," I said.

"Hey."

"So, does Jay have a death certificate?" I asked.

"Yes. It was issued at the hospital and then sent off to be processed. You should be receiving the official copy any day now. Why do you ask?"

I told her about my conversation with the Greensboro Water company.

"Oh, that's rough, Jill. Sorry to hear that. But I'm glad you took care of it."

I could tell she was just glad I was doing something—anything—at the moment.

"Okay. Well, that's all I have," I added, about to hang up.

"Oh wait, Jill. Paul Wellon called again and asked when we would have time to go over Jay's will and affairs."

"Remind me. Who is Paul Wellon?" I asked.

"Mr. Lawyer."

"Oh, right. Can we put him off a little longer?"

"Sure thing. I'll get it done."

"Thanks, Stella."

I hung up the phone. It was just past four when I looked at the clock. I was pretty sure that, pending any big cases, Harry would be home soon. I called and ordered two pizzas for dinner and as I hung up the phone with Domino's, I heard the water turn on in the upstairs bathroom. Harry must have left it on after his attempted shower that morning. A slight smile of satisfaction spread across my face.

....

CHAPTER 12

Things with Harry settled into a routine as they had with Lanie. Every morning I could hear him fumbling around the house as he got ready for work. I would stay in bed until the soft aroma of coffee floated upstairs some time after he had left. Then I would get up and shower and make my way downstairs and fix myself a cup of coffee. I would make a mental list of small things I wanted to accomplish that day. So far, I had finally cleaned the kitchen and established a seminormal grocery-shopping routine. Each day I dealt with another company as I tried to pay bills and get things switched over to my name. I figured I had enough money in savings to pay our bills for a couple months until the insurance money came in or I decided to go back to work. Eventually, the death certificate came in the mail, just as Stella had promised. That cleared the way at many companies and I found myself faxing copies of that document on a daily basis to someone new.

The list grew smaller and one day it merely involved getting the cable reconnected. Only Harry, of course, had noticed. The previous night, as he tried to watch the game on TV after work, he found there was no service. I had taken to fixing a small dinner for Harry and myself. We would sit around the table and eat mostly in silence.

Harry never felt like talking about his day and I didn't have anything to say either. It seemed to be the perfect arrangement.

For that night's dinner I pan-fried two pieces of chicken with red potatoes and some green beans. I had just finished setting the table when Harry came in through the front door.

"Hey," I called as he entered.

"Hey," he called back as he headed up stairs to change. When he finally came down, he was dressed in jeans and a faded orange T-shirt.

"Smells great," he added, coming around the kitchen table to embrace me in a hug.

Well, that's new, I thought.

In the weeks when we had started this fake domestic life together it was the first time he had showed any physical affection for me.

"Rough day?" I asked.

"You couldn't imagine," he said as he filled his plate and carried it into the living room.

"You are eating in there tonight?" I asked, again confused.

"Ya. I hope you don't mind. There's a big game on."

"No, not at all," I said, picking up my own plate and joining him in the living room. "You would be glad to know, then, that the cable was turned back on."

"Oh, I already checked. I called the cable company on my way home to see if it had been done." He didn't take his eyes off the screen.

What?

"Are you checking up on me?" I asked.

"No. Just making sure we would have the game."

"We? Are we expecting visitors?" I asked, again trying to hide my confusion.

"No … I mean … we … you and me," he said as he tuned me out to focus on the football game.

Over the years, I had watched endless games with Jay and Harry always asking a million questions about the rules or calls on the field. Feeling drained from the tension radiating off Harry and his confusing behavior, I sighed and gave up. I had noticed that Harry was beginning to make himself more at home in the last couple days. I could have sworn I saw him bring over a box of pictures at one point to set up in the guest room. I just continued to shrug off his behavior. I was enjoying Harry's company more than that of Stella and Lanie at that moment. Harry never pried into my day or how I felt. All he required was food on the table when he got home and having all the utilities working. For the most part he left me alone. I struggled to keep my eyes open during the game and soon gave in to my drooping eyelids. I was startled awake as Harry struggled to carry me upstairs. I started to squirm.

"You fell asleep. I was just bringing you to bed," he mumbled as he set me on my feet on top of the landing.

"Thanks. I got it," I mumbled and awkwardly walked into my bedroom. I was feeling freaked out by Harry's sudden changes in behavior. I waited for his bedroom light to go off and I crept back downstairs in search of my phone.

"Lanie?"

"Yea, Jill. Are you okay?" she mumbled.

I could see from the kitchen stove clock that it was after midnight.

"Sorry it's so late," I began to say.

Just then, the lights upstairs turned on and I could hear Harry coming back down the stairs.

"Never mind, Lanie. Sorry to call so late." I quickly hung up the phone and reached for a glass of water as Harry entered the kitchen, turning on the light and temporarily blinding me.

"What are you doing?" he grumbled.

"I was thirsty."

I held up the glass. He waited for me to fill it up and followed me back upstairs, lingering in the doorway to my bedroom.

"Are you having any trouble sleeping?" he asked.

"Not really," I lied.

"Need me to stay in here until you fall asleep?" he asked, moving toward Jay's side of the bed.

"No," I nearly shouted. "I mean, you have to work in the morning. I think I will manage," I said more calmly.

"Suit yourself," he said and left the room.

I quickly closed the door and locked it behind him. I hadn't noticed my hand was trembling slightly over Harry's unusual behavior. Was it just tonight? Maybe some case had really gotten to him. I crawled into bed and reached over to turn the light off before deciding it might be more comforting to leave it on and rolled over and went to sleep.

The next morning I waited for Harry to leave for work as usual before climbing out of bed. I crept across the hallway and into the guest bedroom. I could see piles of clothes all over the floor and several toiletry items out on the dresser. I also saw several framed pictures that were not mine, sitting on the dresser. As I got closer, I could see pictures of Harry and Jay and pictures of Harry and me. Some showed the three of us together. I thought it was weird he had brought his own pictures over, but I shrugged it off. I was not one to judge unusual behavior during the previous couple of weeks. I made my way back downstairs and called Lanie.

"What do you mean he's giving you a weird vibe?" Lanie asked.

"I don't know. He has just started to act differently ... almost ..." I paused.

"Almost what?"

"I don't know. Maybe it's just me. I haven't been the most perceptive lately. He's probably fine. It's just me."

"I don't know, Jill. Death of a loved one causes people to do crazy things and it doesn't always happen right after someone passes away. Sometimes these things manifest themselves over time."

"That's crazy. This is Harry. But I could use a change of company. When does the next changing of the guard take place?"

"Jill, you know—"

"Hey, I know. I'm just asking."

"Actually, next week is Thanksgiving, so Stella and I were thinking of coming down to visit."

"Is it really Thanksgiving?"

"Yes ..." She paused. "Have you given any thought to Jay's ashes?"

"Kinda," I said.

"Really?" Lanie couldn't hide the shock in her voice.

"I know I want to scatter them somewhere on Oak Island. I just don't know the details yet."

In truth, I had given it too much thought. It was all I ever thought about. I had moved Jay's ashes all over the house in the previous couple of weeks. They had finally been settled on the mantel, right where I hadn't wanted to put them.

"What if we go at Thanksgiving?" Lanie asked.

"We could do that. It would give me something to set up."

"I'll tell Stella about the slight change in plans. We can all meet at your place on Wednesday evening and then head that way on Thanksgiving morning," Lanie suggested.

"Yea. That would work. How long are you both staying?"

"I'm staying until Sunday but Stella thought she might stay for a week or so after the holiday. She wanted to head to the outlets to start her Christmas shopping, but she said she also had some work she needed to do that involved the Wake library."

"Okay."

Stella was a shopping addict and it didn't surprise me she wanted to start Christmas shopping. The only difference was that Christmas shopping to Stella usually involved her buying more things for herself than others.

"See you in a couple days then." Lanie rushed off the phone, saying her next client was waiting.

I headed back into the office in search of pictures. An idea was starting to form and I needed to find some pictures Jay always talked about. I looked for them for the next hour before I gave up. I had remembered that several months earlier Jay had mentioned that he was packing up some of our books and pictures and putting them into storage. He claimed that he needed more office space for his things. I had suggested we put them in the guest bedroom or attic, but he had insisted that getting a storage space. I thought Harry might know the answers to my questions and decided to wait until he got home.

It was after seven when Harry came home from work. I had given up waiting for him and eaten dinner without putting his food in the microwave to keep it warm. I was curled up on the sofa reading *The Great Gatsby* for the fifth or sixth time while Sinatra crooned quietly in the background.

"Really? You too?" he asked when he came down the stairs after changing.

"Me too, what?" I asked, setting my book down.

"This oldie crap." He waved his hand in the air referring to my musical tastes.

"I happen to like Frank."

"I always told Jay this stuff was for old-timers." He went into the kitchen, looking for his dinner.

"In the microwave," I said as I got up and turned off the music. "How was work?"

"It was good. We caught a big case toward the end of my shift, so I stayed on to help the boys out."

"I talked to Lanie today. We discussed our Thanksgiving plans."

"Oh yea? No one bothered to call and tell me," he said, taking his plate from the microwave. He went into the living room to turn the TV on.

"I'm trying to tell you," I said, trailing behind him like a puppy. "Anyway, Stella and Lanie are coming over Wednesday night and we are leaving Thursday for Oak Island. I'm going to spread Jay's ashes out there." I looked at him.

"I'm coming too then," he said.

"Really? Don't you need to work?" I hadn't thought that Harry might want to come and I wasn't really thrilled at the idea of him coming. Something felt odd about the entire thing.

"I'll get my schedule changed around. I'm coming."

"Fine. You're coming," I confirmed. "Oh, I did have a question. I was looking for some pictures of Jay from when he was a kid and I couldn't find any, but I remember him telling me that some of his best memories with his parents were ..." I trailed off, waiting for Harry to finish my statement.

"Fishing?" He looked confused.

"Yes, that's it! I remember a big white boat and him standing there, but I couldn't place the context. Thanks!" I got up and raced into the office, booting up the old laptop to do some research.

CHAPTER 13

W e all piled into my old Jeep early Thursday morning. Harry was driving and Lanie sat up front to help with directions. Stella and I stretched out in the back with Jay's ashes, which were securely wedged between my purse and pillows on the floor. We had had a lengthy argument earlier that morning over the best place to put them and I finally put my foot down and made a decision that effectively ended the arguing.

"Where are we staying?" Stella asked when we finally hit the road.

"We are staying at this small bed and breakfast by the beach. Jay and I never got the chance to stay there, but we wanted to. The lady who runs the place was very excited to have us and she will be cooking a large dinner tonight," I told everyone, recalling how very excited Mrs. Kendrich had been when I had made the reservations late the previous week. "Then tomorrow we have a fishing boat chartered for four hours in the late afternoon. We are going to try our hand at fishing and then at sunset we are going to spread Jay's ashes in the ocean," I added. Jay often talked about growing up near or on the water and Oak Island had been our get-away, so it was the perfect marriage of his two loves.

"Really? Fishing?" Stella made a face showing her dislike.

"You don't have to go," I said.

Harry mumbled something from the front seat. I kicked the back of his seat with my foot and just smiled at Stella. Harry had grown increasing distant and moody since our conversation the previous week. I was starting to worry about him. Perhaps Lanie had been correct in her assessment. Stella and Lanie settled in and chatted about work as we made the drive out to the coast. As we crossed the bridge into Oak Island, I felt myself relax. The island had always felt like home. Jay and I had even dreamed about getting a beach house out there—someday.

We arrived at the bed and breakfast a little after one in the afternoon. Like most houses near the beach, it was situated on stilts several feet above the ground. The house looked to have three stories and was painted a pale yellow color. A small wooden sign on the side of the house read, "Seaside Escapes." We unpacked the car and made our way up the stairs. Surprisingly, Mrs. Kendrich said that, with us checking in, there would be a full house this extended weekend. We had arranged for Stella and Lanie to share the room with the queen-sized bed and Harry and I would share the room with the twin beds.

Mrs. Kendrich was an older lady in her late fifties or early sixties. She had lived on the island her whole life. She warmly greeted us, giving us a small tour of the house and letting us know that dinner would be promptly at three o'clock. The house was already filled with the wonderful smell of baked goods. I had no doubt that dinner was going to be delicious. We had a couple hours to settle in and freshen up after our morning travel.

"That was the best meal I have eaten in a long time," Lanie said. The rest of us nodded in agreement. We had just finished eating dinner and now sat on the back porch overlooking the ocean. Stella was sipping a glass of red wine. Lanie was finishing her glass of white wine and Harry was nursing a beer. I held fast to my bottle of water as I tucked the blanket Mrs. Kendrich had given me over my lap. I looked out at the view. It was the most calming thing I had seen in weeks. The four of us just sat there in silence as the sun dipped down over the horizon. We all decided to call it an early night and headed to bed. Breakfast was going to be served at nine and then we had a couple hours before we needed to meet up with Jamie Prescott, captain of the *Lady Grace*, who would take us on our voyage.

....

The next morning, after breakfast, I dressed in a warm pair of knee-high socks, jeans and a chunky wool sweater. After lacing up my hiking boots and pulling on a knit cap, I headed off for a walk down the beach, solo. Harry, Stella and Lanie all offered to accompany me, but I needed some time on my own. I mindlessly walked down the beach until I came upon a wooden pier. The pier was mostly deserted with the exception of a few old men fishing. I wandered down to the edge of the pier where the cold wind seemed to cut through my clothes. I leaned over the edge and looked out into the ocean. My only thoughts were of Jay and if I was doing right by him. As I stared in the distance, I could see the sun start to emerge from behind the clouds; the rays warmed my cheeks and the wind seemed to die down. In that moment, I could feel Jay's presence and a sense of peace I hadn't felt in a long time fell over me. Another cloud moved in and the warmth of the sun disappeared from my cheeks, but the peace I felt continued. I knew that this was the right thing.

We met Captain Prescott and the crew of the *Lady Grace* mid-afternoon. They helped us dress in all-weather gear and explained to us that it was unusual to be heading out so late in the day but that they understood my request and were more than happy to oblige.

We all boarded the 55-foot boat and headed out to sea. It wasn't very long before Stella turned a pale shade of green and had to go below deck to lie down. The rest of us tried our hand at fishing when we reached our destination. The chilling wind off the ocean cut around us, but none of us seemed to mind too much. Captain Prescott took his time in explaining each aspect of fishing to Lanie and me. Harry, having fished most of his life, needed little instruction. Lanie gave up after an hour and headed below deck to check on Stella.

At that moment my rod gave a huge jerk. The captain shouted for me to hang on. Harry stood behind me, making sure I didn't go overboard with my fishing rod and line. The crew helped me reel in a large bluefish. It weighed nine pounds. I instructed them to release it back into the ocean but prided myself on my first catch. The crew was still joking with me about my reaction when the captain interrupted to tell us the sun was about to set. I nodded solemnly and went below deck to get Lanie, Stella and Jay's ashes.

Harry, Lanie, Stella and I stood at the back of charter by ourselves. The crew had respectfully declined our invitation to join us and seemed to have disappeared. Stella popped open a bottle of champagne and poured three full plastic cups. Harry declined and opened a beer. I leaned out a little farther over the edge and pulled the top off the canister. Harry stood to the left of me and lifted his beer up.

"To Jay," he said.

Lanie and Stella stood on the other side of me and raised their plastic cups. "To Jay," they said in unison.

"Peace my love," I whispered and tilted the canister into the wind, which whisked around and carried the ashes out over the water.

The three of us stood there watching the ashes dance away in the wind and fall into the water. Suddenly, the boat pitched left and we all went tumbling. Harry caught me right before I fell in.

"I got you," he whispered in my ear as he pulled me back to me feet.

I had a funny feeling in my stomach but brushed it off. We all toasted Jay's honor one more time as the sun sank below the horizon. The captain emerged and asked me directly if it was alright to return to shore. I nodded and we all headed below deck to warm up while we coasted back to shore.

Thanking Captain Prescott and his crew for their assistance in my quest was a humbling experience. As we disembarked the *Lady Grace*, the crew all stood on deck and saluted me. Each of us seemed to be lost in our own thoughts as we headed back to the bed and breakfast. Stella excused herself almost immediately when we got back, saying she had some work to catch up on. Lanie sat with Harry and me for a while longer, drinking and sharing stories, but she soon excused herself as well, leaving Harry and me alone. Harry continued to work on his twelve-pack of beer as we sat and shared stories of Jay. I knew most of them by heart, but I didn't mind sharing them again. It was comforting. Sometime after midnight, I stretched and said I was ready for bed. We had an early morning back to Greensboro and I still needed to pack. Harry indicated he would be up for a little bit. I nodded and left him alone with his thoughts.

It was a little after three in the morning when I heard the door to our room open and close. I sat up slightly and turned the light on, looking at Harry. He looked disheveled as he stumbled around the room.

"Oh, Harry," I said, getting out of bed to help him.

"It's just you and me left," he said as I tried to get him to sit down so I could take off his shoes.

"Yes, Harry. It's just you and me," I said, playing along.

"Do you mean it?" he asked, looking at me.

"What do you mean?" I asked, confused by his statement.

"It's you and me. We can take care of each other. I know we can." He slurred his words.

"What are you talking about, Harry?" I asked, abandoning the idea of taking off his shoes. I now stood and looked at him.

"Jill, I love you and I want to take care of you now." He slurred his words again.

He stood and leaned over to grab my face and kiss me. At first the entire scene played out in front of me as if I were a spectator. It was only after Harry tried to force his tongue in my mouth that I snapped to the present.

"Harry, Jay was my husband," I said, pushing him back.

He swayed a bit and fell back onto the bed. He fumbled, trying to right himself again. "But Jay's gone. The SOB left us both didn't he?" He continued to slur his words.

"You were Jay's best friend. Now what? You just want to slide into his life where he left off? Do you think he left a place holder?" I asked, appalled at where this conversation had led.

"Maybe it's in his will? 'Should I go early, I, Jay Peter Greenfield, leave my wife, Jill Katherine Greenfield, to my best friend, Henry William Conner.' Do you think that's how this works?" I raised my voice as anger set in.

"Jill, calm down. It's not like that. It's just that I loved you too. Jay got you that night at the party and before I knew it, I loved you too. The bastard knew it too and didn't care." He was again on his feet, moving toward me. "Jill, baby ..."

"Baby? ... I'm not your baby."

Harry ignored my protest and continued. "I know we would be happy together. These last few weeks have been so easy. We just fell into a good routine. Aren't you happy?" he asked after a pause.

"Happy? These last week's haven't been happy. They have been the hardest things I have ever lived through. What we had going on, our living arrangement, wasn't real. It was staged. Real love takes work. It takes effort. Jay understood that," I spat back at him as I dodged his attempt to grab me.

"You are over-reacting. This isn't how I meant to tell you. Jill, I know everything about you. Jay told me. Don't you want someone who knows you, cares for you? I can pick up where Jay left off. It will be easier on both of us, being together."

He again reached for me and I tripped over my bag and landed on the bed. Harry was on me before I could react. He leaned down to whisper in my ear. I could smell the beer on his breath and I wiggled to get myself free.

"Baby, this is right."

He leaned over to kiss me again. I tried to get myself loose but was unable. Harry shifted his position, giving me the opportunity to push my knee directly into his groin. He howled in pain and rolled off me.

"You bitch," he yelled.

"You're clearly drunk and delusional. I'm going to stay with Stella and Lanie. Don't you ever, EVER, touch me like that again." I reached down for my bag and stormed out of the room. "We leave at 10," I called over my shoulder as the door slammed.

I made my way over to Stella and Lanie's door and knocked rapidly on it until Stella stumbled to open it.

"What the hell?"

"I'll tell you later, but can I crash here?"

"Sure." She moved to the side to let me in. I crawled in bed with her and Lanie and drifted off to sleep.

CHAPTER 14

T he drive home the next morning was painfully silent. Lanie and Stella had tried all morning to get me to tell them what had happened, but I simply shook my head and said, "Later."

Harry emerged from his room at 10 and climbed into the back of the Jeep, still drunk from the night before. I now sat behind the wheel with Stella on the passenger side and Lanie in the back with Harry, who had passed out, again.

"Are you sure you don't want to talk about it?" Lanie whispered, as Harry slept next to her.

"I do, but can it wait until we get home?" I said, trying to keep my eye on the road.

"Fine," Stella said, clearly annoyed she would have to wait.

"What are you going to do about work?" Lanie asked after a couple minutes.

"I don't want to talk about that either."

"Nice try. You have to talk about something," Stella said.

"Fine." It was my turn to pout. "I don't think I want to go back. The more I think about it, the more I know my heart is not in it. I loved everything about teaching, but what I loved the most was it was part of the life I shared with Jay. He was this high-profile, successful lawyer and I was this kindergarten teacher. Our professions were complete opposites, but we balanced each other out. Now I just don't feel the same way about it. I had been thinking about it for several weeks now, mostly because Principal Bentley had started calling to inquire about my return."

"When are you going to let the principal know?" Lanie asked.

"In the next couple days."

"What are you going to do next?" Stella asked.

"I don't know. For the first time in my life I don't have a plan and it scares me. I know I can't sit at home because I'll go broke very quickly, but I don't know what I can do," I said.

"You could write," Lanie suggested.

"What?"

"Everyone knows you love writing in that journal of yours. Maybe there is something worthwhile in there. You know, share your feelings with the world, kinda thing," Stella said in the only way that Stella could. I couldn't help but think her words echoed what Harry had said weeks earlier.

"Stella!" Lanie swatted at Stella from the backseat.

"What? She won't let us ever read anything so we don't know if it's any good," Stella said defensively.

"She has a point," I said, looking at Lanie through the rearview mirror. "No one has read anything, so we don't know if it's any good. It's more a hobby anyway."

"You could be a lawyer," Stella commented with a smirk.

"Or a psychologist," Lanie added.

"Maybe a stripper?" Stella teased.

"What?" I exclaimed.

"What? I heard they make really good money." Stella cracked up.

"Okay. How about no to all those suggestions. New topic," I suggested. We moved on, chatting idly about nothing of consequence for the rest of the drive home.

....

When I pulled into my driveway, I told Stella and Lanie they could go inside and I would wake Harry. They both looked at me questioningly and trudged inside. I walked around to the side of the car and flung open the door that Harry had been leaning on. He would have fallen out had it not been for his seatbelt.

"What the fuck?" he said as he dangled precariously, trying to right himself.

"We're home," I said in the sweetest voice I could muster. I moved to the trunk and pulled out his bag, throwing it down next to the Jeep while he crawled out of the car.

"Listen, Jill," he started to say.

"No. You don't get to 'listen Jill' me. You were Jay's best friend, but you don't get to take over where he left off. He was always there for you no matter how many times you screwed up and this is how you repay his legacy and his memory. No. I don't think so."

"You got a bit of a temper, don't you?" he mumbled.

"Guess you didn't know that about me. Well, here's another fact you may not know: you're not Jay. You're not even a tenth of the man that he was." I paused for a minute. "I don't know what the hell was going through your head last night. But I do know that I want you to go into my house and get your stuff and leave. I don't want to see you again," I said and started down the driveway away from the house.

"Where the hell are you going?" he shouted after me.

"I'm going for coffee and you better be gone by the time I get back."

"Or what? You are clearly some moody emotional widow who didn't know which way was up last week and now you think you have it all together?"

I caught sight of the curtains moving in the front window. Lanie and Stella were watching.

"I was grieving my dead husband. Remember him? Or did you forget about him when you started making a play for his wife. Think with your freaking head," I said, pointing to my head as I turned again to walk down the driveway.

"I don't know what the hell Jay ever saw in you. I always told him he could do better. He was just always attracted to these poor weak women," he shouted back.

I stopped in my tracks as my blood boiled in rage.

"He could do better than me? Maybe. He deserved the best. But what about you? I know he deserved a better best friend. You proved that last night," I said, still trying to walk away. I heard the front door open and soon I heard Lanie and Stella in the driveway as I continued down the sidewalk.

....

I returned to the house 20 minutes later, coffee in hand. I saw that Harry's car was gone and I sighed in relief. I made my way into the house where Stella and Lanie were sitting on the sofa, glaring at me.

"What the hell?" Stella asked, getting up.

"Pastries?" I asked as I held up the peace offering I had bought at the bakery.

"You better start talking," Stella said as she came over and took the pastries from me. We settled back in on the sofa and I told them everything from Harry's strange behavior in the weeks leading up to

Thanksgiving, his advances the previous night and the whole conversation in the driveway.

"Did he say anything when he came back into the house?" I asked when I was done.

"Oh, he didn't come back in," Lanie said.

"What? That means his stuff is still here?" I asked as a little bit of panic set in.

"Well, it's in a box," Lanie said. "Stella packed it all up after he left."

"I was going to throw it out on the street, but Lanie stopped me." Stella pouted. I burst out laughing over the absurdity of the entire situation.

....

Lanie left the next day and Stella settled into the office to catch up on some work. I decided to do some housework and set about cleaning the kitchen. It took me hours to scrub every surface, but it felt refreshing. When I was done, I took the trash bag out through the garage to the trash bin. On my way back in, I stopped dead in my tracks and stared at the vehicle in the garage. I realized I hadn't been out to the garage in months. I usually parked my Jeep in the driveway, never bothering to pull it all the way in. Jay always stored his car. I dashed back in the house, calling Stella's name.

"I'm in here. What do you need?" she said, emerging from the office. Her Bluetooth was clipped to her ear and she was holding papers. She looked so formidable.

"Jay's car," I stammered.

"Yea. What about it?"

"It's still here," I stated, confused.

"Yea, it is," she said, looking at me, equally confused.

"It just caught me off guard. I forgot about it."

"Okay?"

"What do I do with it?" I asked.

She held up a hand, signaling me to hold on a minute, and walked back into the office. She came out a couple minutes later without her Bluetooth and papers and sat down next to me on the sofa.

"What do you want to do?"

"With the car?"

"With all of it? What are you going to do with all of Jay's things?" she asked again.

"I don't know," and I didn't. I hadn't thought about any of his things. Over the previous couple of weeks, as I cleaned up, I would always avoid touching anything that belonged to Jay.

"Well, before you decide, we should talk to his lawyer. He might have had some wishes for some of his things," she said and I nodded my head in agreement. "I will call him first thing tomorrow morning. Why don't you just sit and read or something. Try and take your mind off of it until then," she said and I agreed. She walked back toward the office to work, leaving me to my own thoughts.

....

I was sitting at the table Monday morning, enjoying my yogurt and granola, around 11, when Stella strolled into the kitchen.

"Late morning?" I asked.

"No. I actually have been up for a while, just working." She made her way over to the coffee I had just recently brewed.

"So, I spoke with Paul Wellon," she said, grabbing a mug from the cupboard.

"Oh yea?"

"He is pretty adamant that we meet with him in person to go over the specifics of the estate. We arranged a date in January, after the holidays." She looked at me to make sure that was okay.

"Sure. Sounds fun," I said sarcastically.

"But he was able to tell me as far as the physical items in this house, Jay's car, clothes and personal items are all up to your discretion," Stella said in a questioning tone.

"What?"

"It's just the way he said 'this house.' It makes me wonder. That's all." She shrugged.

"I can promise you there isn't anything else." I laughed at the nature of her inquisition.

"What are you doing today?" she asked.

"I don't know. I guess I'll look at going through the house and Jay's things." I sighed at the thought of the big task ahead of me.

"Boring!" she said, dismissing my ideas.

"Okay. What are you doing?" I asked.

"Going to the law library," she said, smiling.

"Boring!" I mouthed back at her and we both burst into giggles.

....

Stella left in the early afternoon for the law library to do some research for a case she had back in New York. I didn't understand her need to use this library, as if New York didn't have any bigger or better libraries to use. I didn't question it further. It was probably just another poor excuse for someone to continue to babysit me. Lanie called several minutes after Stella had left to see what we were doing.

"Stella's at the law library like a good girl," I told Lanie.

"What are you doing?"

"Stella talked to Paul Wellon this morning and Jay had no wishes for any of his things, so I thought I might go through some of them."

"Really?"

"It's depressing, isn't it?"

"Do you want help?"

"Don't you have a full case load or something?" I asked, trying to recall our conversation over the last few days about why she had to hurry back to Raleigh after the holiday.

"I did. Things got shifted around and now I'm free most of the week."

"Well, if you don't have anything better to do …"

"Great. I'm already halfway there. See you in a little bit," she said and hung up. I shook my head at my crazy friends and headed up to the attic to find some boxes while I waited for Lanie's arrival.

CHAPTER 15

....

For the next week Lanie and I methodically went through every room in the house and we were occasionally joined by Stella. We made several piles in the living room of things that I thought should be sent to other family members, things that would be donated, sent to storage or things that were simply meant for the trash. It felt very therapeutic going through each room. Every item, regardless of whether it was Jay's or mine, was considered. It was an endless process that left me emotionally drained each night. There were days we laughed, days I cried and days I got angry over everything. Every step of the way Lanie was there to console me and guide me through the process the best way a friend could. By Friday there was just one room left: the master bedroom.

"Last room," Lanie said as we stood in the doorway of the master suite. I nodded as I carried several boxes in and set them down on the bed. The room was a modest size, painted pale blue, with his and her walk-in closets on one side. In the center of the room stood a queen-sized four-poster bed that was given to us as a wedding gift. On the far side was a large, oversized, floor mirror that was flanked by two tall dressers. On each side of the bed was a small bedside table with two matching lamps and on Jay's side of the bed was a blue suede chair.

"What first?" I asked.

"Well, it's mostly clothes in here, right?"

"For the most part."

"What do you want to do with it all?"

"I think I would prefer to donate most of it. The local Goodwill does a program where they take professional clothes and give them to those who are interviewing for jobs or those who can't afford work attire. Jay and I had donated a couple times over the last couple of years. I would like to continue that," I said.

"Okay. Are you keeping anything?"

"I have to keep something," I said tentatively.

"Why don't I go and get us some water and snacks while you take a moment with everything," she said, turning to leave. I stood and stared at the bed for a moment before I made my way into Jay's closet. Everything hung neatly inside, meticulously organized. Jay had always been a little OCD and everything had a specific place. All his suits hung together on oak hangers, dress shirts were all hung by color on the far wall after they came back from the dry cleaners. T-shirts were hung on wire hangers and jeans were pressed and hung below them. All his shoes were arranged underneath the suits, each pair of shoes still in the original box they came in. I walked all the way in and let my hand carefully glide along all the crisp dress shirts before settling on a particular blue one. I pulled down a couple of worn T-shirts and several sweatshirts that were folded on the rack. I carried the items out of the closet and put them on the bed just as Lanie entered the room with a tray full of snacks and bottled water.

"All set," I said, helping her set down the tray.

"You sure?"

I thought for a moment of going through a mental inventory of all of Jay's items.

"I'm sure," I finally said.

With that, she set to work packing up Jay's clothes while I went through my own closet. I found it easier not having to physically pack it all up myself.

"What about these?" Lanie called out to me 30 minutes later.

"What?" I asked as I walked out of the closet with an armful of my own clothes to put in a box. She was pointing to the blue suede chair that sat outside the closet. It still held the clothes Jay had laid out for himself the morning he died.

"Oh those," I said, staring at the outfit. It wasn't anything special but symbolized so much more. "Pack it up," I said after a couple of minutes. Next, I went through the small amount of jewelry that Jay had, mostly watches and cufflinks.

"Where is his wedding ring?" Lanie asked. We had brought it back from the funeral home several weeks earlier and afterward, it had sat in a brown paper bag on the kitchen table for several more weeks. It was only recently I had taken it out of the bag and strung it on my long, white-gold necklace with my engagement and wedding rings.

"It's right here," I said to Lanie, tugging on the necklace around my neck.

"I hadn't realized," she said.

"It's okay. I only recently had to strength to look at it again," I said, tucking the necklace back under my shirt. I decided to send a set of cufflinks to Jay's father and pulled out a watch that I knew Harry would appreciate.

"Really?" Lanie looked at me when I mentioned Harry's name.

"Really. Just because he's an idiot doesn't mean he won't appreciate it. Call me crazy, but I was also thinking of giving him Jay's car," I said. Lanie stared at me and put down the box she was holding.

"What?" she said, dumbfounded.

"The car was Jay's baby. Jay and Harry would spend hours talking about that car until the day he finally bought it and then when he did, they spent hours riding around in it," I explained.

"I still can't believe he bought that car without asking you."

"Me neither." Jay and I were never ones to have big arguments about anything. We could usually settle things pretty quickly with the exception of that car, the Audi A4. He had been out with Harry one night and then just came home with it, claiming they had got a really good deal on it and I didn't need to worry about the cost. I naturally freaked out about how we were going to be able to afford such a luxury car on our salaries. He assured me it would not be a problem. I didn't speak to him for days after that and he finally asked me if I preferred that he return it. This only made me angrier. I wasn't going to be painted as that wife who wasn't going to let him keep his precious toy. Eventually, the whole thing blew over, and he kept the car, but he never again bothered me about trading in my Jeep for something nicer.

"Stella is gonna flip out when she hears that," Lanie said, interrupting my thoughts.

"I know. That's why I have avoided bringing it up so far." I cringed.

"When you going to do it?"

"Soon. I don't want to get rid of all Jay's stuff to get over him, but I need to start moving forward. Does that make sense?"

Lanie nodded and continued packing up Jay's things. By the time Stella got home that night, we had finished packing up everything. The only things left were the piles in the living room, most of which either needed to be delivered somewhere or mailed out.

We decided to head out to Lanie's place in Raleigh for the weekend and do some Christmas shopping. What was meant to be a couple of days turned into almost five and it was Wednesday before Stella and I returned to the house in Greensboro. That evening I sat down and told Stella my plans for Jay's car and several other items. As expected, Stella freaked out and disagreed with my plans. I had to explain my thought process to her several times before she grudgingly agreed. I had only known Jay for five years, but Harry had known him for almost 30 years. They had shared more together than I would ever have the chance to and for that I owed it to Jay to at least leave Harry some memory of him.

On Thursday night Stella followed behind me in my Jeep as I drove the Audi A4 over to Harry's apartment. I hadn't spoken to him since that argument in my driveway after Thanksgiving. He had called and texted several times and each time I ignored him. I wasn't even sure he would be home when we pulled into the parking garage next to his building. Stella would not agree to wait for me in the car and instead followed me into the building but kept her distance behind me as I rang the doorbell to Harry's apartment.

"Hey Bill, is that you?" he said as he answered the door.

"Not Bill," I answered.

"Jill," he said, looking at me. Tonight he was dressed in jeans and a white shirt.

"Listen Harry—"

"I owe you an apology." He interrupted me and I just nodded. "I don't know what came over me. It was all very stupid."

"I'll say it was," Stella said from the hallway.

"Oh hey, Stella. I didn't see you lurking down there," Harry quipped.

"Whatever happened, happened. It doesn't change the fact that I think some distance will be good for both of us," I said.

He looked as if he were about to interrupt again and I held up my hand. "I came here tonight for a completely different reason. I'd like you to come out to the parking garage," I said firmly.

Harry looked at me questioningly and headed back inside to put on some shoes and grab a coat. Silently, he followed me out to the garage. I stopped in front of the Audi A4 and turned to face him. I could see the confusion on his face.

"Is this your idea of a cruel joke?" he commented.

"No. I want you to have it," I said, holding out the keys to him.

"You what?" he said, clearly caught off guard.

"You were Jay's friend long before I came into the picture and I get that and I respect that. I owe Jay to honor that. You both loved this car and I don't. I want you to have it," I said, again holding out the keys for him. He held his hand out and I dropped the keys into them, making sure our hands didn't touch.

"There will be paperwork you need to complete," Stella chimed in.

"Sshhh." I motioned at her.

"Also, I was going through Jay's things and I wanted you to have this as well." I reached into my purse and pulled out the Cartier watch that Jay's dad had given him the day he graduated from law school.

"Jill, seriously?" he said, reaching for the watch and then pulling away.

"Seriously," I said, handing him the red box the watch was stored in. I could tell he was overwhelmed by everything and I turned to leave.

"Jill," he called. I stopped and turned to face him and he engulfed me in a hug.

"Thank you," he whispered, only releasing me after a long while.

"You're welcome," I whispered back and turned to meet Stella, who was now waiting in the Jeep.

....

Stella needed to fly back to New York before the holidays and take care of some cases before everyone scattered for the holiday season. Stella and Lanie were still unsure that I could care for myself. So, I was sent to Lanie's house in Raleigh until Christmas when the two of us planned to fly to New York and visit Stella. Jay and I would have normally spent Christmas Eve at home and then tried to escape to the beach until the New Year. It had become our yearly tradition. This year things were different and my friends were extrasensitive about it. Stella usually spent the Christmas holidays with her mom before jet-setting off to some Caribbean island with her beau of the moment. Lanie on the other hand would spend several days with her family, visiting, before spending time with her girlfriend of many years, Mary Elizabeth. However, Stella had recently informed me that the two of them had decided to split shortly before Jay's death and Lanie hadn't felt right about bringing it up to me and I hadn't asked. Stella decided we would go to a Broadway show and do some shopping and pampering in the city before ringing in the new year in Times Square. It was something we had always talked about doing, just the three of us, but we were never able to schedule it. She felt this was the year to do it and her office was having some sort of party nearby, so we didn't have to wait all day in the cold. We would be able to see and hear the festivities from the party.

CHAPTER 16

....

The holiday season went by pretty quickly and I only broke down twice. The first time was on Christmas morning as the three of us exchanged presents in Stella's apartment. It was Lanie who made me cry. Snowflakes drifted down off the buildings onto the fresh coat of snow that had fallen the night before. It was a very picturesque Christmas morning. Lanie had gotten up early to make chocolate chip pancakes for everyone and we sat on Stella's living room floor exchanging gifts. We had decided this year to forgo buying gifts and instead make gifts for each other, much to Stella's dismay. I had made Stella and Lanie each a "mix-tape" in the form of an iPod shuffle. Stella of course broke the rules and got Lanie and me each a new outfit to wear on New Year's Eve. Lanie, being the most sensitive and thoughtful of us by far, did the best job. She made Stella an emergency office survival kit in the guise of an oversized Kate Spade bag. Stashed inside was an extra set of stockings, Advil, toothbrush, toothpaste, lint brush, hairspray, lipstick, perfume, Band-Aids and a small sewing kit. Stella squealed with delight. For me she had put together a shadow box. The frame was made from re-used lumber white-washed in a pale yellow with a distressed finish. Inside the box was a collection of my life with Jay. Pictures were pinned to the back of the box along with the racing bib from one of our races. Seashells lay next to a gavel

Jay kept on his desk at home and tucked behind that was the name plate from the door to the class I used to teach. I was overwhelmed with emotion over the detail she had worked into this gift. At the back of the shadow box were two small hooks and I looked at her in confusion.

"Whenever you're ready. It's for your rings," she whispered and pointed to the necklace I was wearing with my wedding ring, engagement ring and Jay's wedding ring on it. I nodded.

"Looks like no one followed the rules," Stella commented, looking around at the gifts. We all burst into laughter in agreement. We curled up together on the couch and watched movies until it was time to get ready for our dinner reservations uptown.

The second time I broke down was during the New Year's Eve party. We got all dressed up in the outfits Stella bought us for her office party, which was held in an office building overlooking Times Square. It was an amazing sight. Thousands of people in the streets below were singing and dancing to live music. Stella's firm had gone all out for the party. A live band competed for our attention with the performing bands outside. People mingled and drank and danced the night away until the final 10 minutes. Everyone stopped what they were doing. Champagne was passed out and everyone crowded around the floor-to-ceiling windows and looked out at Times Square. Together we counted down to the new year ... ten ... nine ... eight ... seven ... six ... five ... four ... three ... two ... one ... HAPPY NEW YEAR!

Everyone grabbed somebody to embrace or kiss as they celebrated. I looked around and the enormity of everyone's happiness reminded me of my own unhappiness and loneliness. I reached out and placed my hand on the glass window as I watched the confetti streak down toward Times Square.

"Happy New Year, Jay," I whispered, reaching for the necklace that held our rings. Just then, someone grabbed my other hand and I looked over and saw Lanie smiling back. On the other side Stella tapped me on the shoulder.

"We didn't forget you," Stella said and we embraced.

....

At the beginning of the new year I was again sent to Lanie's in Raleigh for a couple days before Stella was scheduled to fly back down and spend a couple more weeks with me during which we finally scheduled a meeting with Paul Wellon. I tried to assure my friends that I was okay to spend some time alone, but they weren't ready to let me go.

While I was at Lanie's, she confided in me about her relationship with Mary Elizabeth. She wanted to give their relationship another try. I felt bad thinking of how self-absorbed I had been after Jay's death. I had never once stopped to ask Lanie about Mary Elizabeth or where she was. Lanie dismissed my guilt, saying that after seeing what I had gone through with Jay, she had decided life was too short and gave Mary Elizabeth a call. I was glad when Stella arrived several days later to take me home. I felt uncomfortable being a third wheel as Lanie and Mary Elizabeth tried to rekindle their relationship.

Stella and I had just gotten back from dinner one night and were pulling up to the house when we saw Harry in the driveway, leaning against Jay's Audi.

"Stella," Harry said, nodding in her direction as she got out of the car.

"Harry," she replied coolly and shuffled past him. As she passed him, she gave me a look that asked whether she should stay around. I just shrugged and she continued into the house.

"Harry," I said as I approached him. He leaned down to try and give me a hug, but I wasn't receptive and the gesture came off as awkward.

"I drove by the other night and saw the lights on and figured you were back in town," he offered as an explanation for his sudden appearance. "How was your Christmas?"

He had continued to send me texts and leave me voicemails over the holidays. I was advised by Stella and Lanie to ignore them all.

"It was … bittersweet," I answered truthfully.

"Same here. I wish you had replied to my texts and voicemails. We should be relying on each other during this time. We were closest with Jay. We can lean on each other."

"I don't think that's how this works."

"Jill, listen. Last time … well two times ago when we saw each other, I was a jerk. I didn't take losing Jay very well, as you know." He paused to see if I would correct him, but I nodded that he should continue. "I was really stupid and my actions were uncalled for. I need your friendship. It helps me feel connected to Jay, but more importantly, I thought we were better friends than that," he said, looking me right in the eye.

"Harry, I don't know. We were really good friends because of Jay. He brought us together and maybe it's appropriate, with his passing, we drift apart." I wasn't sure if I could be friends with Harry.

"Jill, that can't be it. I need … I want more," he said.

"Harry, I don't know what I have to give," I whispered, looking down at my shoes.

He reached over and put his hand on my shoulder, causing me to look up at him. In that moment I thought he was going to try and kiss me again and so I quickly took a step back, letting his hand drop back to his side.

"I need some more time to figure it all out. Can you give me that?" I asked.

"Jill, I'll give you whatever you want. Just don't push me out," he said, pulling open the door to the Audi. "Goodnight, Jill."

"Goodnight, Harry," I said, waving as he backed out of the driveway.

"What did that bozo want?" Stella asked as I entered the house.

"He wants to be friends." I hesitated with my next statement.

"What?" Stella pressed.

"It seems like he wants more, but I can't tell if that's what he really wants or if he thinks that being with me will be like being with Jay ... in some weird way," I said.

"A very weird way. You need to stay away from him. He's bad news," Stella said, walking over and handing me a cup of tea.

"You're right. He just doesn't seem that easy to get rid of," I said and we settled on the sofa to watch some TV.

"Stella, wake up," I said, trying to shake her awake.

It was past one in the morning and we had both fallen asleep on the sofa watching one of the late night shows. She mumbled something incoherent and rolled over.

"Stella, wake up," I said again, raising my voice slightly.

When I had made my way through the kitchen, locking up the doors and turning the lights off, I had noticed my phone was flashing with a message. There were two voicemails and several texts from Lanie. My heart stopped as a sudden feeling of déjà vu swept over me. Very hesitantly, I listened to the message ...

"Oh my God! Stella wake-up!"

"What? What's wrong?" she asked, starting awake.

"We need to call Lanie right away!" I said, hitting redial and sitting down next to Stella on the sofa.

"Jill?" Lanie answered.

"Yea, Lanie. Stella and I are both here. We fell asleep watching TV." I put her on speakerphone.

"Did you listen to the message?" Lanie asked with excitement.

"I did but Stella didn't," I said, grinning at Stella.

"What? What did I miss?" Stella asked, again rubbing her eyes.

"Mary Elizabeth and I got engaged," Lanie gushed.

"What?" Stella said, fully awake this time.

"Tell us the details!" I said.

"It's really late tonight. What are you two doing tomorrow?" Lanie asked and I looked at Stella. She had become the unofficial keeper of my schedule.

"We have that meeting with Paul Wellon, but we can move that. What do you have in mind?" Stella asked.

"Why don't you two come to Raleigh. We have a wedding to plan!" Lanie exclaimed.

"It's a date," I said.

....

CHAPTER 17

Stella and I arrived at Lanie's apartment in downtown Raleigh just a little past 10 the next morning. We would have arrived earlier, but Stella insisted on stopping to buy champagne so that we could celebrate as soon as we got there. Lanie buzzed us into her apartment and we carried our things up.

"Knock, knock," Stella called as she pushed open Lanie's apartment door.

"I'm back here," Lanie called from the direction of the kitchen.

"Congratulations!" I exclaimed, coming around the kitchen island to give her a big hug.

"Let me see this ring!" Stella said, coming up behind me.

"There is no ring," Lanie said.

"No?" we both asked with confused looks on our faces.

"I'll explain."

"Time for a toast," Stella said, holding up the champagne.

"Where's Mary Elizabeth?" I asked.

"She's on morning rotations at the hospital," Lanie explained as she continued chopping and preparing vegetables for whatever she was preparing. Mary Elizabeth had earned a prestigious position as a cardiology fellow at the Raleigh Hospital after graduating from Duke with her MD. The hospital was, in fact, where Lanie and Mary

Elizabeth had met. Lanie was treating patients in the psychiatric unit and often spent her down time in the cafeteria working on cases or updating her notes. Mary Elizabeth took notice of her always sitting alone and befriended her. Things developed from there.

"So details," I said.

"I know. Last we talked you were taking things slow … rekindling," Stella said make quotation marks in the air with her hands.

"I thought we were doing all that stuff. But last night after I got home from work, there was a note on the front door to meet her at our favorite Italian restaurant, Lucy's, at seven," Lanie said.

"And then?" I asked. I loved romantic stories and the excitement they brought, but Lanie seemed to be dragging her feet getting to the details of this story.

"Drink," Stella said, interrupting our conversation by putting wine glasses full of champagne down in front of each of us.

"Wine glasses?" Lanie asked.

"I couldn't find anything else," Stella said, shrugging.

"Back to the story," I said, trying to steer the conversation back.

"Oh, right. Well, I got to the restaurant a little late because of traffic, but when I finally got there, I couldn't find Mary Elizabeth. I asked the hostess if she had already been seated. The young lady said she had and she could show me to my seat. She led me all the way to the back of the restaurant through this dark curtained section into a private room. I didn't even know there were private rooms at Lucy's," Lanie said, still sounding amazed by it all. "The hostess pulled back this curtain and there was Mary Elizabeth standing in this darkly lit room with hundreds of candles everywhere. She was holding two glasses of champagne and motioned for me to come forward. I was so confused as to what was going on, I did exactly as she wished. She then took my hand and said that things had been up and down for us lately but getting back together made her realize that she wouldn't have wanted to go through that without anyone else and she couldn't picture her life, her future …" Lanie slid a glance in my direction.

"What? No pity glances, please," I shot back at her, motioning for her to continue.

"She said she couldn't picture her future without her best friend and then she took a little box off the table and said she hadn't had time to get a ring but she hoped I would consider spending the rest of our lives together. She gave me the box and inside were her grandmother's diamond earrings." Lanie pointed to the large studded diamonds she now wore.

"How did I miss those?" Stella said, getting a closer look.

"So you said yes?" I asked.

"Yes. I said yes! How could I not? It was the most romantic gesture anyone has ever done for me. We did decide we are just going to do wedding rings not engagement rings. I had given her a diamond necklace a year back and she thought that was enough diamonds."

"You can never have enough diamonds," Stella said, looking slightly disappointed at the practicality of Lanie and Mary Elizabeth.

"I think it's smart," I added, trying to sound enthusiastic.

"So after that, we enjoyed a private dinner and we just talked all night until I called you guys," Lanie said, finally finishing her story.

"Do you have any wedding details?" Stella asked.

"Yes. We want to get married in a month," Lanie said with a straight face.

"What?" I said as Stella spit champagne out across the table.

After Stella cleaned up her mess, Lanie explained that Mary Elizabeth was getting ready to complete a fellow rotation in four weeks and that she would have a small break before she started back up in another more demanding area. They didn't see the need to wait any longer and wanted to start their lives together as soon as possible.

"I guess when you know, you know," Stella mumbled. I think Lanie heard Stella's comment but chose to ignore it. She had stopped chopping vegetables and was focusing her attention on me.

"Jill, we would like you to help us plan our wedding," Lanie said, shifting nervously.

"Me?"

"Yes, you. Every event you plan is flawless and you have planned a wedding before ..."

"You also have a lot of free time," Stella interjected.

"Sure. If that's what you want." I was secretly looking forward to having a huge distraction that had nothing to do with my own personal life, but I was also terrified I might not be emotionally strong enough to go down that road.

"Jill, Mary Elizabeth and I wouldn't ask if we didn't think you could handle it emotionally," Lanie added, reading my mind. I nodded again, not wanting to speak in case my emotions weren't in check.

"There is just one catch," Lanie added.

"Oh, you mean planning a wedding in a month isn't a big enough catch?" I asked sarcastically.

"We want to get married in New York," Lanie said, surprising us both again.

"The hits just keep coming," Stella mumbled.

"Why New York? Shouldn't Stella plan it then?" I asked.

"No, not me," Stella quickly said, shaking her head.

"Well, Mary Elizabeth is from upstate New York and she has a large family that we would like to attend and it's legal there," Lanie said.

"Oh, right." I nodded.

We spent the next several hours going over details and making lists of Lanie's upcoming nuptials only stopping to eat a lunch that Lanie had prepared and to refill on champagne. By the time Mary Elizabeth came home, we were filled with bubbles and laughing uncontrollably. She knew, as did so many of our other friends and loved ones, that once the three of us got going on something, it was best to leave us alone until we calmed down. We often slipped into our own little world, leaving those around us in the dark, much to their frustration.

We calmed down and congratulated Mary Elizabeth and offered her a drink, which she politely declined as she would be back on duty in a couple hours. We then tried to review our wedding ideas and lists with her, but half way through, she raised her hands and said she trusted us as much as Lanie did and gave us carte blanche on all wedding details. She said she had already done the hard part by asking for Lanie's hand, so the rest was just gravy. It made me smile how easily she gushed over Lanie and how at ease they both were. I knew that their journey had not been easy to this point, which made this union seem even more special.

....

Stella stayed several extra days but had to fly back to New York at the end of the weekend. I was again told that I would be staying with the newly engaged couple under the guise of becoming their full-time wedding planner. In all reality, it was a good plan on their part because for the next four weeks I was so busy I didn't have time to miss anything or anyone. There were so many wedding details and out-of-state vendors to organize while balancing the difficult schedules of two doctors there wasn't time in my life for anything else. Before

Stella left, the four of us decided that the wedding would be a black and white event with only touches of frosty blue. After that, all the details fell into place. I made dress appointments and schlepped both Mary Elizabeth and Lanie to multiple dress fittings at different times because they had decided they didn't want to see each other's dresses before the wedding. On Stella's recommendation, I contacted the owner of a small, private, art museum with stellar views of the city. He agreed to rent out his museum space, which would accommodate the wedding and reception for 50 guests. I worked on menus with caterers and bakers, set up a wedding photographer, and contracted a party supply company to supply all the tables and chairs and linens. I helped the brides select last-minute invitations that were sent out via overnight FedEx. I interviewed several justices of the peace before selecting the right one and finally, I selected the frosty blue, floor-length, bridesmaid dresses that Stella and I would be wearing, as well as the tuxedos that both fathers and Mary Elizabeth's brother would be wearing. For several days, I brought home various arrangements of flowers from a local florist whose cousin worked in Manhattan and who would be able to accommodate our order.

Lanie and Mary Elizabeth decided to skip registering for any wedding gifts because they already felt that they had everything they needed and in some cases, two of everything they needed, as they would be merging households after the wedding. Instead, they asked that if anyone felt the need give a gift, it be monetary so that it could help pay for their honeymoon. They had decided to take a four-day cruise in the Caribbean before Mary Elizabeth was due back for her second rotation.

Each night, I would arrange on the kitchen table the notes I had made of my day's progress for Lanie and Mary Elizabeth to look over during dinner and then we would discuss any changes or preferences they had. Oftentimes there weren't any changes, just several nods and a brief discussion about the budget. On the third or fourth night after talking about it, Mary Elizabeth finally decided that money would be no problem and that I should just continue. The brides-to-be only argued once throughout the entire process and that was the night we worked on the seating chart for the reception. Mary Elizabeth wanted only parents to sit at the head table with Lanie and herself while Lanie wanted the head table to be for the bridal party. They finally decided there would be no seating arrangement, only a small reserved table for the brides.

In the evenings, after Lanie and Mary Elizabeth went to bed, I worked on any arts and crafts projects that needed to be completed. It was at night, as I sat sipping on wine, which was usually left over from dinner, listening to the soft melodies of Frank Sinatra or Etta James, that I could unwind from the day. More often than not, my thoughts would drift back to my own wedding and thoughts of Jay. Every detail seemed to remind me of something that he had said or an opinion he had had. One particular evening, as I was gluing black and white cards together that would serve as the menu cards for each place setting, I started to giggle. I was reminded of the time I had stayed up all night working on place cards for my own wedding. They were elaborate black cards that I had written on in chalk. I must have made close to 75 of them and had fallen asleep working on the project. The next morning Jay tried waking me, startling me and causing me to knock the coffee out of his hand and all over the cards. We both just stared at each other and I burst into tears. Jay sent me off to bed and when I got up, he had redone all my hard work from the night before.

On the Tuesday before the wedding, I was finally able to find a small jazz band that had a last-minute cancellation. On Wednesday, with the final details arranged, I packed up Lanie and Mary Elizabeth and we boarded a flight for New York in preparation for their Friday sunset wedding in the city.

CHAPTER 18

···

I had reserved several rooms for the occasion at the luxurious Plaza hotel. Lanie and Mary Elizabeth decided on a suite while Stella and I chose to share a room on a different floor. Thursday ended up being a full day of appointments at the spa, final fittings and a small rehearsal dinner at the Rose Club in the Plaza hotel. At the end of the evening Mary Elizabeth said goodnight and left to spend her final night with her family in a near-by hotel.

"This place is so much nicer than my apartment," Stella commented, flopping down on the bed.

"Most places are," I said just as someone knocked on the door.

"Coming," I said, making my way over to the door.

"Lanie, everything okay?" I asked after opening up the door to find Lanie standing there with a bag in hand.

"I didn't want to be alone," she said.

"Of course. Come in," I added, ushering her in.

"Everything okay?" I asked again.

"Yea. Just wedding jitters, I think," she said, sitting down next to Stella.

"Then don't get married," Stella said.

"Stella!" I exclaimed.

"What? You know that I think marriage is overrated," she added.

"You're such a romantic," I said, rolling my eyes in her direction. "Someday you will find the right person and you will change your mind, and Lanie and I will be there to tell you 'we told you so.'"

"Don't hold your breath."

"Jill, would you do it all over again, knowing what you know now?" Lanie asked, interrupting our childish banter. I paused and stared at her, holding up a hand to let her know I needed a moment as I sat down on the floor, looking between the two of them.

"I would do it all over in a heartbeat," I finally said.

"Why the pause?" Stella asked.

"It wasn't a pause because I was hesitant; it was more for reflection. I mean the best part about life is you don't know the outcome, right? You fall in love, blindly, putting your trust in this other person and hoping for the best outcome. Sometimes things fall apart. People change or they make bad decisions. Would knowing all that cause people to make different decisions? Maybe. But for me, Jay gave me hope. He made me laugh. He loved me and I wouldn't trade those moments that we shared together for a lifetime of not having them. Sure, the last couple months have been painful and sad. But I will always have that time we shared, I will always remember those butterflies in my stomach when we met and his gorgeous smile and that look he got in his eyes when he was being mischievous. Those memories are mine because we had hope."

"Thank you." Lanie leaned down and squeezed my hand and I nodded. I crawled into bed next to the two of them and fell asleep.

. . . .

As the photographer moved people around for the group picture, Lanie leaned over and whispered. "Jill, it's breathtaking." I nodded in agreement, smiling as the flash went off. The whole ceremony had gone off flawlessly and the reception looked to be shaping up as well. Lanie looked radiant as her dad walked her down the aisle only moments after Mary Elizabeth's dad walked her down the aisle. The room had been filled with candles and low lighting which sparkled in the room as the reflection of the sunset bounced off the mirrored and glass surfaces of the museum. The justice of the peace kept the ceremony simple and a handful of tears were shed as Lanie and Mary Elizabeth exchanged hand-written vows. After the ceremony, a small champagne toast was held in the lobby so the staff could set up the glass tables for the reception. Each table had five silver and black and white place settings with large black linen napkins folded in squares. In the middle of each table were large bouquets of white roses and more strands of white light. The rose petals that had flanked the aisle from the ceremony were now scattered around the sweetheart table at the back of the room on the other side of the small dance space. The three-tiered wedding cake sat upon a large glass surface surrounded by more white roses that cascaded down the side. It was next to the jazz band, which started to play softly in the background. It was magical.

Lanie and Mary Elizabeth opted out of a traditional first dance and instead invited everyone to the dance floor as the band played. I moved toward the back of the room, taking in the whole scene. Dancing had traditionally been my favorite part of the wedding reception—well, that and the cake. Couples of all ages made their way to the small space in the middle of the room and swayed back and forth. I jumped when I felt a hand on my shoulder.

"Wanna dance?" Stella asked, holding her hand out to me.

"What are you doing?" I asked, shifting my stance to look at her.

"I'm asking you to dance since I know you're a sucker for this romantic stuff. Come on. I don't bite." I sighed at the ridiculous nature of the whole thing.

"Really, you're too serious," Stella said, taking my hand and dragging me to the floor.

"Stella, really ... I don't need to dance," I said, all the while thinking, "and not with you."

"Yes, you do ... and don't worry I won't try anything. You're not my type," she said, winking at me as I laughed and we started to sway to the music.

"Can I join?" We heard Lanie's voice from behind us.

"The more the merrier apparently," I said as Lanie joined us and the three of us swayed together, now holding hands until the song ended.

"You guys are too much," I said as we headed back to our seats.

"Jill, I know I'm a jerk when it comes to this mushy stuff," Stella said, as we were served our first course, "but I know you. You are a hopeless romantic, but you won't admit it, not on Lanie's day. I know this is hard for you."

"Thanks Stella," I said, reaching for her hand. After dinner, Lanie and Mary Elizabeth cut the cake and shared a couple more dances before leaving early.

"Thank you so much. It was more magical than I could have ever dreamed up," Mary Elizabeth whispered in my ear as she embraced me. Her long black hair was pulled back into an elaborately braided updo, but several pieces had already slipped out of place.

"Enjoy your honeymoon," I said, trying to keep my emotions in check.

"I know you are the two most important people in Lanie's life and while I never asked your permission, I hope you know how special she is to me. I'm not trying to steal her away from anything you three have. I just hope we can all share her," Mary Elizabeth said.

"Of course," I exclaimed.

"Steal away. She's not that special," Stella joked as Lanie joined us.

"You're so sweet," Lanie said to Stella before she joined in another round of thank-you's and hugs before leaving with her new bride.

Stella and I stayed to the end of the reception and saw off the last of the lingering guests before heading back to the hotel.

"Maybe you should take up event planning," Stella said as we were getting ready for bed.

"I don't know. That was really stressful."

"Well, what are you going to do?" she asked.

"I don't know."

"You say that a lot lately."

"I know, but it's true. I was so certain of so many things and now it's all up in the air," I said, waving my hands around my head.

"You look ridiculous. Do that again." Stella laughed.

"I'll pass," I said as I got into bed.

"Night, Stella."

"Night, Jill ... Really good job tonight," she said before drifting off to sleep.

We got up early on Saturday to ride with Lanie and Mary Elizabeth to the airport to see them off on their honeymoon. In reality, I think Stella wanted to ride in the limo they had arranged, as she wasn't someone who was really good with good-byes.

"I don't know how long you both think you can keep babysitting me," I said on the drive out to the airport. I could see them all casting sideways glances at each other.

"What?" I asked defensively.

"Well ... we don't think you should be alone just yet," Lanie said.

"Why?" I asked defensively.

"Well, you have been having really bad nightmares and it concerns us," Lanie said.

"It concerns mostly Lanie," Stella added.

"It concerns us all," Mary Elizabeth said in support of Lanie.

While I appreciated her concern, it was weird hearing that sentiment come from Mary Elizabeth.

"We have kind of worked out a plan for the next couple of weeks," Lanie said.

"When was anyone going to tell me?"

"We are telling you, right now," Stella said.

"Do I get a say?"

"I could lie to you and say yes, but in reality, no, no you don't," Stella replied.

"Fine," I sighed. "What is your grand plan?"

"Well, we thought you could hang out in the city with Stella for a couple more weeks through March. Then Stella has a conference in Greensboro in April. After that, she plans on staying with you for a few weeks longer to work on a case and use the Wake Forest library *again*," Lanie explained.

"Plus we need to reschedule that meeting with Paul Wellon. He's really getting annoyed with me," Stella said, interrupting.

"After that, you can stay with us," Lanie said, pointing to herself and Mary Elizabeth.

"So the babysitting will end when the nightmares do?" I asked. I wasn't even aware I was having nightmares.

"Something like that," Stella said.

"Great. How do I get them to stop?" I asked Lanie.

"It doesn't work that way, Jill. It's something you need to work through," Lanie replied.

"How do I work through something I didn't know was going on," I asked again.

"That's for you to figure out," Lanie said.

"But you're the psychologist," I whined.

"Not your psychologist."

"Are you sure? I feel like you have been doctoring me for months now," I said and everyone burst into laughter.

"Doctoring?" Stella said.

"I was being serious." I pouted.

"Jill, you just need time to heal and process everything. In the meantime we just want to keep an extra eye on you. I mean we really haven't seen a lot of each other in the past couple years, so just think of it as catching up on lost time." Lanie shrugged as the limo pulled up to the airport.

"Whatever you say, doc," I quipped as Lanie smiled back.

We said another round of good-byes as Lanie and Mary Elizabeth headed into the airport.

"I give it six years," Stella whispered as we climbed back in the limo.

"Seriously, Stella. That is so inappropriate."

"No. If I'd said it yesterday, which I wanted to, it would have been inappropriate. Today it's just an observation. They are both way too into their work. It won't last."

"Well, I hope you're wrong," I said as I settled in for the drive back to the city.

CHAPTER 19

....

Weeks turned into months as Stella and Lanie developed an elaborate plan that bounced me around from New York to Raleigh and occasionally my house. Our lives seemed to fall into a pattern. Stella and Lanie were using all their energy trying to keep me busy and preoccupied. I was never alone for long periods of time and never at night. During their time off, every moment of my time was scheduled with museum trips, shopping, hiking, more shopping, movies and eating. In addition to the constant supervision, Harry continued to call, text and e-mail me to get my attention. Several times during my brief stays at the house he stopped by unannounced and stayed awkwardly for coffee or a movie, often under the glare of Lanie, Stella and even Mary Elizabeth, who did not appreciate his company.

By mid-May I confronted Stella and Lanie. The juggling was becoming ridiculous and I needed to try and start piecing my life back together—alone. I argued that they needed to get back to their lives and stop worrying about me. My nightmares were no longer occurring with the same frequency (or so I was told), and I felt I needed some space from my friends. Reluctantly, after a long discussion, they finally agreed under the condition that they would both come down and spend a week with me at the house one final time before leaving me to my own devices. It was during this time that Stella reminded me, yet again, we needed to go see Paul Wellon. I agreed that it was well overdue and I needed to finally deal with whatever estate issues Jay had left. Stella arranged a meeting with Paul Wellon for Monday morning while she and Lanie where both around so we could attend together.

"How long do you think it will take?" I asked Stella.

"I don't know. It depends on what Jay's estate consisted off," she said, trying to navigate the directions to Paul's office she had scribbled down on a napkin.

"Are you nervous?" Lanie asked.

"A little bit. Legal matters seem so official and sometimes confusing. Also I don't really think Jay had an 'estate' to leave behind."

"Well, Paul seemed really irritated with me after being rescheduled for almost seven months. But I assured him you were not in any state to deal with it before now," Stella said.

"Thanks Stella," I said as we finally pulled into the parking garage beside Paul Wellon's office.

....

"Ladies, why don't you come in and sit down." Paul Wellon greeted us and pointed toward a round table and several chairs in the corner of his office. Paul Wellon was much younger than I had expected. He was tall and muscular with dark brown hair and brown eyes and I guessed his age to be mid-thirties.

"How did you and Jay know each other?" I asked as we sat down.

"I was in my final year of law school during his first year at Wake. We shared the same advisor and ended up working on a case study together," he said, picking up some files and joining us at the table.

"I do apologize for our delay in coming to see you. It was completely my fault."

"No problem. You seem to have two really good friends who care a great deal for you," he added sincerely, looking at the three of us. "Now I have a lot of information to cover and I think some of it may come as a surprise to you," he said, clearing his throat.

"Why do you say that?" Stella interjected.

"Well, Jay and I had some pretty lengthy conversations after he set up his investments and started creating his will. He had many plans moving forward and wanted to make sure he was covered legally and he and Jill would be taken care of. He had a couple tricks up his sleeve, if you will. I'm sorry that he didn't get to unveil these to you as he planned." He looked at me earnestly. I just nodded and smiled nervously.

"Well, let's get started," he continued.

"Let's," Stella said. From her tone of voice I could tell she was becoming annoyed with Paul Wellon.

"Jill, Jay left you as the sole beneficiary of everything: the house in Greensboro, both vehicles ..." He paused, checking his notes. "I am to understand you already gave away one vehicle to a Mr. Harry Conner?"

"That is correct," I said, amazed at how accurate his information was.

"It's my job to know these things," he said, reading the surprise in my expression.

"Jay made a lot of investments with the money he made and inherited," Paul continued. I nodded again.

"Now I understand you have an anniversary coming up in June, correct?" he asked.

"That is correct."

"Well, Jay had a surprise for you that I was helping him set up."
He paused, almost giddy with the information he was holding back.

"And that was?" I asked, getting annoyed at his partial statements.

"Jay purchased a house on the beach in Oak Island, North
Carolina. It was meant to be a surprise anniversary gift for you. He
said it was your dream to one day live out there and he wanted to
make that happen." He paused, letting this information set in.

"He did what?" I asked, jumping out of my seat.

"What?" Stella and Lanie echoed around me as they pushed me
back into my chair.

"Jay purchased a house—"

"I heard what you said. I just don't believe it," I stammered.

"The house was bought at the end of last summer and was
deemed a fixer-upper, if you will. We had established a specific fund
for the house remodel and other necessities, but everything was
halted upon his passing," he said.

"How could he ... how could we afford all of it?" I asked,
dumbfounded.

"I assure you, Jill, Jay invested very wisely and you can afford
it. He left you with a sizeable amount of money in addition to the
house on Oak Island," he added as he continued to talk about the
legality of the properties and additional paperwork that would need
to be completed.

"Where is it?" I asked.

"Oak Island ... I have the address written down somewhere,"
Paul stammered after I interrupted him.

"I want to see it," I said. My mind was reeling over the fact
that my husband could purchase a house without my knowledge.
Romantic gesture or not this was a huge decision and secret he had
kept from me. I wasn't sure if I was furious or touched.

"Why of course. But we have many other details to cover," Paul added.

"Can the other details wait?" I asked.

"Jill … Mrs. Greenfield … let me assure you there are matters that need to be attended to. There are stock options, investments and other accounts that need to be maintained and I would recommend hiring a financial specialist."

Stella jumped in. "Paul, I think that maybe this is a little too much information to take in all at once."

"I agree. Why don't we deal with one thing at a time. Is there anything that won't keep a couple weeks more?" Lanie asked calmly.

"No. I guess there is not," Paul said, very frustrated by the turn this conversation had taken.

"Great," Stella said and I nodded.

"Jill," Paul said, now looking directly at me. "Whenever I spoke with Jay, his biggest concern was you. Your well-being, your likes, your future—every decision, every move he made had you in mind. I would like you to remember that as you learn more about all this in the upcoming weeks. I know it can be a lot to learn, especially from a stranger, but there were no secrets or surprises that were ever meant to hurt you. It was all meant to 'fulfill your dreams,' as Jay put it."

"Thank you," I whispered, becoming overwhelmed with all the emotion. Paul nodded and took out some paperwork from a folder that he indicated needed completing so that everything could be moved over to my name. I spent the next 30 minutes completing paperwork as Stella scrutinized every word over my shoulder and Lanie talked with Paul Wellon in the hallway. When we were done, Paul handed Stella a packet of information and shook hands with each of us, wishing us a good day.

The ride back to my house was quiet. I could tell a hundred questions lingered in the air, but no one spoke. When we got home, I went into the house and stood in the living room.

"Jill, you okay?" Lanie asked, coming up behind me.

"I ... I ... I don't know what to do," I confessed, looking at her with confusion.

"What do you want to do?"

"I don't know," I said, sitting down on the sofa with my head in my hands.

"I know what we should do," Stella added, coming in the door.

"And that is?"

"Road trip!" Stella said, tackling me on the sofa.

"Stella!"

"Yes?" she asked from under some pillows that had fallen on the floor when we both fell off the sofa.

"You act like you're five. I can't believe you're a lawyer," I said as I lay on the floor.

"I take that as a compliment."

"Both of you get up," Lanie instructed.

"So serious." Stella pouted at Lanie, causing Lanie to wrinkle up her face.

"No. Incoming," she said as I heard the front door open.

"Anyone home?" Harry called and entered the room.

"We all are," Stella said, pulling herself up and arranging herself on the sofa next to Lanie.

"Harry, I didn't expect you," I said, also getting up off the floor and picking up the pillows.

"Well, it's the only way I get to see you, since you ignore my calls."

"What do you want me to say?"

"Can we talk privately?"

"Sure," I said, pointing toward the back deck. As he walked to the back deck, I turned and looked at Stella and Lanie for help. They both looked back, shrugging their shoulders.

"Harry, I don't know what else we have to say." How many different ways could I tell Harry that I needed my space?

"I heard you met with the lawyer today," he said, completely surprising me.

"How did you know?" I asked, dumbfounded.

"There isn't much that goes on that I don't know about. Plus, he called me a week or so ago to follow up about the car you gave me. Made it sound like there was a lot Jay left you to take care of … investments and such," he said.

"I don't really feel comfortable discussing it all," I replied, instantly feeling defensive.

"Come on, Jill. It's me. Jay was my best friend."

"True, but his investments and whatever he left behind are not." I could feel my anger building.

"Is this how it's going to be between us?" he asked, stepping toward me.

"How what is going to be? And there is no us," I said moving to the other side of the deck.

"I'm just trying to be a friend."

"You have a really odd way of showing it. I keep telling you that I just need some space. Lanie and Stella have kept me under watch since everything happened. I haven't had time to myself to process everything." It was part truth and part lie, but Harry didn't need to know that.

"Jill, come on. We can go for coffee or something. Just you and I hanging out like we used to," Harry pleaded.

"Harry, it's not a good time right now. Stella and Lanie are here for the week and then they are gone. So maybe after that."

"Okay. I'm going to hold you to that."

"Sure," I said while I thought, "I bet you will."

I rejoined Stella and Lanie in the living room. They were both giving me a skeptical glance when Harry left.

"He wants to go to coffee," I said after not being able to take the judgmental looks.

"He wants in your pants, you mean," Stella said.

"Is that all?" Lanie asked, ignoring Stella.

"He asked about the meeting with the lawyer."

"He what? How did he know about that," Stella said, pointing a finger at me.

"Don't look at me. I didn't tell him," I shouted back.

"Neither did I," Lanie added before Stella could accuse her.

"He's bad news ..." Stella said.

"I agree," I said.

"So ..." Stella started to say.

"So?" I asked.

"Before we were rudely interrupted by your husband's crazy best friend, we were talking about a road trip."

"We were?" I asked.

"Don't mess with me," Stella said, pointing a finger in my direction, again.

"Do you think it's a good idea?" I asked Lanie, ignoring Stella this time.

"It's whatever you think," Lanie replied.

"Lanie, you're not helping. The correct answer is that it is the best idea ever," Stella interjected.

"Can I think about it?" I asked Lanie, still ignoring Stella.

"Take all the time you need," Lanie said, getting up from the sofa and making her way into the kitchen.

"Anyone hungry for lunch?" she called back.

"I am," I replied, looking at Stella, who was now pouting back at me.

"Why do you care so much?" I asked her.

"I don't really, but I want to go to the beach." She smiled, got up and heading into the kitchen after Lanie.

"Figures," I muttered to myself as I followed.

CHAPTER 20

....

For the first time in months, I felt as if I were making the right decision and I didn't feel sad. After hounding Lanie and me for two days, Stella had finally convinced us that we should take a road trip to see this mystery house that Jay had bought for me. Stella called Paul Wellon again to confirm the details of the property and we headed out mid-morning on Thursday. Paul had asked to speak with me and warned me that the house was not finished and that Jay had wanted it completed before I saw it. But Jay was dead, so his point seemed moot. Paul confirmed that renovations had stopped in November, shortly after Jay's death, as the future of the property hung in limbo.

....

Stella and Lanie planned a grand road trip adventure for us, which was impressive considering the three-hour drive to Oak Island. Both were optimistic that this was just what I needed: a chance to get away and start over. Stella and Lanie now bickered in the front seat about the best way to get to Oak Island from Greensboro. I sat in the back of Lanie's Volvo convertible, soaking in the sun and letting my mind drift through memories that Jay and I had created on Oak Island.

I knew exactly where the house would be when Paul Wellon told me about it. It was supposed to be a surprise for our anniversary, he had said. Our three-year anniversary was still a couple of weeks away in June, but it didn't shock me that Jay had already been thinking about it the previous summer. He was always thinking ahead, planning our future, carefully crafting every occasion, never leaving anything to chance.

We had spent every free moment since we had met traveling to the small beach town. Sometimes we would pack several cars with friends and stay in one of the many rental houses that lined the beach. Oftentimes it was just the two of us escaping on our own and often we would sleep in our cars overnight. We had always talked about getting a beach house, but I thought it was more in an abstract context. Things like "Someday, when we have our beach house, I want the bedroom to overlook the ocean" or sometimes in the stores I would spot a cute sign or piece of furniture and I would say "Wouldn't this look good in our beach house?" Jay would always smile and nod. I frowned slightly, thinking about how that dream would now always remain just a dream.

"Stop it," Stella said, breaking my thoughts.

"Stop what?"

"You're thinking again. You need to stop thinking and just enjoy this trip."

"I can't help but think of Jay. I mean we are going to the secret beach house he bought me for our anniversary, a house we planned to escape to forever." My voice hitched over the last part. It was too painful. "Maybe we should go back," I thought.

"Jill, you're going to be fine." Lanie reached back and grabbed my hand. "You're so strong, and we are here with you."

"You are both way too serious for this kind of trip. Both of you need to loosen up!" and with that, Stella turned the radio up, drowning out our conversation.

....

Eventually, we crossed the bridge, heading into Oak Island. I couldn't help my excitement. It was slowly building as we neared our destination. No matter what was going on in my life, this place made me feel at home. Jay knew me better than anyone else. This place was so peaceful and it made me happy.

"I think that's it up ahead," Stella said, pointing at a white, one-story bungalow at the end of a long row of brightly painted houses.

"The directions say it's 2828 East Bay Drive. What number does that house say?" Lanie asked.

"I don't know. I can't see any numbers," Stella commented.

"No. That's the house."

"How do you know?" Stella and Lanie asked together.

"Jay and I would always walk by it on the beach and talk about someday owning it," I whispered.

A white bungalow house on stilts with a large front staircase surrounded by scaffolding sat in front of us as we pulled into the short gravel driveway. Scattered around the house were various construction materials and supplies. No one made a move to get out of the car. I couldn't speak and tears started to roll down my cheek.

"Maybe this wasn't a good idea," Lanie whispered to Stella in the front seat.

"No, it's perfect," I stammered.

"Here are the keys. Why don't you go ahead in and we will unpack the car." Stella pressed the key into my hand as she and Lanie scrambled out of the car. I slowly made my way out of the backseat and up the stairs to the front door. The simple brass key fit in the door and I was able to push it open with ease. As I entered the house, I let out a small gasp. Straight in front of me was the most breathtaking view I had ever seen. My legs carried me without any need for direction. I crossed the open space so that I was standing directly in front of what appeared to be newly installed French doors. I reached for the handle and threw open the heavy doors, which opened onto a large wooden deck. I slowly stepped out onto the deck. There in front me of was nothing but the sand dunes and ocean. I was mesmerized by the waves as they crashed down on the beach in front of me. Behind me I heard a soft whistle and I could tell Stella and Lanie were making their way through the house.

"Jill, this is amazing," Lanie kept repeating.

"Really looks deserted. Paul wasn't kidding when he said they stopped right in the middle of construction," Stella commented.

I turned around to face my friends and noticed the interior of the house for the first time. Furniture sat covered in sheets. Stacks of boxes sat piled up. Paint swatches covered the wooden paneled walls. Brown paper stretched out along the floors, covering up new hardwood floors, and building materials lay scattered throughout the main floor.

"Why don't we explore the house and see if there is anywhere for us to sleep tonight? Otherwise, we can still check into that motel we passed a couple blocks back," Stella suggested.

From the outside, I had assumed the house was a one-story home, but now I could see a small staircase that wound its way up to a second floor. Upstairs we found two bedrooms that shared a bathroom and faced out onto the street and a large expansive master bedroom that overlooked the same breathtaking view from the deck.

Attached to the master bedroom was a private bathroom and walk-in closet. The bedrooms were in much the same condition as the rest of the house. Furniture, mattresses and boxes lay scattered throughout most of the spaces.

"At least there are beds," Lanie commented, sounding relieved. Her idea of roughing it was setting up a tent at the local Marriott and ordering in-room service. On Stella's suggestion we opened up several boxes and found brand-new bath towels, linens, pillows and blankets for each room. After setting up several rooms, we ventured into town to grab some supplies from the local grocery store as well as pick up dinner from one of my favorite seafood places on the water. Once we got back home, we set up a picnic style dinner on the deck with our crab cakes, seafood bisque and champagne watching the sunset.

"To us," Stella said, holding up her plastic cup filled with champagne.

"To Jay," Lanie said.

"To hope," I added as we clinked our cups together.

....

The next morning, I woke up to the sun shining and the sound of soft waves crashing down on the beach. Stretching and getting up, I looked around and had to pinch myself to make sure it was real. I had the most spectacular view of the ocean and it had the most peaceful effect on me. I put my hand out of the window as if I could almost touch the ocean from where I stood.

"Thank you, Jay," I whispered. It felt as if for the first time in months I could see through the gray that had surrounded my life. Even in death Jay knew what I would need to get me through my ordeal. I let out a long sigh and smiled as I headed downstairs. The house was still asleep as I opened several more boxes in the kitchen and found a kettle and several other kitchen items I would need to make breakfast. It was past eight when I heard someone shuffle downstairs.

"Smells fantastic," Lanie said, coming around the corner.

"Hungry?" I asked as I finished arranging the last of the French toast and eggs on plates.

"Absolutely," she said, looking for some utensils.

"Coffee?" Stella asked, coming up from behind Lanie.

"Water in the kettle is hot and the instant stuff we bought last night is in the cupboard to the right of the sink," I said, pointing to it for Stella.

"You're up early," Stella commented after she had fixed herself a cup of coffee and sat down on a stool at the island.

"How could anyone sleep with this amazing view," I said, waving my hand toward the ocean.

"Fair point," Stella said, stabbing her French toast with a fork.

"Jill, I forgot how wonderful a cook you are," Lanie exclaimed, taking two more pieces from the stack in the middle of the island.

"I forgot too," I added, finishing off my plate.

"What are we doing today?" Stella asked between mouthfuls.

"It's a beautiful day. Why don't we just enjoy the beach? The rest will still be here," I suggested.

"Sounds fantastic," Lanie said. After breakfast, I cleaned up as Lanie and Stella went back upstairs to change and get ready. I had already dressed in my suit this morning in anticipation of spending the day out in the sand. We sat out on the beach reading, swimming, sleeping and talking until dinnertime. Lanie was the only one of us worried about burning and kept reapplying sunscreen every 45 minutes. For dinner we decided to again try some of the local fare and Stella and Lanie went out to pick up the food while I showered and looked for some additional plates and cups.

"When are we leaving on Sunday?" Lanie asked over dinner.

"Leaving?" I asked.

"Yes. I have to catch a flight back to New York and Lanie needs to get back to her practice and her new wife," Stella said to tease Lanie, who just stuck out her tongue.

"I'm not going back," I said after a couple of moments.

"What do you mean you're not going back?" Lanie asked.

"For the first time in months, I feel at peace. This is where I am meant to be. I just know it," I said, looking eagerly at both Stella and Lanie who were giving each other side-glances.

"I don't know if I can stay—" Stella started to say.

"No. No one needs to stay with me. Jay bought this house so that we would be able to enjoy it and I feel at home here. The house back in Greensboro just makes me sad," I said. Lanie finally nodded while Stella still looked unconvinced.

"Just for a couple weeks … maybe the summer," I added quickly, trying to convince her.

"I don't know," Stella mumbled.

"Look, the house is unfinished. Paul said there were enough funds to finish the remodeling in the account that Jay set up." I still didn't know where he had got the funds, but that didn't matter at that moment. "Someone will need to be here to supervise that, right?" I added, feeling that a more logical reason for my staying would convince Stella.

"I suppose you are right. I will call Paul on Monday to set up the logistics of the fund and find out who the contractor was," Stella said. I grinned at both of them, knowing I had just won a huge battle in gaining back my freedom. We pulled the sheets off the sofa in the living room and I settled in with a book for the evening. I could hear Lanie's muffled voice in the other room on the phone with Mary Elizabeth and Stella sat at the kitchen table, working on her laptop. Shortly after 10 I got up and said goodnight and headed up to my room.

On Saturday morning we awoke to the rumble of thunder and an impending storm that had blown in overnight. After breakfast, Stella and Lanie decided to head into town to do some shopping and look around. I stayed behind and started unpacking some of the boxes. When Stella and Lanie returned, they had several large shopping bags in hand. When I inquired about the shopping trip, they shooed me upstairs.

"Jill, you can come down now," Lanie called up the stairs after several hours.

"You both know I hate surprises," I said, coming down the stairs. As I came into the living room, I stopped in my tracks and my hand immediately covered my mouth.

"Surprise!" Stella and Lanie shouted from the other side of the room. They had rearranged the living room furniture and moved several boxes out of the way, making it look more like a room. In addition, the room was now decorated with accent lamps, throw pillows, photographs and several other items that weren't there earlier.

"I love it," I finally said, fighting back tears.

"No crying," Stella said, handing me a glass of wine.

"You guys didn't have to do this," I said, pointing at all the décor.

"Yes, we did. If this is where you want to make your new home, we want to support you," Lanie said.

"Help you get started in the decorating department. You know we love to shop. We didn't have time to paint but this is what we suggest," Stella added, handing me several paint chips.

"Thank you," I simply said, taking another look at the transformation. We settled in at the kitchen table for the dinner they had again picked up in town and talked well into the night. It felt like old times.

CHAPTER 21

··

I promised Stella and Lanie I would be fine. I again told them
I wasn't ready to go home, back to the home Jay and I had
made. There was so much work to do finishing up the house
and unpacking I knew it would help me keep my mind off
of everything. It also helped that I promised to call Stella and Lanie
at least once a day.

"I don't think my own mother mothered me as much as you two
do," I said Sunday morning as we packed up the car.

"You have the whole summer in front of you," Lanie mused.
Lanie and Stella had spent almost eight months babysitting me and
the separation was turning bittersweet. But I knew as well as they did
that they needed to return to their respective careers and lives. We
arranged that they would come back for a long weekend at the end
of the summer over Labor Day weekend and Lanie promised to bring
Mary Elizabeth.

"Considering ..." Stella left her thought hanging. "It has truly
been the best time I have had in a long time. I can't believe I have to
go back to the real world, for real." For Stella the real world meant
mergers and acquisitions in New York. I wasn't convinced that it was
the real world.

"I can't believe you were able to get all this time off," I said,
thinking of all the weeks they each had spent by my side.

"Roger owes me a favor," she said, winking at me. She was referring to one of the managing partners at her firm.

"Everyone owes you a favor," Lanie commented.

"Hey, I can't help it if I'm good at uncovering secrets." She winked again.

"You mean blackmail," Lanie fired back.

"Lanie, blackmail is illegal. I should know. I'm a lawyer," Stella said, placing extra emphasis on the word lawyer.

"Ladies, do we need to fight now?"

Back in high school Lanie and Stella were notorious for their epic fights over morals, ethics and boys. I can remember this one time when they didn't speak for an entire three months over a boy named Chad Goffrey. Stella claimed they were on the verge of going steady and Lanie claimed that she had confessed her massive crush to Stella weeks earlier and that Stella was trying to date him just to spite her. It was never really resolved, but after weeks of silent treatment, they both came to their senses and things went back to normal.

"You're right. Jill, are you gonna be okay here by yourself? Are you sure you want to stay?" Lanie asked.

"She is going to be just fine. We are just a phone call away." Stella mimicked a phone with her hand as she walked around the car to give me a giant hug.

"Love you," she whispered in my ear. She then quickly turned and got into the driver's seat and started the car. Stella was never good with sentimental things.

"Oh Jill," Lanie whined.

"Lanie, I'll be okay, I promise. I'm not ready to go back." I grabbed her in a big hug before any tears had a chance to escape.

"I love you both. Thank you for everything." Words were never going to be enough for what they had done for me, but they were a start. We waved our good-byes and I stood there and watched them disappear down the road.

....

For the first time in almost eight months I was alone. I turned back up toward the house and stared, wondering what next. Jay and I always had a plan. We were driven, and we were focused on our future. Now here I was, staying in a half-refinished house on the beach, bought for me by my dead husband. I shook my head slowly, not believing the huge turn of events my life had taken, and headed back into the house. I slowly wandered through the living room and kitchen, touching the boxes that still were stacked up in different areas. Stella had hung soft mint-colored drapes over the large windows, claiming that some privacy was needed. I held the material in my fingers and let the materials glide through my fingers as I passed through the French doors onto the back deck and stared out into the ocean. In the distance I could hear people talking and the soft sounds of a guitar. The ocean waves continued to crash onto the beach and I wondered how I would move on. How do you pick up the pieces when your future was stolen from you but you still have your whole life ahead of you? I sighed and sat down in one of the chairs on the deck, taking in the peaceful evening ...

"One step at a time," I thought.

CHAPTER 22

··

I shivered under the cool breeze as I tried to reach for a blanket. Jerking awake, I realized I had fallen asleep on the deck. Standing and stretching, I made my way back into the house, locking the doors behind me. I finally made my way into the bedroom and turned the bedside light out, unable to think about all the events that had taken place. Laying my head down on the pillow, I closed my eyes and willed myself to fall into a dreamless sleep. A noise startled me. Glancing at the clock on the bedside table, I could see that it was just past three in the morning. Deep within the house I could hear creaking and while all reason told me it was nothing, my mind started to race about the many possibilities. Another strange noise made me sit up in bed. Fear and dread invaded my mind and made my limbs heavy. After several minutes, I heard no other sound and lay back down in bed. Staring up at the dark ceiling, I cursed my parents and their love of watching crime stories late at night. As a child I would sneak out of bed and perch myself at the top of the stairs and listen to *Unsolved Mysteries*. Looking back, I knew why I wasn't allowed to watch this show and maybe why my dad liked it too much. Fatigue returned, overwhelming me and causing me to fall back asleep. Suddenly, I heard another unfamiliar noise inside the house. This time I could swear I could hear footsteps. My breathing quickened and my heart raced as I leaned over and turned the bedside light back on. Willing myself to move, I slid out from under the covers and crouched next to the bed. I sat in silence, waiting for another noise. After several minutes, I slowly crawled around the edge of the bed toward the bedroom door. Where was my phone? I could be about to meet a burglar or worse yet a serial killer and I had no way to call for help. Making a mental note that I should start carrying my phone to bed and possibly invest in buying a baseball bat, I pushed the bedroom door open and moved out into the hallway. I reached up from my perch on the floor and turned the hallway light on.

"Hello?" I called out in a shaky voice, "is anyone there?"

No answer. Gaining a small amount of confidence, I slowly stood and continued to move throughout the house. I turned on every light I could find. As I made my way through the living room, the curtains rustled when a slight breeze came through the open window. I froze in place, waiting for any sudden movements. When I felt confident that there wouldn't be any, I moved quickly to the windows, slamming them shut and locking them. Sighing with relief, I grabbed my phone from the kitchen table and made my way back through the house, resigning myself to leave several lights on just in case.

As I climbed the stairs back to the bedroom, I tried to reason with my fear. I knew it was irrational to think that someone was in my house. The crime rate on Oak Island was low and home invasions usually only occurred after the summer months when vacation homes stood vacant. I was in a safe town and a safe neighborhood, but as the adrenaline coursed through my body, I found it harder and harder to convince myself. I went back into the bedroom and stared at the bed. My half was disheveled and the blankets were strewn about. What would have been Jay's side of the bed was still neatly made. I had felt so safe with him by my side. I had never feared noises, let alone the dark. Overcome with fatigue, again, I stumbled into bed, pulling the sheets up. I leaned over for the second time that night and turned the light off on the bedside table. As the soft glow left the room, the house seemed to come alive again. My mind started to race and my imagination ran wild. Leaning over, again, I turned the bedside light on, and checked my phone to make sure it had service. I slipped it under the pillow. The house settled again and I lay back down. Strangely, I felt safe with the lights on. I rolled over and drifted off to sleep.

The sun filtered in through the bedroom windows. I stretched and fumbled under my pillows for my phone. It was still early. I reached over and turned off the bedside light that was still on. Sighing to myself, I rolled over and stared up at the ceiling. I had my whole day ahead of me. Correction: I had my whole life ahead of me, but where did I start? Stretching and getting out of bed, I walked to the floor-length windows that lined my bedroom and, for the first time in months, I knew what I wanted to do. I picked through the clothes that were strewn across the floor and dressed in my running shorts and tank top. I grabbed my Boston Red Sox cap and headed down the stairs. I found my running shoes on the back deck and headed out toward the beach. Moving one step at a time, one foot in front of the other, I slowly made my way down the beach on what would end up being a three-mile run.

My breathing was finally slowing as I stretched on the back deck. I could hear my phone ringing back inside the house. I got up, dashed inside and tried to find it.

"Hello? Lanie?"

"Jill, are you okay?"

"Yea, I'm fine. Why?"

"Well, I called a little bit ago and you didn't answer."

"I was out on a run. I didn't take my phone with me."

"You were running?" Shock sounded in her voice and I can tell she had been sidetracked her from her original purpose.

"Yes. What can I help you with this morning?" I needed to keep her on task.

"Listen, yesterday when we left, Stella got lost—"

"Shocking." How Stella made it from point A to B still amazed me.

"I know, right?"

"I was not lost. Just taking a more scenic route." I could hear Stella in the background sounding like her defiant self.

"Well, anyway, we got lost and Stella missed her flight. We stayed in a local hotel last night and Stella is about to get on another flight this morning from Greensboro to New York, but I have some business in the area that has just come up, so I'm not leaving for another couple of days. Do you mind if I stay at your house?"

I could sense the hesitation in her voice. Did I mind?

"No, not at all. There is a spare key in a hideaway rock by the back porch," I said.

"Do you need me to do anything while I am there?" she asked.

"No, I'm fine."

"Thanks, Jill."

"No problem." I ended the call and made my way upstairs to shower and get dressed.

....

It was after two in the afternoon and I had all the windows open and a soft breeze drifted through the house. After piddling around the house most of the morning, moving boxes from one room to another, I finally decided to move up to my bedroom and unpack the boxes up there. I pulled the first box from the top of the pile and started unloading more sheets and towels. The next box held items that were to be used to decorate the bathroom. I had to laugh to myself at the thought of Jay shopping at all these online stores and selecting all these items down to the smallest detail. The box on the bottom of the pile held pictures and a large canvas of three brightly painted sailboats. I set the canvas down and went looking for a hammer and nails I knew I had seen before Stella and Lanie had had their redecorating party. After locating what I was looking for, I found several cans of paint, each a distinct color. Many were labeled for specific rooms in the house. I stared at the paint cans for a long time and then glanced around the house. For the second time that day I knew what I wanted to do and I searched for my phone and called Lanie.

"Hey, Lanie can you do me a favor?" I asked when she answered the phone.

"Sure. Anything you need."

"Are you still at the house?"

"Ya."

"Can you pack up the following items for me and have them shipped to this address?" I asked as I repeated the address for her.

"Sounds like you're thinking about making that house a more permanent residence," she mused.

"Ya. I think I am." I hadn't thought about it until I spoke the words out loud, but I was and more importantly, it felt right.

"I think that is awesome, Jill. I'm glad you have a plan. What are you going to do with all the stuff here?" she asked.

"I don't know. I just figured out I want to stay here." I laughed. We chatted about some other details and ended the call. I set the phone down and carried the paint can labeled "Master Bedroom" and other supplies up the stairs and set to work.

....

For the next several days my life fell into a familiar pattern. I got up early in the morning and went for a run on the beach, each morning going a little farther and feeling a little stronger. I then either spent the rest of my day painting or unpacking boxes. When I got low on supplies, I would walk several blocks to the local hardware store, which, as luck would have it, was right next to the local grocery store. At night I would sit on the deck and listen to the ocean often-times losing myself in my thoughts. The nights were still the toughest part. I still heard noises throughout the house, which caused panic to set in and keep me awake at all hours. During nights I was able to sleep, I was plagued by horrible nightmares that caused me to start awake, breathless and scared.

....

Finally, at the end of the week, the FedEx truck pulled up with the packages that Lanie had mailed me from the house. Mixed in with all the other packages were two packages I was not expecting. The first had a return label from Paul Wellon's office. I scanned the contents, most of which seemed to be about settling different items in Jay's estate. I made a mental note to call Stella and ask her if she would be able to look through the documents for me. The second package had no return label, but I knew who it was from the moment I opened it. Inside was a vintage wood frame with two pictures. The first was Lanie, Stella and me on the first day of kindergarten. It had faded over the years, but there we stood at the end of Lanie's gravel driveway, holding our lunch boxes and smiling back at the camera. It had been in my living room back in Greensboro. The second photo, taken several days earlier, showed all of us on the beach at sunset. A small note accompanied it.

> *Jill,*
> *Friends are the family you choose. No matter what you need, we are always here for you. Enjoy the house-warming gift.*
> *Love,*
> *Stella and Lanie*

Lanie must have written the note. It was way too sappy for Stella. I carried the picture immediately upstairs and placed it on my dresser. It was the first picture I had displayed in my new house. I grabbed my phone to text my friends.

> *To: Stella Conner, Lanie Alexander*
> *You guys are so sweet. Thank you for the gift.*

Seconds later, my phone pinged back.

> *From: Stella Conner*
> *You're such a sap!*

> *From: Lanie Alexander*
> *Glad you like it. Where did you put it?*

On the dresser in my bedroom. I smiled.

From: Stella Conner
There are many things that should be in your bedroom and that is not one of them.

From: Lanie Alexander
Stella!!

You're hilarious, Stella. I didn't care what Stella thought. Its home was going to be there.

From: Stella Conner
Suit yourself.

I rolled my eyes at Stella and set my phone down. I set my sights on the rest of the boxes that Lanie had packed up for me. For the next several hours, I hung portraits of family, different canvases Jay and I had collected and other pieces that had been up in the attic back home. I also found a home for Lanie's shadow box from Christmas. Finally, I got around to the boxes of clothes Lanie had sent me. Each item was carefully folded and some even had small notes from Lanie pinned to them, commenting on my taste in clothes or how much she liked a particular item over another. After unpacking all the boxes I had asked for, I found yet another unexpected parcel. I tore it open and found another note from Lanie.

Jill,
You used to write all the time. I thought maybe it was time you should start again.
Love,
Lanie

Inside the envelope I pulled out my leather-bound journal, I recognized it immediately. It was the most recent journal I had been writing in at the time of Jay's death. On the last written page was the poem I had read at his funeral. Lanie was right. I used to write in a journal all the time. It was the one thing, I think, that got me through my childhood. I knew she meant well but I could feel my temper flare up. Who did Lanie think she was? Not my mother. I would start writing when I was ready, if I was every ready again. It, like so many other things, just didn't feel right after Jay's accident. I rolled my eyes and tossed the journal and note onto the dresser.

....

The next morning, I walked over to the local grocery store and asked someone at the customer service desk if I could fax some documents. The 20-something-year-old kid, whose nametag read "Zach," looked back at me as if I had three eyes as I tried to explain what a fax was. After several attempts, I asked to speak with his manager. The manager, who appeared to be not much older than Zach, agreed to let me fax my documents after apologizing for Zach's lack of personality, among other things. I shrugged it off and called Stella on my walk home.

"I just faxed you some documents from Paul Wellon's office. Can you read through the documents and let me know what I need to do and what it all says?" I asked.

"First thing Tuesday morning. You know it's Memorial Day weekend, right?" she asked.

"Nope. I had no idea." I had lost track of time ever since the accident.

"Well, it is. Just enjoy yourself. Also, remember that everything is all set with the construction company. I spoke with the owner, Jeff

Powers. He and his workers are starting on Tuesday," she informed me.

"They have been commissioned to finish replacing the windows, paint the exterior of the house, replace the roof, rebuild the deck and do some minor landscaping. It should take roughly two months, they are estimating. This was all under the original plan Jay had laid out for the house." She paused to see if I had anything to add.

"What color are they painting the house?" That was all I had to add.

"It hasn't been decided. Lanie and I decided that you should have the final say," she said.

"Thanks. It's only my house," I snidely remarked.

"Hey, you weren't in any condition to be making decisions for so long," she snapped back.

"Okay. Okay. I get it. I'll pick the color when they get here. Will that work? I don't really have a means to go to them to pick out any colors. I'm without any type of transportation," I reminded her.

"Oh, that reminds me. There was a note in the previous documents that Paul forgot to share. There are additional funds set aside to purchase a vehicle that would stay with this residence," she said, sounding very formal.

"Seriously?" I was stunned.

"I was just thinking of getting a bike," I added.

"You can do that." She paused. "But it's hard to ride a bike in the snow."

I chuckled at her words. She had obviously forgotten how mild North Carolina winters were.

"I have my car back home."

I thought about my old Jeep Cherokee sitting in the driveway back home. Jay had tried so hard over the years to convince me to get something new, something "shiny" as he put it. But it was a good car and it still worked. So what was the point of replacing it?

"On second thought,"—it was my turn to stun—"can you arrange for someone to put my car up for sale and the house too?" I took a deep breath. I hadn't really thought the decision through, but as soon as I said it, I knew it was what I wanted—and needed—to do.

"Seriously?" It was Stella's turn for disbelief.

"Did I stutter?"

"No, but are you ready for that? You have only been there for a couple days. Don't you want to give yourself a little bit more time to think this through?" she said, sounding like Lanie.

"Lanie made me clean out most of Jay's stuff months ago. So it's not like I'm avoiding anything or running away from anything," I argued.

"True, but I never thought you would just sell it. Are you going to go back?"

"Not unless I have too. I have most everything I need or want. There are a couple little things I can have shipped to me, but for the most part, everything else can be donated or sold." My future seemed to be clearer now than it had even been several days ago.

"Sure thing, friend ... only if you are absolutely sure."

"I'm sure. Oh, also, I think I will take you up on the appropriated funds thing. I want a new Jeep, a Wrangler, cherry red. Can you arrange that as well?" I knew I was pushing my luck with Stella, but I wanted to see just how far she would let me go.

"Anything else I can help you with, your highness? It's not like I'm a high-paid lawyer in New York with a full-time job," she said, and I could picture the frown she probably had.

"Please, Stella? You love shopping and negotiations more than anyone I know … and … plus I am rideless, remember? So I can't go do it myself." I added my last point for good measure.

"You do have a point. I'm sure I can get Abbey, my assistant, to help me out on some of your requests." I could hear her mulling over her priorities. "Yea. I can get this done. I'll look over the documents you faxed as well and let you know. You're so lucky we have a history, Jill Greenfield. I wouldn't do this for just anyone!"

I was going to owe her and she was going to let me know it, but I didn't care.

"Thank you, Stella, I owe you!"

"Yes. Yes, you do. Listen, I have to go. I'll talk to you in a couple days. Roger is taking me to the Hamptons for the rest of this weekend." I could hear her smile with delight at being treated to a luxurious weekend.

"Does Roger's wife know?" I asked, raising my eyebrows.

"Don't know. Don't care." Stella never had a problem with being the other women in a relationship. I often thought she preferred it that way because she could avoid getting too attached.

"Alright. Well, be safe. Have fun."

"Thanks, love. Remember, you will have several hunky men there at your disposal on Tuesday. Don't let it go to waste," she said, and I swear I could hear her wink at me.

"Bye, Stella—"

"And Jill," she said, interrupting me.

"Yea."

"It's nice to see you coming back to us," she said softly.

"I agree."

Tuesday morning rolled around quickly and promptly at eight o'clock there was a loud knock at the door. I had just gotten back from my run and as I walked through the house, I wondered if I should be worried about how I looked. Nah. Whom did I have to impress? A burly man in his mid-forties with blonde hair stood at the door, dressed in jeans and button-up shirt and baseball cap.

"Mrs. Greenfield?" he asked, looking up from a clipboard when I answered the door.

"Call me Jill," I replied, extending my hand.

"Jill, I'm Jeff Powers with Powers Construction. We started work on your place several months ago and we got an updated contract to finish up the work," he said.

"Yes, that sounds accurate." With that, Jeff took out the contracts, asking me to sign and initial several statements.

"Great. I would like to walk you through several of these projects and give you a timeline. We are going to try and stay out of your way as much as possible, but some of these projects will be loud and messy."

"It's not a problem."

I didn't want to tell him that I had nothing going on, so they wouldn't be keeping me from anything. For the next hour, Jeff walked me through each project and the estimated time of completion. When we got on the topic of painting the house, he asked if I had chosen a color. I explained to him that I hadn't been previously involved, so I didn't know where we stood on that. He let me know that he would have someone bring by paint swatches, but they would need a decision soon so as not to delay the order.

"It's not a problem" I found myself saying for the second time.

"Okay. Well, I'm going to start unloading my tools. My crew should arrive over the next couple hours and hopefully we can get started before the storm blows in."

"Wonderful." I turned and headed back in the house, glancing at the large black clouds that danced on the horizon. I had several errands I needed to run before the storm blew in. My first order of business was to go buy a bicycle. I had made it the last several weeks without needing one, but since I had decided to make this my permanent residence, I needed another means of transportation. So I headed out toward the local supermarket and hardware store as the construction crew started to arrive.

Mr. Colton ran the hardware store and assured me that my bike could be ordered and would arrive in the next several days. He would assemble the bike himself and give me a call when it was ready.

"How is the construction on your house coming along?" he inquired.

"Wow, word does travel fast around here. They just arrived this morning!" I couldn't hide my shock.

"Mr. Powers and his team do good work."

"How did you know?" My curiosity was peaked. My story was hardly juicy enough to become town gossip.

"You have an interesting story, Mrs. Greenfield, and it's a very small town." He winked at me and then turned to walk into the back room.

Perplexed, I headed home. Most of the dark clouds from earlier had moved on and it looked as if the forecasters were going to be wrong about the weather. At home, the construction workers were in full swing in various areas of the house. I could see roofers moving on the roof, throwing shingles off. Several crew members were unloading what looked to be new windows while several others were unloading new boards for the back deck.

....

Again, I settled into a small routine as the construction workers settled in. I would get up and go for a run and then spend the rest of my day avoiding the work crews. Stella or Lanie called periodically to check in on the progress and see how I was doing. Lanie asked if I had started writing in my journal and I ignored her question. One particular morning, after completing an eight-mile run, I returned home to find the workers had not yet arrived. A quick check of my phone revealed a message from Jeff that none of the workers would be there that day because of the weather. After taking a quick shower and eating some granola, I found myself walking around the house. Over the previous few days I had ignored the last couple of boxes that needed unpacking. Finally, after stalling for about an hour, I turned my iPod on and let the jazzy sounds of Sinatra fill the house, which was normally filled with the sounds of hammering, talking and objects being slammed around. I settled in with the few remaining boxes. The first box was the easiest. It held books that Jay and I had collected over the years. He had told me that he was sending them to storage. Apparently, storage had been code for "I'm shipping them to the beach house of our dreams." I had one more box to go and then I would be officially unpacked. The thought of being done gave me a renewed energy, which quickly faded as I tore open the last box. It was filled with most of my scrapbooks and many loose photos I often had floating around the house. All my memories were staring back at me, haunting me. Not being able to stop myself, I started to pull out the pictures and sort through them.

Time seemed suspended as I made my way through the box. I didn't know if I had sat there for minutes or hours, staring at the wide array of glossy photos. Tears streamed down my checks as I looked into the eyes of my parents. There were photos from my parents during the good times, their wedding, my birth and every milestone in my young life; pictures of Stella and Lanie; and of course pictures of Jay. When I couldn't stand it anymore, I threw the photos down and ran outside, thick tears now streaming down my face. I shimmed down the makeshift staircase the workers had created while they tore apart the deck. I was on the sand and had started running toward the beach when my foot got caught on something and I fell to the sand.

"Son of a bitch," I yelled as pain shot through my foot. I got up and kicked the board out of my way. I could feel the anger building inside me and I didn't know where to turn. From the corner of my eye, I could see that part of the deck had yet to be torn out. I walked over and picked up a hammer and crowbar and started working on the remaining boards. The tears continued to fall and anger overflowed.

"Sure. Mom and Dad bring me into this world only to screw it all up. Dad, you just couldn't resist any type of drug, could you? Just couldn't stay away. Where did that leave you? Jail! Mom, you said we would beat cancer. You said we would beat it!" I was screaming now as I tugged and pulled at those boards, throwing each one to the ground and working on the next. I was screaming at the ghosts of my past.

"And Jay, do not get me started ... till death do us part ... Well, now what? Now what? We had a plan, a future!" I was crying so hard I was having trouble breathing as I kept swinging the hammer. I was no longer pulling boards up. I was just swinging the hammer and repeatedly hitting the boards.

"Now what?" I shouted again.

Somewhere in the middle of my meltdown the rain had started to come down and soak my clothes, but I didn't care.

"Lady, lady." I could hear the shouting in the back of my head, but it didn't register. I was angry and uncontrolled as I continued to shout and yell.

"Lady." Someone was shouting much closer now, and before I knew it, a pair of arms wrapped around me from behind and held me tight.

"Let me go!" I yelled, kicking and struggling to break free. "They all let me down and now they are all gone and what about me?" I shouted again.

"Lady," he said again, more gently this time. But he didn't loosen his grip. I was still thrashing about and yelling. "Lady, calm down, please," he whispered one more time in my ear. I tried to fight him one more time and slowly the fight left me. The tears continued to flow, and I finally gave into the strong arms wrapped around me.

"They all left me... What if it's me, my fault?" That was all I had the energy to say as I slumped over and dropped the hammer, which hit the deck with a loud clatter.

"I'm going to let go now," he said and slowly released his grip on me. I didn't know what else to do. I spun around and buried my face into the shoulder of this stranger and cried until I couldn't cry anymore. I didn't realize what was happening until it was too late. I felt my feet get swept out from underneath me and a strong arm under the small of my back. I was being carried around the house, up the front stairs of my own house and in the front door. He placed me gently down on the sofa, and I sat there in a comatose state.

"Um ... is there someone I can call?" he gently asked me.

"There's no one left." As I said the words, I could hear the hollowness in my own voice. I folded over and lay down on the sofa, closing my eyes and drifting off to into a dreamless sleep.

....

It was dark when I woke up. I could see a soft glow of light coming from the kitchen. I struggled to sit up as the room spun and my head was killing me. A blanket that had lain on the back of the sofa now covered me up and a cup of tea sat in front of me on the coffee table. I reached for the tea. My hands were shaking. The tea was still warm. I took a long sip and steadied myself. Somewhere not too far away I heard a soft guitar melody. Standing up and wrapping the blanket tighter around my shoulders, I followed the music.

Rounding the corner into the kitchen, I saw a shaggy blond, barefoot guy, sitting at the table and strumming the guitar. He was wearing a pair of jeans and white T-shirt. When the song came to an end, I stood there a minute or two longer, observing him. He lifted his eyes to mine and I gasped as I stared into a set of pale green eyes. They seemed endless as they searched mine.

"Two things," I stammered. "Who are you? And I'm so sorry you had to witness that." He paused a moment or two longer and finally replied, "Are you okay?"

"That's a complicated question."

"Shouldn't be," he commented quietly. He put his guitar to the side, stood up and walked toward me.

"My name is Ross Powers. I work for Jeff Powers. He's my uncle."
He extended his right arm.

"Jill," I said sheepishly as I shook his hand. As he stood there in
front of me, I had a better chance to look at him. He was much taller
and younger than I had initially observed.

"What were you doing here?"

"I was bringing by paint swatches." He nodded his head toward
a booklet that sat on the kitchen table. "I came to the front door,
but no one answered, and then I heard the yelling. So I came around
back to investigate, and I found you."

We both knew the scene he had happened upon.

"Thank you. You didn't have to stay."

"Um … I was kinda worried. I don't really come across scenes
like that often. No one seemed to be around and I didn't just want
to leave."

"Often?" I teased, trying to lighten the mood.

"Okay. Ever." He gave me a shy smile and I couldn't help but
smile back.

"Can I make you something to eat or drink?" he said.

I couldn't help but let out a short laugh.

"Let me let you in on a little secret. I live here and I should be
asking you those questions." I smirked.

"Right," he said and turned to pick up his guitar. "I really should
be going. You are going to be okay, right?"

"I'm going to be fine," I lied with a smile. "Where are your
shoes?" I wondered out loud.

"Oh, I left them by the front door. I didn't want to track mud
into your house."

"It was raining, wasn't it?" He turned and looked at me, lifting
an eyebrow in a question mark. "Didn't you notice?"

"Apparently not."

"Did anyone else on the crew witness my meltdown?" I asked quietly, forgetting that Jeff had already called to tell me no one would be coming by because of the bad weather.

"Nope. Just me—"

"Lucky you."

"Your secret is safe with me." He winked at me and made his way toward the door, pulling on a pair of worn Converse sneakers.

"Seriously, Ross. Thank you."

He shrugged his shoulders and turned to leave. Halfway down the stairs, he paused and looked back.

"See you tomorrow, Jill." He flashed a wide grin and turned and left.

I carefully shut the door and walked through the dark house, turning on the occasional light and locking the doors. I made my way upstairs and there in my bedroom sat the large pile of pictures that had started my tirade. I brushed them out of the doorway, moved across the room and turned on the bedside light. My phone sat on the nightstand and when I glanced down, I saw I had three missed calls, one from Stella and two from Lanie. They were probably wondering what was going on with me. I was wondering the same thing as I rolled over and tried to drift off to sleep before the nightmares started.

....

I woke up later than usual. I could hear the Powers crew already at work, banging and hammering. I rose slowly as my head continued to pound from the night before. Just then, my phone rang. Wearily, I reached for it.

"Hello?" I rasped.

"Jill, are you okay?" Lanie shrilled.

"I'm fine."

"Don't give me any of that 'I'm fine' BS. You haven't called in days," She was practically yelling into the phone.

"Well then, honestly, I feel hung over,"

"Have you been drinking? That is really unhealthy … to do alone," she ranted.

"Lanie!" I cut her off before she could go any farther. "I wasn't drinking. I just had an … an … emotional night," I stammered.

"Do you need me to come there?"

"If you need another trip to the beach, you just need to ask. You don't need to make any excuses."

"Jill, you know that is not what I mean," she replied.

"Lanie, I appreciate the offer, but I'm okay … I was just going through a box of photos and everything kinda caught up with me." It wasn't a lie, but it wasn't the whole truth.

"That sounds reasonable," she commented.

Did it?

"But I am going to let you go. My head is killing me and the construction and hammering isn't helping."

"Oh yea, I forgot. How is the house coming along?"

"Really well, but I will be happy when they are all done."

"I can't wait to see it. Oh, and Jill?"

"Yes."

"Don't think you are getting out of this conversation. I'm letting you go for now."

"Not in a million years," I said with a slight frown.

"Okay. Talk to you later."

"Bye."

My body continued to ache and my head continued to pound. I skipped the morning run and instead opted for a day on the beach. The kitchen clock said it was after 10 in the morning and the sun was streaming in through the windows and I could already feel the heat of the day. After making my way slowly through the house and out the front door, I headed toward the beach. I glanced around at the workers as I made my way around the house. A few waved and said good-morning, but no one looked familiar. I was beginning to think that maybe I had dreamed the entire incident the previous night. Maybe I was finally losing my mind.

....

I settled in on the beach and stretched out on the towel, the soft sound of the waves crashing down soon lulled me to sleep. I woke with a start. I was disorientated and unsure of where I was. The sun was much higher in the sky and I could feel the sweat sticking to my body. Slowly opening my eyes, I found myself in the same position I had fallen asleep in. Several families had congregated around me, and I wondered how long I had been asleep. My head no longer pounded. I smiled and sat up.

"I was starting to worry that someone needed to check your pulse, see if you were still alive?" a voice said behind me. Startled, I turned around and came face to face with those pale green eyes from yesterday.

"Ross, what are you doing down here? I thought you said you worked for your uncle?" I was confused.

"I do. But I try and catch the waves during my lunch hour," he explained.

"Of course you do." It was only then I noticed he was sitting on a brightly colored surfboard.

"I was just finishing up my lunch anyway. Didn't mean to disturb you," he said, holding up his arms to show he meant no harm.

"What time is it anyway?" I asked.

"A little after two," he replied.

I had been asleep for almost four hours.

"What do you do for your uncle?" I asked, changing the subject. He didn't seem like the roofing type.

"I usually run errands, some office work. In return, he lets me stay at his place here on the beach."

"And what do you do when you're not surfing or running errands?"

"I hang out, write music, chill."

Could this kid be any more of a hipster? I stood up and brushed the sand from my legs.

"I'm going to go down for a swim." I felt the need to explain my exit.

"Cool. I'm sure I will see you around." He stood up and grabbed his board. "Oh wait! Did you have a chance to look at those paint colors?" he asked, pausing to look back at me.

"Nope. I forgot about them to be honest. I'll look at them this afternoon and let Jeff—"

"You can just let me know. I'll be around here somewhere most of the day," he said and strolled off.

"I'm sure," I said out loud to no one in particular as I headed down to the surf.

....

"Stella, I can't understand what you are saying. Slow down." I had come back up to the house and showered when I noticed I had three missed calls. I was now sitting at my kitchen table, with a large cup of coffee, staring at the paint swatches Ross had brought by the previous evening.

"Jill, he left it all to you."

"Left what? Who?" I still wasn't following Stella.

"Jay. He left it all to you," she stammered.

"Tell me something I didn't know. You were there when Paul Wellon explained all that the first time."

"No. You don't understand."

"Then start making some sense."

"Jay's mom left him a sizeable amount of money when she passed away. He invested that money into different stocks, companies and real estate." I had known Jay was always tinkering with his portfolio, brooding over every move and investment. It normally didn't interest me, so I would let him ramble on and on about his investments, most of which I usually tuned out.

"Right. I knew that."

"Did you know that he was worth millions?"

I could feel the room start to spin.

"Are you sure?" I finally replied.

"I doubled-checked the paperwork and then made a couple of phone calls. I'm sure."

"Was I that clueless? I didn't know about any of this," I whispered back into the phone.

"Don't be melodramatic. He was setting things up to ensure you both had a comfy lifestyle." She paused. "Jill, your name is on all these documents. He made sure you would receive full ownership of everything if something happened to him."

We had lived such a modest life up to that point. Some months we were working pay check to pay check and we struggled as everyone else did, paying off our student loans and credit cards ... or so, at least, I had assumed.

"Jill ... are you there?" Stella asked.

"Um ..." I mumbled back.

"Earth to Jill ..."

"I just ... I don't know what to say."

"Well, there's is more."

"More?"

How could there be anymore?

"Seems like Paul was holding out on us when we met with him."

"Is that legal?" I asked.

"He didn't lie. He was just creative in some of his wording. I should have seen it then," Stella said. She hated being taken by surprise, but she loathed having someone pull one over on her.

"Anyway, he released most of his notes about conversations he and Jay had."

I braced myself again as she paused. Learning my husband was not the man I thought he had been was becoming very taxing.

"Jill, he loved you. I mean, he really loved you."

It was not what I thought she was going to say. Now for the second time in a matter of minutes I was confused.

"I really don't understand," I confessed.

"Jill, Jay set up the accounts and the money to create a lifestyle where you would be able to quit your job teaching and follow your passion. He knew that the two of you had a plan and a future but he wanted to ... amend that plan ... if you will."

"What is my passion?" I was trying to rack my brain about any conversations that I might have had that would have indicated I wasn't happy or that I wanted to do something else.

"I was happy, Stella. Everything was perfect."

"Jay knew you better than you knew yourself. It's so romantic," she squealed. Only Stella would think large sums of money were romantic. "You are always the last one to figure it out. You're so oblivious." She paused, turning serious. "He had this money and he never told you so you didn't have to worry. He wanted to give you the world and he wanted you to follow your dreams ... He wanted you to write."

"Write? I'm not a writer. I'm a kindergarten teacher ... Well, I was a kindergarten teacher."

"Jill, you didn't have to be married to you to figure it out. Lanie and I have watched you scribble away in those journals of yours since we were kids. You were always happiest sitting by yourself, lost in some train of thought, writing."

It was true. I used to tell my mom I was going to be a writer. That dream died when my mom did.

"Anyway, it looks like Jay had read through some of your stuff and thought you had it."

"He did what? If he wasn't dead, I would kill him," I said. That was the only condition Jay and I had ever had. He had promised never to read or flip through any of my journals. I considered them my most private thoughts and I didn't want anyone to invade them.

"There's that feistiness I have missed," Stella exclaimed.

"I feel so betrayed."

"Stop it. He was creating this life for you. You were going to live on the beach and write books while he mergered and acquisitioned all day."

"That's not a real thing 'mergered and acquisitioned,'" I commented dryly.

"Bottom line is you were never going to have to worry about anything. He was going to take care of you."

"I never asked for all that."

"Doesn't matter. It's all yours and it's all here in black in white and legally binding. Paul wanted to wait a while before he laid it all on you. He thought the shock of Jay's death and finding out about the beach house was probably all you could take last time."

"He's probably right. I don't know if I can still really comprehend this all."

"Well, I can and you're going to be fine. You will be treating me to the best lobster dinner Oak Island has to offer after this. Anyway, I have started to take care of the initial paperwork for you. I have asked Roger if we can take you on as a client, as well. You know, so we can make sure everything is managed properly. I didn't think you wanted to deal with all the paperwork and to continue to manage the portfolio." She rambled on and on about details and initial meetings. "Since your information was already provided on the documentation, I took the liberty of transferring a small amount of money into your account so you can get by and we will straighten out the rest when you come and meet with the financial guys and me in a couple weeks."

"When exactly?" I asked, as this trip was news to me.

"No rush. I figured you can come up here for a couple days. We can straighten this out and then we can head back to the beach together and meet up with Lanie for our Labor Day trip."

"Yea. That sounds great."

"You gonna be okay? You sound down and this is really great news."

"Just a lot to take in, you know," I replied.

"I have no idea, but I'm excited for you."

"Thanks, Stella." We talked pleasantries for a couple more minutes, catching up on her nonrelationship with Roger, before finally ending the call.

The idea of being financially stable was comforting, but the feeling that Jay was hiding all these secrets from me was disconcerting. Did I really know the man I had married? If he was capable of hiding these things from me, was there anything else? On the other hand, he seemed to have devoted so much time and energy ensuring that we—I—was going to be happy. I wished I could have told him I was happy with our life. I was happy with the way things were.

A knock on the door brought me out of my reverie.

"Ross," I said, opening the door.

"Jill, sorry to bother you at the end of the day like this, but my uncle—I mean Jeff—wants to know if you have a paint swatch for him. He has to get that order in so everything can stay on schedule."

He shrugged his shoulders. He was dressed casually, wearing ripped Cargo shorts with a vintage concert tee and the same Converse sneakers from the other night.

"Of course. Come in."

I stepped aside and gestured for him to come in. "I have the swatches on the counter; I was just getting around to looking at them, to be honest."

"Need any help?" he asked.

"Actually, I would love some."

We made our way to the kitchen and stared at the couple of swatches I had pulled out before Stella called.

"That's quite an array of colors," he said, running his hand through his shaggy hair. In truth, there was no rhyme or reason behind the color selection. I had pulled colors in shades of blue, green, orange, white, pink and gray.

"Any advice?" I asked.

"Are you trying to blend in or stand out?"

"Neither."

"Well then, what color speaks to you."

"Speaks to me?"

"You know. What color makes you feel ... something," he said turning toward me and looking directly at me. It felt as if his eyes could see right through me and he would surely uncover everything about me at any minute.

"I can tell you what doesn't speak to me." I reached across and pulled the pink and gray paint chips to the side.

"Okay. That's a good start ..." He paused and thought a moment before continuing. "Are you going to name the house?"

So many beach houses were identified in the area simply by a name or phrase the owners had given them, such as His & Hers, Southern Comfort, Weekend Getaway, Beach Breezes. I had toyed with several names over the last couple years, thinking about the day when we could finally own our own beach house and be able to name it.

"I hadn't really thought about it," I lied.

"Really?" he looked at me with a quizzical look, not quite believing me. I aimlessly walked to the set of windows that overlooked the ocean. It was another perfect evening. The sky was turning all types of orange and pink as the sun started to set. The ocean was still like glass and the breeze was blowing the tall grass ever so slightly. I felt so relaxed, so still at that very moment.

"Eirene" slipped out before I knew I was even thinking about it. "It's named after the Greek Goddess of ..." I stammered, turning to face Ross.

"Peace."

"Yea. Not many people know that," I said with a slight smile.

"Shocked I knew that?"

"Yes, actually."

I was floored. Not many took the time to learn Greek Mythology anymore. I found a passion for it while in college and took every elective course I could on the subject.

"I could tell. You don't have a very good poker face." He chuckled.

"I'll keep that in mind."

"So back to colors." He gestured to the table.

"What color makes me think about peace?" I asked.

"Yea, something like that." He shifted his position and glanced and his watch. I glanced at the clock on the wall and saw it was well after eight in the evening.

"Oh, I'm keeping you from something, aren't I? I'm sorry," I babbled on.

He was a young, handsome guy, who probably had much better things to do than discuss paint colors with some half-crazed older woman.

"No. You're fine," he said as he reached across the table and spread out three paint colors. "Seems to me like you could do with a few less options." He pointed to the colors he had selected. I doubted he knew how right he was.

"I like the slate-blue color," I finally said after staring at the colors for several minutes.

"Me too." He smiled and reached across the table for the paint chip just as I did. As our hands touched, I could feel an almost palpable energy between us. I quickly withdrew my hand and looked up to see if he too had felt it. As always, he looked calm, cool and collected.

I thought I might be losing my mind.

As he collected the rest of the paint swatches, we made some small talk and I walked him to the door.

"Thanks for coming by and getting that done. I would hate to mess up your uncle's schedule," I said, leaning against the doorjamb as he stood on the porch.

"He will be fine. He just panics for no reason."

"Goodnight, Ross."

"Have a goodnight, Jill. I hope you get some rest."

I must have given him a look that warranted further explanation. "Well, it's just that my friends and I often hang out on the beach at night and I have noticed the lights on at all hours of the night. Seems like you're burning the midnight oil a lot."

"Yup. Just burning the midnight oil." I didn't want to reveal that I was paranoid and scared of the dark.

"Night," he said, waving to me as he made his way down the steps to the navy Ford F150 with "Powers Construction" painted on the side parked in the driveway.

Nightmares continued to plague my sleep. I always awoke in a panic, feeling terrified but never remembering anything that actually occurred in the nightmare. On this particular morning, I gave up on sleep just after three in the morning and sat out on the porch, watching the sun rise just a little before six. I knew what day it was without even looking at the calendar: June 28. This would have been Jay's and my third wedding anniversary as well as Jay's thirty-second birthday. When we had picked our wedding date, I asked Jay repeatedly if he minded that our wedding day fell on his birthday. In truth, it was the only day the venue had open for the next year.

"Have you as my birthday present every year? I couldn't imagine a better way to celebrate," he replied simply and with that, ended any discussion on the subject.

But now I felt as if any life I had breathed into my sails had been deflated. I had been dreading this day for weeks, unsure of how I felt about it and most importantly how to deal with it. There were several times when I reached for the phone to call Lanie or Stella, but each time, I couldn't follow through. How did I explain the void that Jay's love had left in my life? I would have done anything to get just five more minutes with Jay, to be able to look into his eyes and hold his face in my hands. The pain still hurt and often left me breathless.

Could I make them understand how he once floated through my dreams and now I felt as if he haunted them, slowly driving me crazy. I would have sat out on the porch all day in my almost-vegetative state had it not been for the large rain drops that had started to fall. I dashed inside and heard my phone chime, indicating I had a voice message. Ignoring the phone, I headed back upstairs and climbed into bed, pulling the covers over my head. I was soon lulled to sleep by the sound of rain on the roof above me.

....

Several hours later, a loud knocking noise woke me from my dreamless sleep. Disorientated, I was unsure of where the sound was coming from. Slowly it dawned on me the construction workers were continuing work on the house. The morning storm had blown through but gray clouds continued to linger in the sky. Sighing, I rose from bed and decided to take a late afternoon run. Checking my phone, I saw that I had several missed messages. The morning message had been from Lanie, who had called two additional times. Stella had texted several messages, and Harry also called to leave a message.

"All the normal players," I thought.

I ignored them all. Instead, I set off down the beach on a very slow, methodical run, and with each step, I could feel the tension and sadness trying to leave my thoughts, clearing my mind completely, or so I thought. It was toward the end of the run that my mind started to wander, drifting to thoughts of Jay and the accident. I tried to run harder as the images flooded my thoughts. Tears escaped and blurred my vision. My breathing was soon irregular as I struggled to keep up my frantic pace. It wasn't long before my knees gave out, and I suddenly collapsed on the beach. Running had always been the greatest escape and it now had failed me. I continued to sit in the sand as tears streaked down my face. I looked up at the sky for a clue or sign, something to indicate that everything was going to be okay. There was nothing. The peaceful feeling I had found weeks earlier had gone and my emotions were now wreaking havoc on my life. With what little motivation I had left, I found my way back to the house.

A hot shower and clean clothes did little to improve my mood as I sat at the kitchen table, drinking coffee. I sent a blanket text back to my friends that I was okay but didn't feel like talking with anyone, before they panicked and decided to do something drastic. Then, for the first time in a very long time, I felt the need to express the thoughts that were now continuously scrawled through my mind. I rifled through my dresser and found the journal Lanie had sent to me weeks earlier. Unable to relax in the house, I put on Jay's Wake Forest sweatshirt, grabbed a blanket and headed out to the beach, journal in hand.

Settling into one of two green Adirondack chairs that I had carried down to the beach several days prior, I curled up with my journal. Carefully, I thumbed through the previous entries. Stella's words floated back to me: "Lanie and I have watched you scribble away in those journals of yours since we were kids. You were always happiest sitting by yourself, lost in some train of thought, writing … Jay thought you had it."

All the people in my life seemed to know more about me than I did. That much seemed true. I owed it to Jay, to all of them really, to try. I could feel the excitement pulse through me. What was I afraid off? Failing or succeeding? I started to write in the journal. The words just flowed. Thoughts I had been bottling up since Jay's accident, months and months of emotion, were finally ready to be put into words.

"Jill?"

I heard the soft sound of my name in the distance, breaking my train of thought. Ross was jogging up the beach with his surfboard.

"Hey, Ross," I replied, closing my journal and resting it in my lap.

"My friends and I were just finishing up surfing and I saw you still sitting here. Thought I would at least swing by and say hey."

"How was the surf?"

"Awesome. You surf?" He combed his hands through his wet hair.

"Nope."

Someone farther down the beach called Ross's name, distracting him for a moment. He looked back at me, his green eyes searching mine, causing some unnamed emotion to stir inside.

"Did you want to sit?" I asked, unsure if he was lingering to be polite or if he really wanted to stay.

"Do you mind? I didn't want to interrupt," he said almost shyly.

"You're not interrupting. I could use the company," I said, unsure why.

He waved his friends on and sat down on his surfboard, facing me.

"You could sit in the chair."

"Nah. This works just fine." He smiled and for a couple of moments an awkward silence lingered between us.

"Have you surfed a long time?" I finally asked, breaking the silence.

"My whole life. There is something exhilarating and soothing about the ocean all at the same time, but it mostly takes my mind off of everything else."

"Running has the same effect for me," I said.

But I was thinking, "Except for today."

"You run?" he asked.

"I try to every morning, but it doesn't always work out that way."

"That's cool. I hate running."

I let out a giggle.

Feeling the tension break, we talked freely about various things with the comfort of two old friends. The sun had long set and we both sat in the glow of the lights reflecting off the many houses that lined the beach.

"I should get going. It's getting late and I have to work in the morning," Ross finally said after I had yawned for the third time.

"I understand, Ross. Thank you for the company tonight," I said, getting up and gathering all my things.

"Jill?" Ross asked as I headed back up to the house.

"Yea?"

"It doesn't last forever."

"What?" I asked, confused.

"The sadness. It's consuming and heavy but keep fighting. You'll get through it." He turned and headed back down the beach.

Rendered speechless, I made my way back to the house.

....

"We have been sooo worried about you," Stella said.

"I know, but I just needed my space today," I replied, having finally called Lanie and Stella back after missing two more calls from them.

"You can't shut us out," Lanie said.

"I wasn't. I just didn't have the right words to explain to you guys what today felt like to me.

It should have been a day of joy and celebration, but instead I feel like it set me back several months."

"We want to be there for you. You can always lean on us," Lanie said.

"I know but I needed a change … a change in perspective."

I thought back to Ross and how this stranger had come into my life with no expectations.

"What did you do?" Stella asked tentatively.

"I'm not gonna lie. It wasn't an easy day. The sadness is so overwhelming, but a friend helped take my mind off of it all," I said before realizing the questions that would follow such a vague statement.

"What friend?" Lanie asked.

"What? Are we suddenly not good enough?" Stella sounded angry.

"No, no. It's just that you are both so entwined in my whole life it's hard to just lose myself in casual conversation with you. Ross doesn't know anything about me or my story and so it was just nice to sit and talk about nothing and everything without any evaluation of my feeling or state of well-being," I stammered.

"Who is Ross?" Stella asked.

"Ross works for Jeff Powers. We have met several times and we bumped into each other on the beach today."

"But you're sure you're okay?" Lanie pressed.

"Yes. I'm okay … I'm fighting through the sadness," I said, quoting Ross and smiling to myself.

"Okay. We are just worried, Jill," Lanie finally said.

"I know and I appreciate it, but this is my fight now." I paused not wanting this conversation to drag on all night. "I love you both, but I need to go."

"Love you too," Stella and Lanie echoed before hanging up the phone.

Glancing at my phone, I saw that I had another text from Harry.

From: Harry Conner
Jill, I miss you.

To: Harry Conner
We all miss him.

From: Harry Conner
How do you get through?

To: Harry Conner
Have a little hope.

I went to bed, dreading another night of haunting nightmares. As I climbed the stairs, I could hear Ross's advice in the back of my head. Did I have any fight left in me? Was I brave enough? Taking a deep breath and letting it out slowly, I knew deep down inside there were things out there still left to fight for. I just needed to figure them out.

CHAPTER 26

···

M r. Colton called several morning's later and apologized for the delay with the delivery of my bike. He said it had finally arrived and was ready for me to pick up. I set out for the hardware store a little after 10. When I arrived at the hardware store, I could see the mint-green bike with white-walled tires set up outside the shop. After paying for the bike and assuring Mr. Colton I didn't need a helmet, I set out back home. Halfway back to the house, I decided I wasn't ready to return to the house and took a right and headed out to explore the island. After weeks of being confined to my walking radius, I was ready to explore my surroundings. I spent the rest of the morning exploring the island and revisiting several of my favorite locations. I had just pulled up to the stop light several blocks from the house and was waiting for traffic to pass when a truck pulled up next to me. The driver rolled down the passenger window and called out to me, "Fancy meeting you here."

"If I didn't know better I would think you are stalking me," I said to Ross with my best deadpan expression while he grinned back at me from inside the truck.

"Need a lift?"

"No thanks. I just got my new ride this morning." I pointed to my new bike.

"Very trendy. Now you look like one of those hip tourists."

We both burst out laughing. I knew for sure that I was the least hip person on the island.

"Listen, what are you doing this evening?" he asked.

His question completely disarmed me.

"It's not what you think," he quickly added.

I was glad he couldn't tell what I was thinking.

"Don't look so horrified."

Okay. Maybe he knew exactly what I was thinking.

"My friends and I are having a bonfire out on the beach, just a small get-together, you know, to celebrate the Fourth. I wanted to see if you wanted to come." He glanced over at me, his eyes twinkling.

"It's July 4?" I clearly needed to get a better grasp on time as the year was slipping away from me.

"Last time I checked."

"Um ..."

"I'll make it supereasy on you. We are going to be on the beach, maybe 150 yards down the beach from your place. Stop by if you like. We will be there around sunset."

"I'll think about it," I stammered.

"Cool."

The light changed. Ross waved at me and he was gone.

....

"You should go," Stella chimed in.

"I don't know. I mean, what do you know about this guy?" Lanie asked. As always she was ever practical about every situation.

"He's more like a kid," I replied.

"How young is young? He's legal, right?" Stella asked.

"Stella!" I tried my best to sound offended. "I don't know, early twenties?"

"You're young," Lanie countered.

"I'm almost 30." I felt as if I had aged 10 years in the last several months, making me feel 10 times older than I actually was.

"We are the same age and we are not 30 … 28 is 28 … not 30," Stella shrilled. "Additionally, it's the Fourth. Go out and have some fun. Enjoy yourself. He didn't ask you for your hand in marriage and there will be other people there. I say go for it. You could use some social interaction." Stella offered her opinion a little more calmly.

"For once, I agree. You need to get out, make friends, be social," Lanie chimed in, changing her tune quickly.

"Okay. I'll think about it," I finally said.

"Don't think about it. Do it. Why call us and get us all riled up if you aren't going to follow our advice," Stella complained.

"To get you all riled up," I snapped back.

"Mission accomplished."

"Bye, ladies. I'll keep you posted." I hung up despite their protests.

....

I stood in my closet for 30 minutes, wondering what to wear before deciding that the whole situation was ridiculous. I was sure that I was nearly 10 years older than Ross and probably most of his friends. What could we possibly have in common? He had probably just invited me since he felt sorry for me, or better yet, so I wouldn't call and file a noise complaint against them. I finally decided that I would just stop by and say hi and then return home. After settling on a pair of cut-off shorts, loose-fitting cotton V-neck and my L.L. Bean flip-flops, I grabbed Jay's Wake Forest sweatshirt off the sofa and headed out the back door. Most of the new decking had been completed, which made my walk to the beach much easier.

....

I could see a group of people ahead as I stepped onto the beach. A small glow flickered in the distance where everyone sat in a circle. The soft hum of a radio could be heard and the occasional laugh or shout.

"Jill."

I looked up. Ross was jogging toward me.

"Hey, Ross." I waved as he got closer.

"I'm so glad you decided to come," he said as he reached me.

"Listen, I'm not sure …" I started to repeat the million of excuses I had come up with when I had stood in my closet.

"Let me introduce you to everyone," he said and grabbed my hand and led me over to the group. I felt faint butterflies in my stomach as our hands touched but quickly dismissed the feeling as just nerves. As soon as we reached the group, he dropped my hand and started pointing out different people in the group. Each person waved back, politely and went back to doing what they were doing. The only person I recognized was the surly young man named Zach from the local grocery store.

"Do you want anything to drink?" asked a slender girl in jeans and a slinky tank top.

"Sure."

Were they even old enough to drink? But drinking would make this easier, right?

"I'm Mandy," she said introducing herself to me as she handed me a beer. I'm sure that Ross had already mentioned her name, but I couldn't remember. I settled in between Ross and Mandy and listen to the stories and music as I sipped on my beer.

"So, Jill, do you live here?" Mandy asked.

"Yea. I live in the house just over there." I pointed in the general direction of the house.

"Oh, is that the place your uncle's working on?" she asked Ross.

"Yea," he replied, not paying attention to our conversation and returning to the conversation he was having with the dark-haired guy next to him, who, I thought, was named Mark.

"Do your parents own that place?"

It took me a minute to realize that Mandy was still addressing me. I nearly choked on my beer.

"No, no. I own that place."

"Really?"

I wasn't really sure how to reply. Did I tell her my dead husband gifted me the house as a surprise? Mandy didn't give me the chance to reply.

"Do you live there all by yourself?"

"Yup."

"It's such a large place. Do you get lonely?" She was just full of questions.

"Sometimes." I wasn't sure how long this line of questioning would continue and how much longer I would continue to answer.

"Do you have a boyfriend?" Mandy blurted out.

"No," I whispered back.

She slid her eyes across to Ross and back at me. She must have thought there was something going on between us. I would need to assure her there was nothing but pity going on between us as soon as she let me speak.

"So you and Ross met while he was working on your house?"

"Correct."

"Wait. Isn't that the house ... April, what did you tell me?" she shouted to the girl across the fire. "That's right. Now I remember. April had told me how the owner of that house—I'm guessing, your husband—bought that house as a surprise. How romantic! What happened?" She had clearly never got the full story from April.

"He died," I whispered.

Looking up I saw that all conversations had now stopped and all eyes were now clearly on me and my tragic reply.

"Oh my God! Did you guys know that?"

Mandy again looked at her friends across the way. Everyone shifted in their seats, clearly uncomfortable with where this conversation had gone.

"Mandy, why don't we talk about something else? I'm sure if Jill wants to talk about it she will bring it up," Ross said, turning his attention back to our extremely awkward conversation.

When I glanced up, I could see the concern reflected in his eyes. Mandy switched gears and started talking about other local town gossip.

Ross continued to look at me and mouthed, "Are you okay?"

I nodded slightly, reflecting on all that had occurred. Ross knew my story. This recent revelation did not at all surprise him or the rest of the group. They all knew my story. I was the sad women who lived alone in the beach house that her husband had bought her, only to die before he could present it to her himself. The thought depressed me as I finished my beer.

....

"I think they are about to start the show," Zach said, turning up the radio as the announcer finished thanking all the sponsors for supporting the firework display. Everyone got up and shifted around to get a better view of the distant pier where the fireworks would be shot off. Ross moved closer to me and leaned in to say something just as the fireworks started. I asked him to repeat what he had said, but he shook his head and said it could wait. In all reality, I loved fireworks. I thought they were the most romantic thing. They made me feel like I was a child again. Jay never really cared for fireworks but always agreed every year to attend some ridiculously overcrowded fireworks show because it excited me.

The display continued to boom over us as patriotic music played on the radio. The soft crackle and fizzle melted into the night sky as another loud pop accompanied an entirely new display. A collective gasp or sigh could be heard from the group as everyone became entranced by the display. Ross again shifted his position next to me and his hand brushed mine. I looked into his eyes, and he smiled a shy smile before taking my hand. Another electric sensation ran through my entire body, causing me to break his stare and focus my attention back on the firework display.

....

After the display, several people got up and left, but for the most part everyone stuck around, talking and continuing to drink.

"Ross, when are you going to play?" Mandy whined, and several other people around the circle also jumped in, encouraging Ross to play.

"Alright. I left my guitar in the car. I'll be right back."

There was general applause and a cheer from the group as Ross let go of my hand to get up and took off on a jog down the beach.

"He's so talented," Mandy commented, again leaning in next to me.

"I haven't really ever heard him play."

That was mostly the truth. I knew he played that one night at my house, but I was not in my right state of mind that night. I shuddered and tried to put the thought out of my mind.

"Oh, he's really talented. He played all the time growing up, even went to school for music," Mandy added. She was really into knowing everything about everyone it seemed.

"He had a couple gigs and auditions with some big-name bands," Mark chimed in from across the bonfire.

"What happened?" I asked, drawn into the enthusiasm for Ross and his talent.

"His mom got sick," Mandy whispered.

Several people looked uncomfortable for the second time that evening and started other conversations. I wondered if Mandy's sparkling personality was always this direct.

"Is she okay?" I asked.

"No. She died. Breast cancer. I guess you both have that stuff in common."

"That stuff?" I asked, shocked at how she could know that my mom had also died from the same horrific disease.

"You know, losing someone close to you," she said and turned her attention to something someone else had said.

Mandy seemed to have a knack for delivering unsettling information, either that or the sentiment of it all was completely lost on her. I decided on the latter. Yet she was more accurate than she could have ever known.

"What—" I had so many questions and Mandy seemed more than eager to share.

"Ross," someone in the group called out.

I looked up and saw him jogging back to the group, guitar in hand.

"We were worried that you might have gotten lost and where never coming back," I quipped as he sat down.

"And leave you here to fend for yourself? Never." He winked at me and adjusted his guitar.

Over the next several hours, Ross played the guitar, taking requests from almost everyone in the group. The fire began to die down and people started to get up and leave. Soon the only ones left on the beach as the embers burned down were Ross and me.

"Anything you want to hear?" he asked, bringing me back from my thoughts.

"Um ... I'm not really good with music," I stammered, caught off guard by his question. It was true. I liked my classics, but I was not a music aficionado by any means.

"It's fine. Just tell me your favorite song."

"You're that good you know them all?"

"Try me."

"Alright ... New York—"

"Oh, the Jay-Z song."

"No. 'New York, New York,' the Frank Sinatra song." I sighed.

"I was just kidding. I know that song ... Just relax. You're too serious."

He started to play. The melody engulfed me. As the last of the embers died down, Ross softly sang the lyrics to no one in particular and I truly felt as if we were the only two people in the world at that moment.

"You're really talented," I commented when he was all done.

"Thanks, but it's just a hobby," he said, brushing off my compliment.

"You're way too good for it to be just a hobby."

He gave me a sly grin and stood up. "It's late."

"Oh, right. Sorry. I didn't mean to keep you. Thanks for a nice evening."

I stood up and started back toward the house.

"Wait up. Let me walk you," he called after me.

"It's right there."

I paused and pointed in the direction of the house. He jogged up next to me, guitar over his shoulder.

"Humor me. Consider it peace of mind."

"Suit yourself."

After several quiet moments, he cleared his throat.

"Listen, Jill, I'm really sorry about Mandy. She really doesn't have any tact and I—"

"Ross, it's not your fault. It was bound to come up in conversation ... eventually. But let me ask you a question. Why did you invite me tonight? You barely know me. You're young. You have your whole life ahead of you and I'm older and ... broken."

It came out much more serious than I had intended. Ross paused before answering as we reached my back deck.

"Ever since that first night, I can't stop thinking about you."

He was close to me now, looking directly into my eyes. I was pretty sure I had stopped breathing.

"Bad things happen ... to everyone ..." He paused and closed his eyes for a moment as pain flashed across his face. "But you are not broken." He leaned in closer and kissed me softly on the cheek. "Goodnight, Jill." He turned and headed back down the beach leaving me frozen in my place.

"Night," I mumbled several minutes later when he was already too far down the beach to hear me.

As per my nightly ritual, I walked through the house, locking up all the doors and turning on several lights. As I made my way upstairs, I glanced at my phone and I could see it was after two in the morning. I sighed and walked to the window, staring out into the dark abyss. What was I doing? My life had taken such a twist that I never imagined myself here in this moment. Was I ready to get involved with someone so soon after Jay had passed? He was the love of my life. Is there enough room in one person's heart for more than one person? I knew I was overthinking things. It was just a peck on the cheek, but it also meant so much more.

....

That night was no better than other nights. Nightmares continued to haunt my sleep. I hadn't been asleep for more than an hour when the first one ripped me from sleep in sheer panic. Letting my breath slow, I got out of bed and headed downstairs. On the kitchen counter sat my journal from the other night. I stared at the journal as thoughts continued to flood my mind, overwhelming me. Having no other release, I grabbed the journal from the counter and sat down on the sofa and let everything I was thinking and feeling flow onto the pages and just like the other day, the words came easily and freely. Losing track of time, I wrote until the sun began to rise and my eyelids grew heavy.

....

At first I thought I was dreaming. The knock sounded as if it was in the distance, but after several moments, it became louder. I opened my eyes slightly, feeling a bit disoriented, only to find Ross and his uncle standing on the back deck, staring at me through the glass door.

"Ah," I yelled out with a start, knowing I had fallen asleep on the sofa while writing.

Ross seemed to chuckle over my reaction while Jeff seemed embarrassed for startling me.

"One minute," I called out through the glass and held up one finger.

I quickly raced upstairs and grabbed my bathrobe. I glanced in the mirror, did some minor adjustments to my hair and quickly brushed my teeth. Gathering my composure, I raced back downstairs and opened the back door, letting Ross and Jeff into the house.

"Mrs. Greenfield, I'm so sorry about—" Jeff started to say.

"No. It's okay, and I said to call me Jill." I waved my hand to indicate their interruption was nothing.

"Looks like you were burning the midnight oil again," Ross joked.

"It's actually the first time in months I was actually burning the midnight oil, as you say."

Ross looked as if he had a follow-up question but refrained from asking it since his uncle was there.

"Jill, I just wanted to update you on our progress. We are almost done with the deck. The roof and windows have been completed. We will be painting the house starting tomorrow—"

Jeff was interrupted by the melody coming from my phone. I held up my hand quickly.

"I'm so sorry. Can you excuse me for just one minute?" I asked.

"Sure," they both echoed.

I quickly scanned the kitchen for my phone and located it on the table. I grabbed it, punched the button, and walked into the other room.

"Make yourselves comfortable," I called over my shoulder.

"Who is making themselves comfortable? I take it the beach rendezvous was a success?" Stella said over the line.

"Um … I was just speaking to Ross and Jeff."

"Who are?"

"Jeff, as in Jeff Powers, who is doing all the construction on the house, and Ross is his nephew," I whispered.

"Why are we whispering?" she whispered back.

"I didn't want them to hear me."

"Anyway, all very fascinating, but I have some serious business to discuss with you," Stella said, getting into what I referred to as her "lawyer mode."

"Okay." I tried to focus my attention on whatever she had to tell me.

"I need you to come to New York in the next couple of days. It seems that the paperwork Paul Wellon sent us is time sensitive and I need you to come sign some documents."

"Can't you fax them?" I asked. The idea of traveling after spending months being shipped around by Lanie and Stella was not appealing.

"No, we need to go over other things and get some accounts set up, etc.," she said and I could hear her drumming her fingers on a hard surface.

"Where are you?" I asked, trying to place the call in context.

"My office. Why?" she asked, distracted.

"No reason. You were saying?"

"You need to come to New York," she said again with a little bit more annoyance in her voice.

"Yea. I guess I can do that."

I wandered back into the kitchen and put the water on to boil so I could make some coffee.

"I can book you on the first flight out of Wilmington in the morning. It will have two layovers, or there is a direct flight from Raleigh," she said.

"There is just one problem with your diabolical plan. I don't really have a means to get to the airport at either location."

"I can take you," Ross chimed in from the living room.

"That's right. Ross would be more than happy to take you." Jeff echoed his nephew's sentiment.

"See. Ross can take you," Stella mimicked on the phone. "Who is Ross? Oh, is he the guy from the beach? He's in your living room? Very interesting."

"Yes, very interesting."

Looking at Ross, I asked, "Are you sure you can take me?"

"Yup. No problem."

"Do you have a preference for Wilmington or Raleigh airport?" I asked him.

"Whatever." He shrugged.

"Raleigh it is," Stella said, making the decision. She always liked to fly from larger airports, claiming the accommodations were much nicer.

"Sure. Fine. You can text me the details."

The kettle on the stove started to whistle. I turned it off and motioned to Ross and Jeff to see if either of them would like a cup of tea or coffee. Both respectfully declined.

"How long am I staying in New York?" I asked Stella.

"Three days."

"Very precise."

"Well, I have a lot of work right now. I can't get too distracted."

"Same arrangement as always?" I asked.

Prior to Jay's accident, Stella and I had a standing agreement that whenever I came to visit in New York, we would always check into a hotel and treat ourselves to a girls' spa day. Her first apartment had been so small, we just couldn't fit. She now lived in a nicer apartment on the upper West Side, but we still had our tradition.

"It's been too long. Yes ... and you're treating ... I was thinking the Fairmont or Trump Tower—"

"Do I need someone to pick me up when I get back?"

"Oh, actually, you do not. I have arranged or will have arranged by then for your new Jeep to be ready and waiting for you at the airport upon your arrival." She was very proud of the work she had done.

"Fantastic. See you tomorrow," I said, trying to end the conversation.

"Pack light," she said and we hung up.

I immediately turned my attention to my guests, who were still waiting for me. "Very sorry about that. I have some business to attend to in New York suddenly and I will be out of town a couple days." I looked at Ross and Jeff.

"Everything okay?" Ross asked.

"Yes. I think everything is fine and thank you for the ride tomorrow. I'm not sure what time the flight is yet."

"New York? Ross lived in New York for several years. He went to music school there. He could recommend several places for you to stay or eat while you're there," Jeff added, obviously very proud of the time Ross had spent in the Big Apple.

"No. I'm sure she has her own plans, Unc," Ross said slightly embarrassed by his uncle's comment.

"I didn't know that," I said, trying to hide the fact that I had already heard that information from his friends.

Ross called me out. "Terrible poker face. Yes, you did."

"You got me," I said, holding up my hands in defeat. "Anyway as soon as I get more information, I will let you know." I tried to direct the conversation back on track.

"No problem. Let me give you my number so you can just call or text me."

We spent the next couple of minutes exchanging numbers and finalizing the last of the house renovations with Jeff. After they finally left, I ate a quick breakfast and laid down for a nap.

....

It was close to six when I woke up from my nap. I tried to check my phone and found that the battery had died at some point during the day. I found the phone charger and plugged it in, letting it charge while I showered and started to pack a bag. My stomach started growling and I made my way down to the kitchen. I opened the fridge to find it mostly empty. The couple of items I did have didn't appeal to me. I decided to go out and get something to eat in town. I grabbed my phone, turning it on as I headed out the front door where I almost collided with Ross.

"We need to stop meeting like this," I commented as I straightened myself up.

"Sorry. I hadn't heard from you yet about the flight and I tried to text you, but you didn't reply and I was on my way by the house so I decided to stop and ask."

"Oh, my phone died." I held up my phone. Just then, a flood of messages came in on it. I glanced through them and saw the text message from Ross, two from Stella, finalizing flights, and an e-mail from US Airlines, confirming my reservation.

"Looks like my flight is at 9 a.m."—I quickly did the math in my head—"which means we need to leave here at 5:30 a.m ... I'm so sorry ... You didn't sign up for that."

"No problem. It's exactly what I signed up for." Ross grinned at me. We stood there for an awkward minute before Ross asked, "Were you going somewhere? You looked like you were in a hurry."

"Oh, I was on my way to grab something for dinner."

"Where are you going?"

"I haven't decided yet."

"Mind if I join you?" he asked.

It still shocked me that he wanted to spend any time with me, but the idea of having company was welcoming.

"That would be great."

"I know this great local place not too far from here. We could walk." He pointed out the direction, just down the way.

"I had no idea there was something down there," I said, shocked by the information.

"Most people don't. Island secret." He winked and we started out toward the restaurant, talking the entire way there.

....

The restaurant was only a couple blocks from my house and sat right on the water. It was painted teal and had a silver metallic roof. A neon sign that read "Rusty's" hung overhead. A line of people stood by the order window and others milled around, sitting on picnic benches and high-top tables overlooking the ocean. We ordered our meal and sat down at one of the open picnic tables. Everyone who walked by us stopped to talk to Ross.

"You are popular," I commented at one point between visitors.

"Sorry. My uncle is the only contractor on the island and everyone loves him."

"Him or you?"

"Him. I've been working for him on and off since I was 16. I guess people know me by now." He brushed his popularity off and we continued our meal.

"That was the best seafood I have ever had on the island," I said after I cleaned my basket and licked my fingers clean.

"You must have liked it." Ross laughed as he looked at my empty basket.

"What? I'm a healthy eater," I said, defending myself.

"Hey Ross! Hey Jill!" a voice shouted behind us.

I turned around to see who could possibly be calling my name. Standing in line at the order counter was Mandy and several other people from the bonfire the other night.

"Incoming," Ross whispered to me conspiratorially. I moved down the bench to make room for everyone.

"Fancy meeting you at Ross's favorite place," Mandy said as she sat down next to Ross. We were joined by Mark, April and another guy whose name, I thought, was Jake.

"Are we interrupting anything?" Mark asked Ross.

"Oh, is this a date?" Mandy blurted out.

"No. It's not a date," Ross answered, shaking his head.

I could feel my cheeks go red and I looked down at my empty plate.

"Well, that's good because I would hate to interrupt anything like that. But it's about time you started dating again."

At first I thought Mandy was speaking to me, but when I looked up I saw that she was looking directly at Ross. Perhaps I had missed something earlier, but it looked as if Mandy had a thing for Ross.

"In due time," he casually replied, stealing a glance in my direction.

"Have you had the ice cream?" April interjected, saving me from an awkward conversation.

"No. I didn't realize they had ice cream."

"They are known for their ice cream. You have to have some," April exclaimed.

And with that, they all launched into a deep discussion about their favorite flavors and how Rusty's ice cream compared with name brands.

"Ready to go?" Ross asked quietly across the table 20 minutes later. I nodded my head and stood.

"Hey, we are going to have another bonfire tonight on the beach, if you're interested," I heard Mark tell Ross.

"I'm not sure I can make it tonight. I've got an early morning," Ross said.

We said our good-byes and were about to head back to the house when I stopped by the order counter. Ross stopped a couple feet ahead when he realized I wasn't by his side. He turned and gave me a questioning look.

"Ice cream. My treat," I said very matter-of-factly.

"Ice cream it is," he said.

After I had ordered a large chocolate waffle cone for myself and a large birthday-cake-flavored cone for Ross, we headed back to the house.

"How do you know all those guys?" I asked once we were finally out of earshot of Rusty's.

"I've known most of them since I was little. My mom and I used to live on the island, not too far from where my uncle lives now, actually."

"So you have lived here your whole life?"

"No. Shortly after I turned 13, my mom and I packed up and moved to Nashville. I was really into music at that time and my mom figured that I needed to be closer to everything in order to follow my dreams."

"She sounds like a great mom," I said, thinking of my own mom.

"She was a great mom."

"What happened?"

"You don't already know?" he asked and I blushed at being caught in my little lie.

"Mandy may have mentioned something briefly the other night," I confessed.

"Shocking," he replied with a small, sweet smile and I had to stifle a giggle. "Mom got diagnosed with cancer several years ago." His voice became serious. "By that time we had already lived in Nashville several years and I had just started my freshman year at New York University. She decided to move back here to the island to be closer to my uncle Jeff. They were really close. By my second semester she was much worse. I took the semester off to spend time with her before she died. She made it to the end of summer but made me promise I would go back and finish my degree. So after she passed, I went back to NYU, always coming back in the summers to Oak Island and then eventually finished up my degree. I graduated last May and I moved back down here and I'm staying with my uncle until I figure out what's next." He sighed when he was finished, but he wasn't sad. It just seemed that was the way life was. By this time we were standing on my porch.

"Sounds really similar to the way I lost my mom as well," I said, telling him about my mom's own struggle with cancer and her ultimate loss to it. He looked surprised and raised an eyebrow when I was done.

"Do you want to come in?" I asked him, not wanting the conversation to end.

He looked at me and hesitated a moment before finally agreeing.

"Make yourself at home," I said as we walked in. "I'll be right back."

I dashed upstairs to grab a sweatshirt and plug in my phone. When I came back down, he was over by the far wall, examining the photos and books that lined all the shelves.

"Some collection you got here." He nodded toward the books. I simply nodded in agreement.

"So what do you do
?" he asked turning to face me.

"Well, at the moment, nothing actually. I used to be a kindergarten teacher."

"Did you like it?"

"Loved it but after—" I stopped, suddenly feeling very awkward. Could I discuss my dead husband with my new ... friend?

Suddenly, Ross was in front of me. He lifted my chin up so that he could look me straight in the eyes. "I can't begin to comprehend the loss of a loved one like a husband, but it happened to you. Don't ever feel the need to hide that. It's who you are. It's part of your story." His voice was very quiet as he spoke. He was so young, yet his words made him seem older and more mature than most people I knew. A single tear slid down my cheek and he reached up and carefully wiped it away. "You don't have to talk about it."

"Yes I do." I sighed as I took a seat on the sofa. "I loved teaching, but after Jay's accident I just couldn't go back. That just seemed like part of a life plan that didn't exist anymore and I couldn't go back to that school and have everyone look at me and pity me all the time."

"Makes sense, but now what?" His words echoed my own thoughts.

"That's a great question. I have no idea." I shrugged. "Can I fix you a cup of coffee or tea?" I asked, changing the subject.

"Coffee would be great. Doesn't look like we are going to get much sleep."

"I don't usually, anyway."

I busied myself in the kitchen, making a cup of tea for myself and a cup of coffee for Ross.

"Oh yea, burning the midnight oil and all … do you mind explaining that?" Ross asked. Of course he had remembered.

"It's nothing really. I just don't sleep well, alone in the house and all."

I looked over at him and he could tell my answer was not really an answer. He patiently waited for a better explanation.

"I'm terrified of the dark," I mumbled.

"You're what? I couldn't hear you."

"I'm scared of the dark," I mumbled again, clasping my hands over my face.

Slowly he made his way over to my side pulling my hands from my face. I stared into his eyes and he carefully moved a wispy piece of hair back behind my ear. The space between us was electric and I found myself holding my breath.

"I'm almost 30 years old and I sleep with the lights on," I explained, finally breaking the tension and exhaling.

"You must have a reason," he said.

Just then, the water began to boil and I turned my attention to fixing our beverages.

"You didn't laugh."

"Was I supposed to?"

"I expected you to. I'm sure I would have laughed if Stel—my friends told me that."

"Explain it to me and I'll decide if it's funny or not," he finally said after several minutes.

"Here. Let's sit on the sofa and I'll try." I motioned for him to sit as I brought over the steaming mugs.

"What's this?" he asked as he picked up my journal from the floor.

"Oh, it must have fallen off the sofa earlier when I was sleeping."

Was that really this morning? It seemed to have been ages before that.

"It's my journal."

"You're a writer?"

"Maybe. More like aspiring. Think of it as a possible second career option." I really didn't want to talk about the journal or my absurd fear of the dark but something about Ross made me feel comfortable.

"Can I read something?" he asked, still holding the journal.

"No!" I shouted and launched myself across the sofa to grab the journal from him.

"A simple 'not now' would have worked," he said dryly before breaking into a grin.

"Sorry. I just recently started back up again and I don't know where it's going, if it's going anywhere."

"Maybe someday, then," he said, picking up the coffee mug and drinking from it.

"Someday."

"So this fear of yours?" he asked, bringing the conversation back around.

"My mind gets the better of me at night. I hear crazy noises and let myself get freaked out that I might be getting robbed or a serial killer is lurking around the corner. I know it's highly irrational, but the only way I fall asleep is turning the light on. It also helps with the nightmares."

"Nightmares?"

"I don't always realize I am having them, but my friends, Stella and Lanie, told me I have been having them since Jay's accident. I guess they keep me up at night too. The light just … it helps me see what's real whereas in the dark I can't tell where reality ends and my nightmares begin." I stared out toward the ocean.

"That doesn't sound crazy. Seems to me like you have a good reason for doing what you're doing. Does anything help with the nightmares and fear of the dark?"

"With the nightmares? I'm not sure. Lanie—she's a psychologist—says they are getting better and I just need time. The fear of the dark developed more recently." I paused not knowing how to explain myself without sounding too insane. "I have never lived alone, never really spent any nights alone, ever, until I moved into this house. I always slept well with others around. I felt safe protected and now for the first time I'm out on my own and I feel vulnerable, exposed. I mean, what if something does happen to me? Who would know?" I dropped my voice to a whisper.

Ross just nodded and reached over and squeezed my hand. Then, to move the attention away from myself, I launched into an assault of questions about Ross. What were his musical tastes? Did he write his own music often? What did he want to do in the future?

And with each answer, he surprised me more and more. He seemed more like an old soul than a 22-year-old.

"Will you teach me to play?" I asked when there was a lull in the conversation.

"Teach you to play what?"

"The guitar."

"You want to learn?"

"It's on my bucket list."

"Sure. When do you want to start?"

"How about right now? I seem to have some free time."

"You're serious?"

"That is one thing you should learn about me. I'm always serious. It's a character flaw." I smiled at him and he chuckled.

"There's just one thing to learn about you?"

"For now." I smiled back.

"Okay. Let's do this." He got up to retrieve his guitar from his truck.

"You always have that handy?" I teased when he got back.

"Never leave home without it." He winked at me.

We settled in on the sofa and he showed me the different chords, explaining the general hand positions. I didn't know if it was the exhaustion from the day, the soft strumming of the guitar, or how safe I felt, knowing he was there, but soon I couldn't keep my eyes open and I fell asleep in the middle of my first lesson.

....

"Jill, it's time to wake up." A gentle hand touched me on the shoulder. I sat up with a start.

"Did I miss my flight?" I looked around bewildered.

"No, but we need to leave soon."

I looked around the room and saw his guitar learning against the table.

"I'm so sorry. I didn't mean to fall asleep. I'm a horrible student," I lamented.

"No problem, but that doesn't really boast my confidence as a good instructor if I can't keep my students awake."

"Did you get any sleep?" I asked as I stood and folded the blanket he had placed over me.

"I don't require much sleep in general, but yea, I dozed in the chair over there for a while," he said pointing toward one of the chairs by the fireplace. "When I wasn't sleeping, I listened to you snore and then when it was quiet enough, I just played the guitar." His back was to me at that moment and I couldn't tell if he was being serious.

"I don't snore," I said defending myself.

"Prove it," he said as he turned and faced me, a large grin on his face. "No. You didn't snore. But I did make breakfast, if you are interested."

"Really?"

It was only then that I realized the room was filled with the aroma of coffee, eggs and toast.

"It was slim pickings but I put something together." He motioned me into the kitchen.

"You cook too. Is there anything you can't do?"

"Nope. I'm amazing," he deadpanned.

"So you seem to be," I thought.

We ate breakfast with the ease of a couple who knew each other. There was no need to talk the entire time and we both sat in comfortable silence as we finished up eating.

"I'll clear the dishes if you want to go freshen up and grab your bag," he said as he reached for my plate.

"Really amazing."

I dashed upstairs, quickly showered, and put on the clothes I had laid out the day before. I threw some last-minute items in my bag and made my way downstairs. Ross was waiting by the front door. His guitar was leaning against the wall.

"Let me help you with that," he said, reaching for my bag.

"Thank you, but I got it."

"I locked the back door already," he added.

"Great. Then I'm ready to go." We made our way outside and I locked the front door. I turned to face him and hesitated for a moment before handing him my keys. I could tell he was surprised. "In case you or your uncle needs to get into the house for anything while I'm gone."

"Makes sense. I thought you were asking me to move in and I was gonna tell you to slow down. I'm not that kinda guy," he joked as we loaded his truck and headed for Raleigh.

....

"Have a great time in New York," Ross said and gave me a big hug as we stood on the sidewalk in front of the departures-drop-off area at the airport.

"I will," I said, thinking that Stella would see to it. "Thank you again for driving me."

"Are you sure you don't need a ride home?"

"No. I got that covered."

Ross looked slightly disappointed, but I was excited by the prospect of having a car again.

"When are you getting back?"

"Um … I think I land at 3 p.m. so I should be back to the island around 7 p.m."

"Awesome. I'll see you in a couple of days." He turned to leave.

"Ross?" I said, grabbing his arm as he brushed past me.

"Yea?"

"I had a great time. Thank you."

I stood on my toes and kissed his cheek and then turned and headed into the terminal without waiting for a response. I made it through security and was at my gate in record time. I took a moment to check my phone and saw several missed texts from Lanie and Stella, which I replied to. There was one missed call from Harry, which I ignored, and right before I turned off my phone, a text from Ross chimed in.

From: Ross Powers
We will finish that conversation when you get back. Have a great trip.
—R

I smiled broadly and felt giddy as I boarded my flight. Not realizing what my seat number was, I missed the first call for my zone but quickly recovered when I saw the seat that Stella had booked was in the first-class section. She never ceased to amaze me. She had gone all out for this trip. The pilot informed us of our flight path and time for our short flight that morning. I was asleep before the stewardess had finished the safety instructions.

CHAPTER 27

....

We landed in New York 10 minutes early. I grabbed my bag from the overhead bin and made my way through the airport. I had arranged with Stella to meet curbside. As I made my way through the airport, I noticed a man dressed in a suit, holding a sign that had my name on it. At first I didn't think anything of it as I walked by, making my way curbside, but after standing on the curb for several minutes, I wondered if Stella had changed our plans. I turned my phone back on and found several text messages from Stella, confirming that my hunch was correct. She was unable to make it but had sent a limo service to pick me up. Sighing, I made my way back to the man in the suit.

The driver dropped me off in front of the Waldorf-Astoria hotel. I was able to check myself in and made my way up to the suite that Stella had reserved. I had also learned from Stella's messages that she was caught in a meeting until lunch and I was on my own until then. She had planned for us to have lunch near her office, after which we would have several meetings. I took the opportunity to change into something more businesslike and made my way toward Park Avenue where her office was. I reached the lobby of her office building before noon and took a seat and watched all the people walking in an out.

"Jill."

I heard my name called from across the lobby and looked up to see Stella striding toward me. She was dressed in capri, black, suit pants, skinny belt and light blouse with tall high heels.

"Looking good," I commented as we embraced.

"I must say so are you! You're so tan and not so gloomy," she said in the way only she could. She led me from the building down a couple blocks to a little bistro where we sat out on the street after we each ordered a deli sandwich. She spent most of the lunch quizzing me over the house renovations and how my decorating was going. At one o'clock promptly we walked back to her building where she signed me in and we rode up to the thirty-second floor.

"Do I get to meet Roger?" I whispered to her in the elevator.

"No. He's on vacation in Saint Tropez with his family."

"I really don't understand—"

"Not here," she said firmly as the doors opened up. She led me down a long hallway to a conference room that had a magnificent view of the city. The room was already set up with several binders and folders sitting at five different spots. Stella indicated that I take a seat at the very large conference table while she informed the others we were ready. All the formality of the meeting was starting to make me nervous. I felt as if I should have done some homework or prepared my own presentation.

Stella walked back into the room with another woman, who was dressed in a very expensive-looking dress. She introduced herself to me as Laura and said that she would be taking notes during the meeting. The next person to enter the room was a tall man with dark hair and a dark complexion. His name was David, and he informed me that he was a senior associate in the finance department of the firm. Last in the room was an average-looking man who seemed to be about 10 years older than everyone else. His name was Scott and he was the senior partner in the finance department. Stella took a seat by me, grabbing my hand under the table and giving it a small squeeze.

"Mrs. Greenfield," Scott started to say.

I started to correct him and Stella stepped on my foot under the table and shook her head. So I stayed quiet.

"Ms. Conner has asked that we take your portfolio on as a client of this firm."

I did my best to look professional and I tried to sit as still as possible. Having been around mostly five- and six-year-old children during my professional career, I now had a new appreciation for those times when I had told them to sit still.

"You must understand that this is a highly unusual situation. We normally don't take on this kind of matter." I had no idea what he was talking about, but he continued to tell me how highly regarded Stella was and that, after looking at my documentation, as a favor to her, they had decided an exception should be made. I could only think that something in the paperwork must have been worth a lot of money, as Stella had suggested on the phone. I remembered her once telling me that the firm wouldn't consider new clients unless they netted at least several million dollars in assets. As I sat and mulled that over, I realized what that meant for the portfolio that Jay had accumulated.

"How much?" I blurted out, startling everyone at the table.

"Excuse me?" David said. He was now eyeing Stella and probably questioning my mental stability.

"Sorry, but how much is the total estate worth?" I said with more reserve.

"With both properties in North Carolina plus the money from the insurance policy and various investments that Mr. Greenfield made, we estimate that your entire net worth is now a little under $23 million," he said with a straight face.

"Holy shit!" I whispered to myself as I leaned on the table and put my head in my hands in disbelief.

"Jill, are you okay?" Stella sounded alarmed as she put her hand on my back.

"Sorry. It's just I had no idea and it's *so* much money … Are you sure?" I asked, looking at David.

"Checked it myself … twice," David said and part of me thought he didn't believe it himself.

"I didn't mean to interrupt. You can continue," I said.

David and Scott nodded and they explained how the firm could protect my assets while helping me to further invest and grow my portfolio. The firm would take me on as a client and Stella would become my legal counsel. They expressed concern over the relationship that Stella and I had and whether or not it would be a conflict of interest should any problems arise in our friendship. Stella assured me that she had drafted a contract that included a clause in which I could excuse her as counsel at any time and the firm would immediately appoint another lawyer who met my standards. When both Stella and the finance guys were done, my head was swimming with figures, numbers and terms that I was unfamiliar with. The group decided to give me a 10-minute break before continuing, during which everyone, including Stella, left me alone in the large conference room. I wandered over to the window and looked out over the city. How my life had changed in less than a year! Never in my wildest dreams would I have imagined this. I leaned my head against the glass and let out a big sigh.

"Overwhelming, isn't it?" an unknown voice said behind me. I twirled around to find myself face to face with another man. He was dressed in suit pants and a button-up dress shirt with the sleeves rolled up to his elbows. His tie was loosened around his neck and his sandy-brown hair seemed to be a little long for firm standards. His dress and demeanor reminded me of Jay and I instantly felt comfortable.

"Andrew Conklin," he said as he crossed the room and shook my hand.

"Jill Greenfield."

"Well, Jill Greenfield, have they told you my role here?" He smiled at me and gestured for me to sit down. I shook my head no. He took the seat next to me, turning to look directly at me.

"Your friend Stella hired me as a third party consultant. I have no stake in any of this. I'm here to explain in more normal terms what went on earlier and to make sure you understand everything and are comfortable with the terms. While we are going through this, let me know any questions or concerns you may have and we will discuss them and try and draft some new terms."

"Are you a lawyer or finance guy?" I asked.

"A little bit of both. I started my career as a lawyer, but after several years all the mergers and deal making got to me, so then I went back to school and became a finance guy. That wasn't really my thing either, but I found the world of consulting and explaining legal and financial terms to people who are not lawyers and finance people to be enjoyable." He leaned back in his chair and smiled at me.

"Sounds indecisive, if you ask me."

"It cost me a lot of money to come to that conclusion as well," he said, winking at me.

"Are you ready to get started," he asked, pointing to the paperwork.

"Ready as I'm gonna be."

With that, Andrew began to explain all the investments, legal contracts and various options. I would stop him often, asking questions or asking for further clarification.

The conversation with Andrew came naturally and I was able to talk openly about my fears and apprehensions of suddenly inheriting so much wealth. He listened to my concerns and offered up frank advice. It was almost two hours before we finished our session. At the end, he rose from his seat and stretched his hand out. "It was a pleasure to work with you this afternoon, Jill Greenfield."

"The pleasure was all mine and please call me Jill," I said, returning his smile.

His energy was contagious and I felt empowered at that moment.

"Oh, then you must call me Drew," he said. "Are you sure you're okay with all the changes and how the contract stands?"

"Yes, I'm sure."

"Great. I will explain all the amendments and changes to the group who look to be nervously waiting in the hallway. They will either agree or disagree. If they agree they will make the changes and then all you need to do is sign your life away." He winked at me. "If they disagree, you can walk away and find new representation both legally or financially or you can sit down again and try and renegotiate the terms."

"I didn't realize this was such a negotiation."

"Everything is open for negotiation," he commented.

I saw Stella fidgeting in the hallway. She wasn't known for her patience. Drew saw me glance at Stella and he motioned for her to come in.

"And?" she said as soon as she entered the room.

"The verdict is that Jill has agreed to most of the terms set out by the firm. There are some amendments and changes that you will need to review. If you accept the changes, it seems that you will have a new client, Ms. Jill Greenfield." He grabbed my hand and held it up as if I had just won a boxing match. I let out a giggle and Stella smiled.

"My associates and I will review the changes but I think we are open to anything Ms. Jill Greenfield has suggested." She sounded so professional. She took the changes out to David and Scott and the three of them filed into another conference room across the hallway leaving Drew and me alone.

Drew and I chatted about our families and different backgrounds. He grew up an army brat, living in a new location every other year, experiencing different parts of the country and globe. His parents were still happily married and retired on Long Island. His older sister was widowed and living in New Hampshire with her teenage daughter, and his younger sister was studying to be a doctor at Wake Forest, of all places. He knew the basics of my present story but I talked about my childhood and my friendship with Stella. It turned out Drew and Stella had met at a conference several years ago and even went on a couple dates, but when things didn't work out, they stayed in touch and Stella often called upon him for consulting work.

"Jill," Stella called from the doorway as she and David and Scott filed back into the room.

"Yes?"

"My associates and I have looked over your changes and we accept all the changes. We will have a new contract drafted before you leave for you to sign if you are still interested."

All three of them looked very tentatively at me. I looked back at them and at Drew, who smiled and nodded in my direction. I felt relieved the day was over.

"I agree," I said, nodding my head. Not knowing if it was appropriate or not, I walked over to Stella and gave her a big hug. "You could have warned me," I whispered in her ear.

"You would have never come," she whispered back and maybe she was right.

I shook hands with David and Scott, who both assured me I was making the right decision and they looked forward to working further with me. Then they left the room.

"Let's drink!" Stella said as soon as they were gone. I let out a laugh. Leave it to Stella.

"Ladies," Drew said, nodding his head in our direction as he left the room.

"Wait, Drew," Stella called. He popped his head back in the office. "Drinks at Flannigan's at eight?"

"Wouldn't miss it." He winked in our direction and was gone.

"That was exhausting," I said when everyone had left.

"Are you okay?" It was the first time Stella my friend had appeared since we got off the elevator.

"How about I tell you at dinner—your treat—exactly how I feel about being ambushed by this meeting and the information," I said, grabbing her arm.

"You're the mulit-multi-millionaire. You should be treating," she teased back.

I stopped abruptly in my tracks.

"Get it all out of your system before we get on the elevator. You are never to refer to me as that again or mention this whole thing," I said with a serious face.

"You got it, but seriously, you're paying for the hotel this weekend. I can't afford it on my paycheck."

"Sure. Why not?" I said and we both started giggling as we got on the elevator.

CHAPTER 28

....

We headed over to the Waldorf to change and freshen up before dinner. While Stella was in the shower, I called Lanie and told her all about my day. She had no idea that Stella had arranged such a day but was glad that a third-party consultant was present to make sure my best interests were at play. She asked about how I was handling the whole situation and understood when I said it was overwhelming. We then talked about how her work was going and how she was managing to catch up after being sporadically out of the office over the previous several months. She also said that Mary Elizabeth had been given some time off and would be able to join us at the beach. We finally talked about the beach house before ending the call.

"How's Lanie?" Stella asked, emerging from the bathroom.

"Stressed but doing well."

"I asked her to join us for a couple days and she said she couldn't get away."

"I believe it," I said, walking over to the bed and flopping onto it. "These beds are fantastic, by the way." I sat up and looked at Stella with a wide grin.

"I know." She walked over and grabbed a pillow and threw it at me.

"How many times have you stayed here?" I asked.

"A few times, always in great company." She smiled.

"Skank," I said.

"You're too serious, Jill. You need to lighten up." She paused. "Speaking of lightening up, tell me about this Ross guy." She sat down cross-legged on the bed and faced me.

"Worse transition ever!" I exclaimed. "What's there to tell? He works for his uncle's construction company. He plays the guitar. Even went to NYU for music. His mom died from cancer and now he lives on his uncle's sofa." I covered the basics, with Stella less was more.

"Boring," Stella said. "What does he look like? Do you like him?"

"I told you this already. He's tall, maybe a little taller than six feet. He has blonde shaggy hair, tan, muscular ... he looks like a surfer. I enjoy his company. He's a great musician and he's easy to talk to ... but I don't know ... he's young. I don't know if he even likes me that way," I paused. "What am I saying...'likes me that way'. I feel like I'm in high school again and dating ... ugh. I never thought I would have to worry about dating again. All that awkwardness at the beginning, trying to figure out the other person and then if it doesn't work, you have to start over ... Anyway, it's too soon to start thinking about dating. I just lost my husband."

I buried my head in the pillow. Stella tugged at my shirt, making me sit back up.

"You lost Jay almost 10 months ago. There isn't a magical time when you're supposed to put yourself out there, but I think it's time. Jay wouldn't want you sitting around alone, mourning him. You are still young. You have your whole life ahead of you. So whether it be this Ross guy or someone else, someone is going to come along and sweep you off your feet and you need to be open to it."

"If I don't mourn him for as long as I can, who will?"

Stella looked at me and sighed. "It's not about mourning his life; it's about celebrating it, remembering him in the little things you do as you move forward. You have to find a balance." She stood up and walked back to the bathroom calling over her shoulder, "This talk is too serious. We are going out and having fun tonight!"

....

Stella always attracted attention whenever we went out and that night was no exception. She wore a tight red dress with tall, nude, platform pumps. Knowing I didn't own anything that would meet her standards, she had taken the liberty of bringing me several outfits from her own closet. I wore a sleek black dress with equally ridiculous pumps. Stella straightened my naturally wavy hair and attempted to do my makeup. I thought I looked like a streetwalker when she was done, and I took the time to redo it while she pouted in the other room. We went to dinner at a trendy restaurant called Blue. After seeing Stella, the wait staff moved us to a better, more private booth in the back and gave us a bottle of complementary champagne. By the end of the dinner, two different waiters had slipped her their numbers.

We grabbed a cab and headed across town to Flannigan's for drinks. We made our way to the bar where Stella ordered us each a martini. When the bartender got back with our drinks, he informed us that the nice gentleman at the end of the bar had picked up the tab. I rolled my eyes and we both started giggling. After several minutes, Stella was looking around the bar.

"Looking for someone?" I asked.

"Yes, Drew. He was supposed to meet us here." She sounded annoyed.

"Are you trying to start something back up with him?" I asked, confused. Last I knew, Stella was enjoying her current arrangement with Roger.

"Not starting something up with me but with *you*." She emphasized the last word.

"What about Ross?" I asked. I didn't even know if there was anything with Ross.

"You said you weren't sure where that was going and a little friendly competition never hurt anyone. I saw how into you he was today."

"Who, Ross?" I asked, not following her conversation.

"No. Drew. Speaking of which—" She waved her hand and called out, "Hey Drew over here."

Drew made his way through a sea of people and joined us at the bar.

"Ladies." He nodded and tried to get the bartender's attention.

"Let me." Stella leaned over the counter and waved down the bar and immediately got the bartenders attention. She ordered another round of martini's and a beer for Drew. We grabbed a pub top and chatted about the day and the weather. In the middle of our conversation, Stella's phone rang and she excused herself.

"Looks like we find ourselves alone again," Drew said.

"Looks like it." For some reason I didn't find myself as comfortable with Drew at this moment as I had earlier in the conference room.

"How long are you in town for?" Drew asked.

"Just a couple days. I just moved into a new house and they are finishing some work on it so I want to get back and make sure everything is well." In truth, I felt anxious about being away from the house in Oak Island.

"Is that the beach house?"

"You remember?" I was slightly impressed.

"I remember more about you than the house."

"Do you, now?" I said, shifting uncomfortably.

He tried to say something else but Stella came back, and she was fuming.

"Problem?" I asked.

"Oh you know. That was Roger's wife on the phone. She wanted to call and let me know that she was the only women he needed in his life and I should stay away." She was shouting now.

"Who does she think she is?" she asked, almost spitting her words.

"Well, she is his wife," I said.

"Ouch!" Drew said. He finished his beer and flagged down a waitress, indicating we were going need a round of shots and a new order of drinks, quickly. She nodded and headed off toward the bar.

"She is so nosy, going through his phone and finding all these messages. Oh, and Roger, he didn't have the balls to call me himself." Stella fumed as her phone rang again. She looked down and mouthed "Roger" as she answered it and stepped off away again.

"Stella loves her drama," Drew commented.

"She feeds on it," I agreed.

"That's what ultimately broke us up, you know."

"Drama?"

"Yes, her constant need to be in the middle of everything and everyone. She can't ever just leave anything alone."

"She is not perfect, but she means well, usually."

Stella headed back to our table.

"Things better?" Drew asked, as the waitress returned with our drinks.

"Roger called to apologize for his wife's drunken tirade. He said it won't happen again and I told him he was right. It was never going to happen again because I'm done." She shrugged.

"But a minute ago …" I stammered.

"A minute ago the wife was calling me and that pissed me off, but Roger called to tell me he had told his wife that he didn't love her anymore and he was leaving her," Stella said.

"For you?" I squeaked.

"I don't know. I didn't let him get that far. I told him things were moving too fast and I didn't think that it was working anymore … and then I hung up."

"To Stella," Drew said, holding up a shot, shaking his head.

"To Stella."

"Forget me. To Jill and her future," Stella added, taking the shot and following it up with her drink.

We stayed and drank at the bar until closing time. When I went to close out our tab, I was informed that every drink we had had that night had been covered by someone else in the bar. It seemed the drunker Stella got, the friendlier she got with half the bar. Drew insisted on helping me get Stella safely back to our hotel as she was barely able to stand on her own at this point. I reluctantly agreed as he hailed a cab.

"Thank you so much, Drew," I said as he gently laid Stella down on the bed in our suite. She had passed out in the cab, and Drew carried her up to our room.

"No problem," he said as we moved toward the door.

"She can be a little overwhelming."

"She's Stella. I hope she finds someone who can harness her in one day."

"Me too."

"Listen, Jill, it wasn't the evening I had hoped for, to be honest. But if you are ever in town again let me know. I would like to take you out to dinner, maybe get to know you better." He leaned down and kissed me on the cheek. I just nodded, afraid to speak and say the wrong thing.

"Well, Stella's got my number. Goodnight, Jill."

After he left, I leaned against the door, not believing what was going on. First Ross, now Drew. What was going on? My mind was spinning with too many thoughts to be able to go to bed at that moment. I changed into my pj's and grabbed my phone, sending several texts to Lanie, explaining what had happened at the bar. I knew she was already asleep, but she would get them in the morning. I thought about Drew and how handsome he was, but ultimately he made me a little uncomfortable. It just didn't feel right. After checking on Stella one more time, I crawled into bed, staring at the ceiling. My thoughts drifted to Ross. I wondered if he was on the beach tonight, playing guitar with his friends, and in an unguarded moment I decided to text him.

To: Ross Powers
What did you play tonight?

Not expecting a reply, I had rolled onto my side and pulled the covers up when my phone chimed back.

From: Ross Powers
A couple original songs.

To: Ross Powers
Sorry I missed that.

From: Ross Powers
Can't sleep?

To: Ross Powers
Missing home.

From: Ross Powers
Then come back.

I smiled at his reply and I could feel the butterflies in my stomach and teenage excitement over our conversation. The realization set in that I was missing more than home.

To: Ross Powers
Soon.

From: Ross Powers
I'll be waiting … Goonight, Jill.

I couldn't wipe the smile off my face as I fell asleep holding my phone.

....

The next morning as Stella was in the shower slowly getting ready for our day at the spa while trying not to throw up. I decided to check my e-mail, which I had long ignored. As her Mac booted up, I munched on some fruit and toast that had come to the room at eight in the morning as a result of the order Stella had placed the previous day. After logging into my e-mail, I realized just how neglectful I had been. I spent the better part of the next hour replying to friends and family about my well-being and future plans (or lack thereof). There were also several e-mails from Harry. The first couple expressed his apologies for his actions, but the last e-mail from him had angry undertones over my sudden disappearance and inability to return his calls and text messages. I rolled my eyes and hit Reply to his last e-mail.

> *To: Harry Conner*
> *From: Jill Greenfield*
> *Harry, all is well. Stop worrying. I have been out at the beach, recovering. I am trying to pick up the pieces. You should too. Please give me some time.*
> *—J*

I could hear Stella turn on the hairdryer in the bathroom as I glanced at the clock. We still had enough time to make it to the salon on time. Feeling emotionally drained from all the correspondence, I logged out of my e-mail and started to surf the web. My mind wandered to thoughts of Ross, which trigged my curiosity about his budding music career. Feeling slightly guilty, I typed his name into the search engine. What the search revealed shocked me.

"Stella!" I shouted.

"What?" she said, emerging from the bathroom. "No shouting." She held her head as she slowly moved in my direction.

"You don't look good. Are you sure you are up to going today?" I asked, distracted by Stella's pale greenish hue.

"I'll be fine. I just need some good greasy food. None of that healthy crap," she said pointing to the food on the cart that had been delivered.

"You ordered it," I said defensively.

"I know but that was yesterday before I got so drunk." She plopped down next to me. "What got you all excited?"

"Oh, right! Look at this. It's Ross," I said, opening up a picture of him at what appeared to be an awards ceremony.

"Ross?" she questioned.

"The guy from the beach." I would need to slow down for Stella to process this conversation this morning.

"Oh." We sat in silence as I clicked page after page of information.

"He's kind of a big deal ... and really cute," Stella finally said, winking at me as she got up from the bed and headed back to the bathroom, mumbling something about being sick.

"I had no idea," I said, looking back at the site that showed a professional-looking headshot photo of a younger Ross Powers. Underneath the photo, the bio included his song-writing accomplishments, many of which I recognized from other bands. He had played back-up and toured with several other well-known bands and had won a slew of awards and other accomplishments. The final line in the bio mentioned his mother's passing and his near-disappearance from the music industry after having had such success at a young age. I sat back on the bed, overwhelmed by all the information. We didn't know each other well, but still, it seemed too big a part of his life for him not to have mentioned it to me. His friends had clearly downplayed his success when they mentioned it at the beach.

"Are you ready?" Stella called from the bathroom, breaking into my thoughts.

"Almost," I said, climbing off the bed and closing the Mac as I headed into the bathroom to finish getting ready.

....

"Jean Marc is the best there is," Stella said as the cab dropped us off in front of the spa and salon. Stella had arranged for a full day at one of the trendiest salons in Manhattan, Fresh Face. Of course, she knew someone who knew the owner and was able to get us both into the exclusive salon. Our agenda included massages, pedicures, manicures, facials and haircuts and styling by Jean Marc himself.

Throughout the day we were ushered from room to room as we were rubbed, massaged, scraped and polished. But whenever I had a moment to myself, I found my thoughts drifting to Ross and his career and all that he had given up. The more I dwelled on it, the angrier I got about his hiding out on Oak Island when he was obviously meant for greater things.

"Earth to Jill."

"What?"

"I asked if you wanted to grab an early dinner and then maybe squeeze in some shopping after all this?"

"Yea, sure. That's fine."

"What's going on?" she asked and then mouthed the word *Jay* at me.

"No, actually I was thinking about Ross. But now that you say that, I feel terribly guilty," I said in a small voice. The fact that I was thinking about another man and not Jay tugged at my heart strings. It upset me that as the days came and went and the more time that passed, I thought about Jay less and less. I didn't want to replace Jay in my memory, but I didn't know how to make room for both the past and the future. Stella didn't say a word. She just raised her eyebrows at me as we made our way to the check-out counter.

"The total is what?" I asked when the girl behind the counter repeated our total bill to us. I felt faint.

"Relax," Stella said, pulling out an envelope and handing it to me.

"What's this?" I asked, puzzled.

"It's your new black AMEX card," she said proudly.

"Do I really need one?" I asked, clearly missing the fact that Stella was implying the card was prestigious.

"Of course. Anyone with your status does." She rolled her eyes at me and took the card from me and handed it over to the girl at the counter, who had been listening to our conversation.

"When did I get it?" I asked Stella as she waved down a cab outside the salon.

"My firm set it up for you at the beginning of the week." She smiled.

"I ..." I started to stammer.

"You are financially sound Jill. This card can open a lot of doors for you."

"What doors do I need opened?" I questionned the impact a shiny black card could have on my "status," as Stella put it.

"You never know and you just need to deal with it now. Your circumstances have changed and you need to adapt, be resilient," she snapped at me and then directed the cab driver to a diner several blocks away, called Moonlight's. We sat in silence for the rest of the drive and through most of our meal.

"I'm sorry," Stella finally mumbled.

"For what?" I asked, not sure if Stella had anything to be sorry for.

"I shouldn't have assumed you would want that card."

"It's not the card, Stella. It's all of it, the money, the lifestyle, financial advisors. I'm not sure who I am anymore, I didn't ask for any of it," I said, trying to find the right words that would explain how I felt so that Stella would understand.

"I get it. It's a tremendous gift that Jay left for you."

"Tremendous is an understatement," I muttered.

"Let me finish. Jay left you this gift. He worked hard to get everything just right and you need to start accepting it. Anything else would be an insult to him."

"I know. It's just a lot," I said, pouting slightly.

"No pouting … no one who finds out they just inherited $23 million ever pouts … ever. You up for shopping?" she asked, changing the subject.

"Of course," I said after a moment. I know Stella had done a lot for me over the last couple of months and even put herself out on the line professionally, getting me set up with the financial advisors at her company. I needed to move on.

After dinner, we went shopping at several of Stella's favorite boutique stores. At every store we entered the staff knew her by name and asked how she was doing. They then would pull out racks of the trendiest clothes for the upcoming fall season. She nodded and negotiated at each store, getting the best deals and latest gossip at the same time. When we were done shopping, we headed back to the hotel, each of us carrying several bags of new clothes, and we decided to call it an early night. The following morning, I needed to stop by Stella's office to officially sign off on the final contracts and documentation before catching my flight back home.

CHAPTER 29

....

My flight was delayed 30 minutes in New York. When we finally landed in Raleigh, I grabbed my bag and made my way to the curbside valet. Stella had confirmed prior to my departure that my new Jeep would be waiting for me. The valet told me it would take a couple minutes for them to retrieve it and that I could wait on the bench outside. As I sat down, I checked my phone and found several text messages and a voicemail. The voicemail was from Harry, checking on how I was doing, *again*. I had a text from Stella, asking if I had seen her favorite pair of earrings from the previous night. I replied that I had not. I also saw that I had a text from Ross I needed to reply to.

From: Ross Powers
Hey, Jill, are you still arriving home today?

To: Ross Powers
Just landed in Raleigh, waiting on car.

Within seconds, I got another message.

From: Ross Powers
Cool. I will leave your house key under the mat.

To: Ross Powers
Sounds great.

I texted back, feeling a twinge of disappointment over not having a reason to see him that night. I sat on the bench, wishing I could think of something interesting or smart to say back, but I had nothing. Just then, the valet announced that my car was on its way up. I stood up, putting Ross out of my mind and focusing on the excitement over my new car. It would be the first car that I would own that would be brand new. All my previous cars were older used models that I would drive until they wouldn't drive anymore. When I saw the Jeep pull into the valet area, I had a big smile on my face. I thanked the valet and set out to remove the hardtop cover. I got stuck and the valet offered his assistance. I made sure to give him a big tip and then I settled into my new car, taking time to adjust all the settings. Finally, I plugged my music in and hit the road.

The open air and long drive were refreshing. It gave me time to think about my trip to New York and all the events that had taken place. When I wasn't thinking, I was singing to the music at the top of my lungs. I felt so free, free of everything that was happening around me. It was well after seven when I crossed the bridge to the island. I could feel my heart beating faster and my excitement build as I got closer to the house. I turned down the street and I could see the sun was starting to set. Reds, oranges and yellows painted the sky. I pulled into the gravel drive. I was putting the Jeep in park when I looked toward the house and couldn't hide my surprise.

There in front of me was my house, my home. It looked as if the construction crew had finished while I was away on my trip. All the scaffolding and equipment was gone and what little yard there was had been landscaped. Inside, I could see that the lights were on, sending a welcome glow down onto the street. Halfway up the front steps, I saw a sign hanging from the bottom of the deck and my hand quickly rose to my mouth to stifle my emotion. The sign, a solid piece of oak, had been inscribed with the name *Eirene* and the outline of waves in the background. It had been painted white with slate-blue lettering to match the house. It was so simple and yet so perfect.

I knew it had to be Ross as he was the only one who knew about the name, but I had more questions than answers. I found the key to the front door and entered the house. I set my bag down by the stairs and wandered through to the kitchen, where, on the kitchen table, sat a small vase of flowers with a card. I picked up the card, and a tear slid down my cheek. I had cried so much in the last couple months, but, for once, I knew these tears were tears of joy. My heart swelled with hope and happiness as I read the note.

Welcome Home.
—R

It said all it needed to say and I believed it. I was home.

....

I had so much energy and excitement I didn't know what to do next. The night was still young and filled with so many opportunities. I grabbed my phone and texted Ross.

To: Ross Powers
THANK YOU! You're amazing.

I hit Send and waited. Normally, Ross's replies were really quick. There was no reply this time. After giving up waiting, I took my bag upstairs and changed into something more comfortable. Feeling inspired, I looked for my journal and found it sitting on the coffee table. I sat down and started to scribble away. It was a dangerous occupation, writing. One was always bound to lose track of time. I probably would have written all night had I not been distracted by the chime of my phone, indicating I had a text message. I got up and looked at my phone.

From: Ross Powers
I know.

I found myself grinning over his response and shaking my head all at the same time.

To: Ross Powers
Where are you?

From: Ross Powers
Front door.

No way! I put the phone down and ran to the front door, flinging it open. There on the porch stood Ross. He was dressed in jeans that hung low on his hips and a weathered red polo with the collar flipped up and he had a pair of Converse sneakers on. His shaggy hair still looked damp as if he had just gotten out of the shower.

"Hi," I said, suddenly feeling shy when I looked into his green eyes.

"You look beautiful," he said after several seconds, causing me to blush.

"Thank you," and for a moment we just stood there staring into each other's eyes. The time apart seemed only to draw us closer together as I felt that nervous energy dance between us.

"I brought dinner and entertainment," he said, breaking the tension. He held up a brown paper bag in one hand and his guitar in the other.

"Perfect," I said, letting him in the house. He grinned at me and made his way toward the kitchen.

"What's for dinner?" I asked, following behind him. I could feel my stomach rumbling as I had neglected to grab dinner on my drive home.

"Rusty's," he said, setting the bag on the counter and leaning his guitar against the chair by the kitchen table. He turned to look at me, asking me some question, but I didn't hear him. I looked into his eyes. I had so much to say to him. I needed to thank him for so many reasons, some of which I couldn't even put into words. In that instant I crossed the kitchen, put my hands on his chest and reached up on my toes and kissed him.

He body-registered his surprise but only for a second. He wrapped his hands around me and the kiss deepened. When he finally released me, I felt weak at the knees.

"Well, that happened," he said and grinned at me.

"So it seems." I grinned back.

"Dinner?"

"I'm starving."

"Tell me all about your trip to New York. How is Manhattan these days?" His voice indicated a little bit of sadness.

"Do you miss it?" I asked as I pulled some plates from the cupboard.

"The city?"

I nodded at his question and we moved to the kitchen table.

"Maybe a little bit. The city is alive. It never sleeps. It's a drastic change from Oak Island."

"I feel like you're stating the obvious," I replied.

"So you go off for a couple days and suddenly you become a jokester?" he said with a laugh. I couldn't help but chuckle back and we fell into a casual conversation. I filled him in on most aspects of my trip to New York.

"So I saw your new ride in the driveway," he said casually.

"Oh yea! It's nice. I always told myself that if I ever got to live on the beach, that was the only car to have."

"It's a sweet ride ..." He paused.

"What?" I knew he wanted to ask something but was hesitant.

"Well, it's just that I never really pictured you driving a Jeep. I kinda saw you in something fancier, like a Volvo or Lexus."

I couldn't help but laugh when he had finished.

"There's a lot you don't know about me, but no, those cars aren't really my thing. That would be Jay's thing or Stella's but not mine."

When I finished I looked to see if my mention of Jay bothered him and he didn't flinch or react. He just continued to listen attentively to what I had to say. We had finished dinner by this time and the sun had long set. I got up to clear the table and Ross turned on some more lights.

"So, entertainment?" I stood in front of him with my hands on my hips.

"I thought we might take another try at those guitar lessons," he said, grabbing the guitar and making his way over to the sofa.

"I'd like that," I said, taking my seat next to him and for the next several hours he patiently showed me each chord on the guitar, carefully moving my hand into the exact position needed. It was well after midnight when I started to yawn.

"I should get going. It's late."

He stood to leave. I also stood and walked him to the door.

"What are you doing tomorrow?" he asked.

"Well, last time I checked, I'm still unemployed so ... nothing of importance."

"A group of us are going up to Oceanside. Didn't know if you would like to join us?" He seemed nervous and fidgeted a little bit with his guitar.

"What's Oceanside?"

"An amusement park. Several of us try to go as a group every summer."

I hadn't been to an amusement park since I was in high school.

"Actually, that sounds like a lot of fun." I could tell my answer surprised him. "On one condition ... we take the Jeep!"

"Awesome. I'll be by here around nine. It's a short drive up the coast." His enthusiasm was so contagious. But I was just as excited. I loved everything about amusement parks and thrill rides, but as Stella, Lanie and even Jay got older, everyone started to shy away from going to the parks, saying they were too busy.

"Goodnight, Jill." Ross leaned down and gave me a quick kiss on the lips.

"Night, Ross," I said as I watched him walk down the stairs and get into his truck and drive off.

....

CHAPTER 30

The next morning promptly at nine Ross was at my door, dressed in shorts and a T-shirt. I had, after much deliberation, decided on a pair of jean shorts and a faded, grey, vintage tee, opting for comfort over style.

"Ready?" Ross asked when I opened the door.

"Ready. I'm actually really excited about this. Where are your friends?" I asked, expecting him to be with several people.

"They are driving up in separate cars. It's just you and me," he said as we made our way down to the cars.

"Do you know where we are going?" I asked when we reached the Jeep.

"Yup. Been going my whole life."

"Great. Then why don't you drive," I said, tossing him the car keys.

"Seriously?" he asked, looking at me.

"Knock your socks off," I said, climbing into the passenger seat.

"Cool," he said, getting in the driver side.

As we made our way up the coast, we talked nonstop. He asked about Stella and Lanie, as he had heard me mention them several times. I asked about his mom and growing up on the island as well as his time in Nashville. I tried several times to ask about his music, but the conversation always drifted in another direction. When we arrived at the amusement park, the parking lot was already filling up with people. We quickly found Mandy, Mark, April, Zach and several others and made our way in. When I got to the counter to pay for my ticket, I realized that I hadn't grabbed my wallet from my other bag after the trip to New York. The only card in my bag was the black AMEX Stella had given me. Hoping not to draw any attention to myself, I slipped the card to the teller while the others paid for their own tickets.

"Ms. Greenfield?" the teller asked.

"Yes?"

"As an AMEX card holder you automatically get tickets to tonight's concert."

"What concert?" I asked as Ross walked up behind me.

"Problem? Do you need me to pay?" he asked and I chuckled to myself at his statement. If only he knew how ridiculous his question was at that moment.

"J. King and Foray," the girl said, answering my question.

"I know J. King," Ross said with a confused look on his face.

"I apparently have qualified for tickets to his show. How many tickets?" I asked the girl.

"Normally, it's two, but let me call my manager. Someone with your card status should qualify for more," she said, grabbing the phone and calling someone.

"What's the hold up?" April asked as they all gathered around me.

"Jill got some free tickets to the concert tonight," Ross said.

"How?" Mandy asked.

"Not sure," I said, trying to downplay the whole situation.

"Ms. Greenfield, we can accommodate your whole group in the VIP section. It will also include a meet and greet before the show. We ask that you and your group be at the south gate no later than five this evening," she said, handing me back my card and a slip to sign.

"Do we need the physical tickets?" I asked.

I heard several people in the group whispering behind me as they got a look at my card. Under my breath I cursed Stella Conner and her love for flashy things.

"No. We have your name down on the list. Just show up."

"This is so cool," I heard someone comment behind me.

"Thanks," I mumbled and turned to the group, all of whom where now gaping at me.

"What?"

"Was that a black AMEX?" Mandy asked.

I finally gave in. "Yes. You want to see it?"

"Of course!"

I took the card back out of my pocket and they passed it around. They all knew what it was but they were too polite to ask how I qualified for one. Even Mandy was mum on the issue. Ross stayed at the back of the group, strangely quiet all of a sudden. After the "oohs" and "aws" over the card were done, I put it away and we continued into the park.

"Are you okay?" I asked Ross as we walked through the park. April and Mark were leading the way toward one of the roller coasters.

"I know him," he said again.

"Who? J. King?"

"Yea. I used to work with him," he said, lost in his own thoughts. I thought this was my window. It wasn't the ideal place, but it was now or never. I waved the group on ahead and pulled Ross to the side.

"Ross, I know," I blurted out.

"Know what?"

"I know about your music career, the songs, the tours, the awards," I quickly confessed.

"How?"

"Well, your friends ..."

"Mandy?"

"Perhaps." I wasn't ready to throw anyone under the bus. "But when I was in New York, I looked you up. Your career was amazing! You have more talent than most of us will ever have. What happened?" I asked directly, hoping he wouldn't ignore my question.

"My mom got sick."

"That was then and now?" I asked. I could feel the irony in my conversation. I was telling him he needed to move on, but I hadn't done the same in my own life.

"I don't know," he said, looking past me into the distance.

"I think you do and if you don't want to tell me, that is okay. But let me ask you this: do you still love music?"

"Yes."

"Love performing?"

"Yes."

"Do you picture yourself doing anything else?"

"Nope," he said, looking at me now.

"I think you have your answer then. You can't hide forever. Trust me. I know," I said, taking his hand and giving it a squeeze.

"It seems like a lifetime ago. I wouldn't even know how to get back in the game."

"Well, you don't have to make that decision now. Let's enjoy today and see what happens," I said, trying to be as "chill" as possible, but inside I was freaking out.

"You're right ... and Jill? ... You're awesome," he said as we started walking to where his friends were now in line.

"I know," I said, smiling.

....

We spent the next several hours waiting in lines, riding rides and eating the best amusement park food. It was the most fun I had had in a long time. Mandy, as it turned out, was scared of most rides and instead took pictures all day, making a picture documentary of our journey. It was almost five when I asked the group if they wanted to attend the concert. A unanimous yes followed my question. I looked at Ross to see if he was okay and he nodded. With that, we headed over to the gate the girl had instructed us to go to, and we waited.

"Jill?" Mark said.

"Yea?"

"Don't take this the wrong way, but you're way cooler than I thought you were going to be," he said, making me laugh.

"Thanks, I think."

Just then, my phone rang and I answered without looking at the screen.

"Hello?" I said, motioning to Ross that I would just be a minute.

"Jill! What the hell is going on?" Harry shouted at me from the other end.

"Harry, I didn't recognize the number," I said with a frown.

"Yea. It's probably the only reason you answered. You would know I got a new number if you had ever bothered to reply to me," he snapped.

"What do you want, Harry?" I snapped back, walking farther away from the group.

"Jill, I just saw the house had a sold sign out front ... Where the hell are you? I heard this rumor you were living in a beach house ... one that Jay bought you." He accused more than he asked. I hadn't realized the house had sold, but Harry was unable to see the surprise register on my face.

"Not that it's any of your business, but yes I have decided to move. I couldn't stand to live in a house I shared with Jay when he wasn't there to share it with."

"Are the rumors true? Are you living in a house on the beach on that island?"

"Who told you that?"

"Peter called to tell me that Jay had made some smart investments and left you with a boatload of money and a house."

"Of course he did," I thought.

"Well, if Peter told you that, why are you asking me?" I asked, annoyed.

"So it's true."

"Does it matter? It's not really any of your business."

"You're wrong. You are my best friend's wife, so that makes it my business," he said heatedly.

"Harry, you need to drop this. Jay is gone. I am moving on."

Ross came up behind me, putting his hand on the small of my back, startling me.

"You okay?" Ross asked.

"Who is that?" Harry asked.

"Harry, I don't think this is healthy. You need to leave me alone. Put Jay to rest and let me move on," I said, ignoring his question.

"Where the hell are you? Who are you with? Why are you keeping all these damn secrets," he asked, becoming more agitated.

"Good-bye, Harry," I started to say.

"Jill, you bitch. Don't hang up on me," Harry shouted back.

"Good-bye," I finally said, hanging up the phone and turning to face Ross, who now had a concerned look on his face.

"Before you ask, I'm okay," I said, wondering how to explain it all. "Just an old friend who is having some trouble moving on."

"You want to go?"

"No. I'm good."

"Okay. They are ready to let us in," he said, pointing toward the group and some official-looking woman with a clipboard.

"Right. Let's do this," I said as we walked back to the group.

. . . .

The woman checked my credit card at the gate and verified our names on the list before letting us in. Once inside, we were ushered backstage to a large tent that was set up to look like a lounge where we were told to wait. April and Mandy were talking excitedly about meeting J. King and seeing the concert. I could not have named one song that he sung, but I was glad they were excited. We waited for what seemed like an hour before a large security guard came in and took us to another tent. The second tent was set up much like the first one, but bottled water, sharpie markers and J. King posters were set up in this one. I knew that J. King had arrived by the sudden squealing and shrieking from Mandy and April.

"Oh my God!" they gushed as he walked in with several other people. When the security guards motioned that they could go up and get their picture taken, they rushed up to the singer. J. King was older than I expected. I thought he might be a teenager, but he looked to be about my age. He wore ripped jeans and a tight-fitting cotton shirt under a black jacket. A pair of sunglasses hung from the collar of his shirt and he wore a pair of black combat boots that matched his jet-black hair. After Mandy and April had their pictures taken, body parts signed and posters autographed, the rest of our group went up to meet the singer. Ross and I were last in line.

"Ross? Ross Powers?" J. King said as we approached him.

"Hey, man," Ross said, holding his hand out to shake the singer's hand.

Instead, J. King got up and wrapped Ross in a hug. "How the hell are you?" J. King asked, clearly shocked by running into Ross.

"Things are good."

"I heard about your mom and I'm so sorry."

"No problem," Ross said, shrugging his shoulders.

"Jane? Do you know who this is?" J. King called to a woman who was standing off to the side. She shook her head and looked as confused as the rest of us.

"This guy wrote 'When She's Gone' on my last album," he gushed.

I could hear the group whisper behind me. This was quite the exciting trip for them.

"Who is this with you? Your girlfriend?" J. King said, pointing to me. Ross started to correct the singer.

"Jill," I said, interrupting Ross by sticking my hand out to shake J. King's hand. Instead, he wrapped me up in a hug as well.

"She's a cutie," J. King said, looking at Ross.

I could feel my face go red with embarrassment. I excused myself and made my way over to the group as Ross and J. King spoke quietly in the corner. After about 20 minutes, Jane walked over and whispered something to the singer. He hugged Ross one more time, waved to us and excused himself. One of the security guards escorted us to the front-row seats that J. King insisted we sit in for the show.

As soon as we were seated, Mandy and April jumped all over Ross with a million questions about his connection to the singer.

"I wrote that song maybe two years ago. No big deal," he said, shrugging it off.

After several minutes, they realized Ross wasn't going to say anything more on the subject and they turned their attention to the opening band that was taking the stage.

"So, girlfriend?" I said, turning to look at Ross and interrupting his thoughts.

"So sorry about that," he said, running his hand through his hair.

"No. It's okay. I have been called much worse today," I said shyly and Ross casually slipped his hand next to mine until our fingers were intertwined.

"Ross Powers?" a voice asked.

"Yea, that's me," Ross replied.

As we turned to look, Jane from the tent casually strode toward us. "J. King has asked that you join him onstage tonight. His guitarist just got sick back stage and we don't usually travel with a backup."

"I don't know …," Ross started to say.

I squeezed his hand and gave him a slight nod. He looked up at me and we stared at each other for several beats as if we could read each other thoughts.

"Alright, yea, I would love to play," he said.

"Great! If you could follow me," she said, obviously relieved to find a replacement guitarist for the band.

"Give me one minute."

"Of course," she said, stepping to the side.

"Are you sure? Will you be okay by yourself?" he asked, looking at me.

"I'm a big girl. I'll be fine. I'll be with your friends."

"That's what I am afraid of." He laughed.

"I will be fine. You go. Don't worry about me."

"You amaze me," he said, leaning over to kiss my forehead. He waved to his friends, who, as soon as he had left to make his way backstage, rushed over. All of us jumped up and down and squealed with excitement.

CHAPTER 31

··

We waited for about an hour before the lights dimmed and the announcer told the crowd to stand and welcome J. King and the Foray Band to the stage. J. King came onto the stage dressed as we had seen him earlier and immediately began singing. I scanned the stage for Ross and saw him standing between the drummer and several backup singers. He had somehow changed and was now wearing ripped jeans and a tighter black cotton shirt that had "J. King" printed on it in white. I couldn't take my eyes off him. J. King danced and sang several more songs and I found myself drawn to Ross the entire time, the way he moved, how he played, even as he sang along with the backup singers. J. King had been on for about an hour and half before he paused and spoke to the audience.

"How you doing, North Carolina?" he asked the crowd who yelled back.

"I wanted to let you know that you are all in for a special treat tonight. My good friend Ross Powers has joined me onstage tonight." He pointed to Ross, who waved from his spot onstage as the audience yelled and applauded.

"He was a good sport tonight, sitting in for Jerry, who normally plays the guitar but got sick at the last minute. Ross is extremely talented and he's going to sing the next song," he said to the hushed crowd.

"Ross, come up here." He motioned for Ross to join him. Ross casually walked to center stage as if he had done it a thousand times and embraced J. King, who handed him the microphone and then sat down on a stool by the backup singers.

"What's up, North Carolina? How are we doing tonight?" Ross asked the crowd who cheered.

"This next song is a song I wrote recently after meeting someone new in my life," he said, looking down into the audience until his eyes locked with mine. "You should always have hope," he said as he began to play. For the next three minutes I stood rooted to my spot in the audience, unable to breath. I felt like the only one in the entire park. He finished up his song, glancing in my direction one more time before he was done. J. King walked back to center stage and hugged Ross as the audience went wild. Remembering where I was, I joined April and Mandy who were jumping like crazy, yelling and screaming. J. King finished up two more songs before thanking the audience and disappearing from the stage.

The lights came on and people started leaving the concert area. Jane appeared from the side of the stage and motioned for us to follow her backstage. Obediently, we followed her to yet another tent that we had not been in before. This one looked more like a hangout area for the band and singer himself. Sofas were arranged in the center with chairs, and several musical instruments were lying about. As we entered the tent, Ross, J. King and several other band members were already standing there. April and Mandy and the guys rushed past me to congratulate Ross and talk with J. King again. I stood back taking in the whole scene. Ross was truly a musician who should be touring the world. I smiled and shook my head at the strange curves life throws at you.

"Jill."

I heard Ross call my name as he waved me forward. I walked toward him, trying to tell him how much I loved his song. Instead, he stepped forward and put both hands on either side of my face. Looking me eyes, he leaned in and kissed me.

"I meant every word," he whispered to me afterward and embraced me. It was as if the scene in the tent didn't exist for that moment.

"I know," I whispered back, looking into his eyes.

"Come. Let's celebrate," he said, taking my hand and leading me back to the group who were all celebrating, mingling and chatting.

....

It was well after three in the morning when Ross pulled up outside my house.

"What a crazy unexpected day," I mused out loud and Ross looked at me and nodded, obviously lost in his own thoughts as well.

"Jill, I can't thank you enough."

"Me? What did I do?" I was confused.

"If it wasn't for you getting those tickets to the concert, I would have never had the chance to reconnect with J. King," he said.

"The card opens doors for you." I could hear Stella's words in my head.

"It was kismet," I finally said, getting out of the Jeep. Ross walked around the Jeep and grabbed my hand and walked me to the front door. He leaned down and kissed me again when we reached the door.

"Good night, Jill," he said and turned to leave.

"Ross?" I said, tugging at his hand. I wasn't ready to let go. "Do you want to stay?" I asked shyly.

He stopped and turned to look at me, his eyes searching mine until he saw something that convinced him of something.

"I would like that," he said and followed me in.

I walked around the house and turned on a couple of lights per my nightly ritual. Ross watched.

"Don't judge," I said, feeling defensive.

"No judgment here," he said, raising his arms in self-defense.

We climbed the stairs to the bedroom and I headed into the bathroom to change. When I emerged from the bathroom, Ross was lying on top of the blankets on Jay's side of the bed. I stood and took everything in. My past and present were colliding in ways I never thought possible.

"Come," Ross said, patting my side of the bed, and then he held the blankets up so I could slide in under the covers.

"I'm sorry. It's just a lot to take in," I said, trying to keep my emotions in check.

"We are just sleeping," he said, reading my emotions, and I nodded, climbing under the blanket and snuggling up to his chest.

"May I?" he asked, pointing toward the bedside light. I nodded and he leaned over and turned the bedside light off. He rubbed my back slowly as I listened to his heart beat and the slow rise and fall of his chest as it lulled me off to sleep.

....

The sun filled the room completely when I opened my eyes the next morning. Sometime in the middle of the night we had shifted, and I was now on my side and Ross was curled around me sound asleep. I smiled to myself and slowly eased myself out of bed, trying not to wake him. I saw that it was a little past nine in the morning. What a crazy 24 hours it had been. I grabbed some running clothes out of the drawer, wrote a quick note, leaned it against the clock in the bedroom and then made my way downstairs. I put on my running shoes and headed out for the beach. The steady and methodical movement made it easier for me to organize my thoughts. It was almost an hour later when I climbed the back steps to the porch and made my way into the house.

"How was the morning run?" Ross asked, startling me when I entered the house.

"Slow." I leaned against the counter, looking at him.

He was seated at the kitchen table with a large cup of coffee in front of him. His blonde hair was sticking up in random places. "Are you checking out my bed head?" he asked, catching me staring at him and I giggled. He got up and made his way toward me at the counter, pinning me before kissing me.

"Good morning to you too," I said between kisses.

"Fantastic morning," he mumbled before backing up and looking at me.

"I really need to shower," I said, remembering my run.

"I need to go home and change anyway."

"Do you work today?" I asked. I had long given up trying to keep up what day of the week it was. Without a steady job, it seemed impossible to keep dates straight.

"Nope. Took the day off. I was hoping to spend the day with you."

"I like the sound of that." I kissed him on the cheek and headed toward the stairs.

"I'll be back in an hour or so … with lunch," he said, looking at the clock on the wall.

"Sounds perfect," I called as I headed upstairs.

....

"It was the most amazing time," I gushed to Stella and Lanie after I had showered and dressed.

"Sounds like something out of a movie," Lanie commented.

"Is it serious?" Stella asked.

"I don't know, but I do really like him and I think he really likes me too."

"I'm happy for you," Lanie said again.

"It's okay, right?" I asked.

"What's okay?" Stella asked.

"It's okay I'm starting to see someone else, right? I'm just having a hard time allowing myself to be happy. I feel like after what happened with Jay I should maybe still be mourning."

"Jill, everyone processes death differently. There is no set time to mourn anyone and he will always be a part of your life on this earth, but you now have to follow your heart, again," Lanie said, repeating some of the same advice Stella had already told me earlier.

"I can tell you've been back at work." I chided Lanie, and Stella laughed.

"Funny," Lanie said.

I heard a knock at the door.

"Come in," I called.

"Is he there?" Stella asked as Ross strolled in, wearing board shorts, a white cotton tee and a pair of black wayfarer sunglasses. He was carrying two, large, brown paper bags.

"Yup," I said, waving Ross in.

He nodded in my direction and headed for the kitchen.

"I can't wait to meet him in a couple weeks," Lanie commented. "I can't believe the summer is coming to an end," I said.

"Believe it, sister," Stella said. "I could really use a vacation. Roger got back from his and won't leave me alone. He has already sent me like three or four bouquets of flowers and chocolate truffles—you know, the one's I like from the Sweet Shoppe near where I work."

"Sounds awful," Lanie said.

"Well, I have to go. I will talk to you both in a couple days," I said and hung up.

I wandered into the kitchen and watched Ross prepare lunch from the food he had brought.

"Hey there," I said, wrapping my arms around him from behind.

"Hey," he said, softly turning around to face me.

"Stella and Lanie?" he guessed.

"Yup," I said. "Can I help you with anything?"

"Nope. I'm almost done anyway. Most of it came prepared," he said, pointing to the bags. I looked closely and saw that they were imprinted with the name of a local deli that I recognized. We sat down at the kitchen table and talked about the previous night as we ate our lunch. Ross shared his excitement over performing again and being onstage. He tried to explain to me how it felt to perform in front of a large audience. He then talked about his decision to leave the music industry after his mom had passed and how lifeless he had felt. I nodded in sympathy as I tried to clear the table, knocking over my drink and spilling it all over my lap.

"I'm such a klutz. Let me go change really quick," I said and walked to the stairs. I was almost done cleaning up when I heard a knock at the front door.

"Can you get that?" I called down to Ross. Moments later, I heard raised voices.

"Who the hell are you?" I heard Harry say from my living room.

"Who are you?" I heard Ross ask back.

"Harry?" I said as I rushed to the living room. Harry's clothes were wrinkled and his hair was longer, shaggier than the last time I had seen him. He looked as if he had put on some weight and his normally clean-shaven face now sported a two- or three-day stubble.

"Who the hell is this, Jill?" he asked, turning to face me and pointing to Ross. "Is this the guy I heard on the phone yesterday?"

"Harry, what are you doing here? How did you find me?"

"I'm a cop, Jill. I can find your new address pretty easily. You made me do it. You kept ignoring my calls, texts and e-mails. Then you go and sell the house out from underneath me, you just can't do that."

"Yes, I can and I did," I said, moving to stand in front of Harry. "Harry, you shouldn't be here. I don't want you here," I said more forcefully.

"Who is this kid? What is he, like, 12? Jay dies and you run off to the beach and shack up right away with this kid. Nice way to honor his memory. I always told Jay he could do better."

"Listen, buddy, I think that the lady asked you to leave," Ross said, putting himself between Harry and me.

"Lady? I don't see any ladies here, just this gold-digging whore." Harry slurred his words.

"Have you been drinking?" I asked.

"What's it to you?"

"What are you doing to your life?" I asked, moving to Ross's side.

"I'm trying to honor my friend the best way I know how and you have gone and fucked it all up. We should be together. We could have lived in that house or sold it if you wanted. We were a good fit,

276

Jill, you and me. That is what Jay would have wanted." He grabbed my arm.

"Let go," I growled at Harry, trying to pull my arm back.

"Let her go," Ross said, putting his hand on Harry's arm, the one that held mine.

"Back off, kid," Harry said, looking at Ross. He suddenly let me go. I stumbled backward and slammed into the wall. Harry tried to step forward to catch me, but Ross blocked his way. This only made Harry angrier and he swung wildly at Ross, catching him in the gut.

"Stop it," I yelled, getting up.

Things were quickly getting out of control. I tried to put myself between Ross and Harry just as Harry took another wild punch. It landed squarely on my left cheek. I fell backward into Ross, who was getting up. Everything went black.

....

"Jill?" I heard Ross call my name but my body wouldn't respond. I heard people all around me. Some seemed to be shouting while others were whispering. I felt a slight squeeze of my hand before I drifted off again.

....

"Jill?" I heard Ross call my name again, but I was still unable to make my body respond in the way I needed it to. I thought I heard Lanie's voice among the other voices that surrounded me. I felt a sharp pain in my cheek and I faded off again.

I opened my eyes but could only see clearly from the right side. It looked as if I were in a hospital room, but I was unsure of how or why I was there. Looking around, I saw Ross and Lanie talking to a doctor in the doorway.

"Hey," I croaked, trying to get their attention. Both Lanie and Ross turned at the sound of my voice. I could see relief rush over Ross's face. Lanie walked over, grabbed my hand, and sat in a chair beside my bed.

"Jill, you gave us such a scare," she said. Her eyes were swollen and red.

"What happened?"

My mouth was very dry and I tried to reach for the water that was sitting on the rolling tray next to my bed. Ross saw what I was trying to do and reached for the water, adding a straw and holding it up for me to sip from.

"Thank you," I whispered and he nodded back.

"Mrs. Greenfield, I'm Dr. Baker." The man I had seen them standing with moments earlier approached my bed.

"Call me Jill," I mumbled.

"Jill, you sustained a pretty big impact to your jaw. You were knocked unconscious and suffered a concussion. In addition, your jaw has a slight facture. There is some severe swelling on your cheek and near your left eye, as well as a couple stitches, but there will be no permanent damage. We are going to keep you here overnight for observation, but I don't see why you shouldn't be good to go home in the morning," he said, checking several more charts before leaving.

"What happened?" I asked again when the doctor left. I could see Lanie and Ross glance at each other before Ross spoke.

"What do you remember?"

"I remember Harry showing up at the house and there was a fight, but I don't remember being hit," I said. I tried to recall details of that encounter, but I kept coming up blank.

"You got in between Ross and Harry during the fight and Harry ended up hitting you pretty hard in the cheek," Lanie explained.

"When you got knocked down, you ended up falling on top of me, knocking me down as well. But Harry kept trying to pick you up. He kept calling you his wife and that he needed to take you home. Every time I tried to stop him, he got crazier and all he wanted to do was keep fighting," Ross said.

It was only then I noticed the bruises on Ross's face and several stitches above his eye.

"Oh my! I'm so sorry, Ross," I whispered.

"This is not your fault," he said fiercely.

"Anyway, after about 10 or 15 minutes of dealing with Harry, Ross finally convinced Harry they needed to call an ambulance."

"I didn't want to leave you to go find one of our phones in case he tried to grab you and make a run for it," Ross added.

"Harry ended up running out of the house after he saw all the blood. I think he thought you were dead," Lanie whispered, horrified by the idea.

"I was then able to call for help, and when they arrived, I called Lanie," Ross said. "I remember you telling me she lived in Raleigh. I thought you would want her here with you when you woke up." Ross sat down on the other side of the bed and held my other hand. "It just all happened so quickly," Ross said in disbelief.

"I called Stella, but I told her not to rush down here until we knew something further," Lanie added.

"Did anyone find Harry?" I asked. Ross and Lanie again shared a glance before Lanie cleared her throat.

"Yes, they did. They found him about two blocks away from your house. He was suffering a major psychotic break and they took him into involuntary custody. He was convinced that you and he were married and going to move into that house in Greensboro together in order to honor Jay's memory. He thought all of Jay's belonging and possessions including you should be under his purview. In some weird way he had convinced himself that it was the only way to keep Jay alive, if you will," Lanie explained, sounding very clinical.

"What's going to happen to him?" I asked, horrified by the whole thing.

"He is heavily sedated right now and he is being treated for injuries sustained while he resisted arrest. He will get medical treatment and then deal with the legal implications of everything. But the most important thing is he can't hurt you anymore. Also the police will need your statement about the entire thing but said it could wait until morning."

Lanie's phone rang. "Stella," she answered and walked out of the room.

"Ross, I can't even begin to ..." I turned to look at him and tried to apologize.

"Jill, please stop. You did nothing wrong here. Harry is the one that is sick here. I'm just sorry I wasn't able to protect you from getting hurt in the first place." He bowed his head down.

"Ross, look at me," I said as forcefully as I could in my weakened state. "Thank you for staying with me."

He nodded his head.

Lanie came back into the room. "Stella is going to stay in New York, although she already has legal council set up for both of you if needed,"

Both Lanie and Ross hung around and idly chatted for another hour before I finally drifted off to sleep.

CHAPTER 32

....

I must have slept all night because when I woke up, it was a little after seven in the morning. Lanie was asleep on the small sofa in the hospital room. I looked around for Ross and couldn't find him. Feeling disappointed, I struggled to sit up in my bed.

"I sent him home," Lanie said from her spot on the sofa, startling me.

"You didn't need to stay," I said, feeling bad she had spent the night in the hospital room.

"Yes, I did. I had orders from both Mary Elizabeth and Stella not to let you out of my sight." She sat up. "You know, that Ross, he's a pretty special guy—cute too," she added after several seconds.

"You think so?"

"His concern for you was so genuine and he wasn't going to leave here last night until the nurse said that only one of us could stay. I was then able to convince him to go home and get some rest and that he could be by your side when I brought you home today." She smiled. "I don't know how you got so lucky twice in your life, but I think love found you out on that beach. Jill, he's your next forever love."

"It's too soon to tell that," I said, slightly embarrassed by Lanie's bluntness.

"Time will tell, but someone is looking after you," she said.

The rest of the morning went by slowly. First, two officers came by to take my statement. I learned nothing more about Harry or his condition. Dr. Baker came by again and checked on my vitals and told me he would release me as long as I went home and rested and that I would need a follow-up appointment in a week or so. Another doctor and nurse came by to sign my release papers. The nursing staff insisted that I be wheeled to the curb where Lanie had pulled her car around. She drove me from the Wilmington hospital back to Oak Island. When we pulled up in front of the house, I saw Ross's truck parked outside. He was sitting on the front steps.

"Welcome home," Lanie said, smiling, and parked the car. Ross walked over and helped me out of the passenger's seat.

"Hey," he said leaning down close to me. I expected a small kiss, but instead he insisted on carrying me into the house and settling me on the sofa.

"You both don't have to baby me," I said when we were all in the house. There were no signs of a struggle, so someone must have cleaned up the mess.

"Jill, this is amazing," Lanie said, walking through the house, examining the finished projects.

"I agree," I said, sitting up to look at her. Lanie stayed for a couple more minutes before heading back to Raleigh, but not before she had given a list of instructions to both Ross and me about my care.

"Promise me you will take care of yourself," she whispered to me as she sat down on the sofa next to me.

"I promise," I said, squeezing her hand. She got up and quietly spoke to Ross in the other room before leaving.

"Bye, Jill," she said on her way out the door.

"Bye, Lanie," I called over the edge of the sofa. I heard her car pull out of the driveway and I lay back down on the sofa, letting out a sigh. Ross emerged from the kitchen, carrying a cup of tea for me, which he placed on the end table. He took a seat on the coffee table across from me and reached for my hand.

"Jill ..." he started to say.

Suddenly, my stomach lurched forward. I had a bad feeling about this conversation.

"Yesterday was not the day I expected. I realized that there is still so much I don't know about you."

I swung my feet around so that I was now sitting on the sofa, facing him.

"Ross, yesterday was an awful day. It was unexpected, but I'm so glad you were here with me. I would hate to think of what would have happened if you hadn't been here." I shuddered at the thought "But I understand if it was too much. There are a million reasons for you not to stay, too serious, too crazy ... you don't owe me anything. You don't have to stay." I rose and walked to the back door and stared out to the ocean. My head protested slightly.

"Jill." Ross came up to me and softly caught hold of my hand. He slowly turned me so that I faced him. "If you let me finish ... There may be a million reasons for me not to stay, but I only need one: you. I was going to say before you interrupted me that since meeting you, my life has been far more interesting. I know it's only been a short time and I don't know everything about you, but I want to. I think I'm falling in love with you, Jill Greenfield," he whispered, kissing me lightly on the forehead.

I was not sure what had just happened. I had been sure he was about to break up with me and go running for the hills. Now, instead, he was declaring his love. Did he expect me to do the same? Did I even know how I felt about him? Everything seemed so fuzzy still that it was hard for me to concentrate on this conversation.

"Ross, I ..." I tried to sort through my feelings for Ross, but nothing worked.

"Nope. Not today. You take your time sorting through every-thing. You need to heal. I just wanted you to know I wasn't going anywhere and whenever you are ready, you can let me know how you feel. In the meantime, back on the sofa with you." He whisked me off my feet and settled me into the sofa again. He lifted my legs, sat down on the sofa, and lowered them back down on his lap. He started to hum a soft melody and I soon fell asleep.

....

It was dark outside when I finally stirred. I could hear the soft melody of Ross's guitar as I opened my eyes and sat up. Ross was now sitting across from me in another chair. He strummed the last chord of the song he was working on and looked up at me.

"Hey, sleeping beauty, you hungry?" he asked with a smile.

"I'm starving."

"Great. You stay there. I'll go heat it up." He put his guitar down and headed toward the kitchen.

"Heat what up? I didn't think I had anything."

"You didn't. I asked April if she would be willing to stop somewhere for me and bring it here. She dropped the food off several hours ago, but I couldn't bring myself to wake you."

Ross reheated two bowls of homemade chicken noodle soup from one of the local restaurants and we ate in the living room in comfortable silence. When we were done, Ross handed me my phone and told me that I needed to call Stella.

"I promised her that you would call when you woke up and after you ate," he said sheepishly.

"You spoke with her?"

"Believe it or not, I have spoken with Lanie and Stella several times in the last 24 hours. They care a great deal about you. You are all very lucky to have each other. That kind of friendship and loyalty these days is rare."

I nodded in agreement. I spent the next 30 minutes on the phone with Stella, assuring her that I was okay. Yawning, I turned to Ross, who declared it was time for bed. After much protest, he let me walk to bed. He again pulled back the cover and let me slide in while he got on top of the blankets, letting me curl up on his chest.

"You probably haven't gotten any sleep in days," I mumbled.

"Don't you worry about me. My nights have been just as wonderful as my days," he whispered as I fell asleep.

....

I woke up the next morning trying to remember everything that had occurred over the last few days. My body ached as I stretched my legs and moved slightly, trying not to wake Ross.

"I hope you're not thinking of sneaking out of bed again," he said from beside me.

"You're awake?" I said, surprised, and rolled over to look at him.

"Just barely. How are you feeling?" He looked concerned.

"I'm achy and sore, but my head isn't pounding." I gingerly touched my check. "How are you feeling?"

"Me? I'm fine."

"I'm not the only one who took a hit. You took a few swings that got stitches and bruises too," I added, reaching up and letting my fingers lightly touch his cheek.

"True, but you're the only one who got knocked out," he mumbled, grabbing my hand and kissing me on the nose.

"Breakfast?" he asked

"Yes, but let me cook," I said, looking back at him.

"Are you up for it?"

"Yes. Please let me feel useful."

"Okay, but we will probably need to go to the store. Your fridge is pathetic."

We lay in bed a little while longer, chatting, and then I got up and dressed while Ross went downstairs and made coffee for both of us. After that, we drove to Ross's uncle's place so he could change and grab a couple of items before heading to the grocery store. When we returned home, I was more tired than I thought I would be. I napped on the sofa while Ross ended up making something to eat, more as an early lunch than breakfast. We decided to sit on the beach and enjoy the peaceful late summer afternoon. For dinner, I was finally able to show my cooking skills, making Ross steak and potatoes while I enjoyed a simple salad and more soup from the previous night.

The sun started to set and Ross and I found ourselves on the sofa. We first talked about Harry, and I explained my friendship with him as well as his odd behavior since Jay's death. Ross asked several questions about Jay, which I answered before his phone rang. He excused himself for a moment to take the call.

"The group is going to be out on the beach this evening if you are interested," he said when he came back.

"Oh," I said, not sure if I wanted to see anyone.

"Actually, they specifically asked for you to come."

"Really?"

"What? They took a real liking to you. You're easy to like." I finally agreed that it would be nice to see everyone and enjoy the summer for as long as we could. I changed into jeans and a cotton shirt and grabbed a blanket off the sofa as Ross grabbed his guitar and we headed to the beach. I could already see the group gathered around the bonfire as we approached. I was thankful it was already so dark that my injuries wouldn't look as bad.

"Jill! Ross!" April called us as we approached. Several people got up and gave us hugs and asked us how we were doing. Apparently, the island was abuzz with the encounter at my house and everyone already knew all the details as if they had been there themselves. Mandy and April fussed over our injuries before letting us settle in around the bonfire. Zach appeared with the ingredients to make s'mores and soon the conversation became a steady hum of stories and chatter as everyone toasted marshmallows and enjoyed each other's company. In no time, as usual, people asked Ross to play, and he happily picked up his guitar and started to play. After a while, he asked me if I had any requests. I thought back to my research in New York, discovering all the songs he had written and picked one I could remember. He raised his eyebrows at my request but said nothing and just started to play.

"I love that song," Mandy commented when he was done.

"I know. That group is one of my favorites," Mark commented.

I was shocked that no one had made the connection to Ross and was about to say something when Ross shook his head at me. Apparently, he wasn't forthcoming with his friends either.

"I have to get going. I have an early shift at the grocery store," Zach said, rising, and as if on cue, we all stood to leave, one by one. Ross grabbed my hand and we strolled quietly back to the house. On the porch, I stopped to look out over the ocean. Ross cleared his throat.

"You really did your research, didn't you?" he asked in a playful voice.

"I told you I did," I said, turning to face him.

"I have known those guys for years and none of them have ever figured it all out. They know bits and pieces, but most of them think I couldn't hack it. Yet you figure it out in weeks," he said, shaking his head.

"What can I say? I wanted to know," I said, shrugging my shoulders. "Ross I think it's time for you to leave Oak Island," I added hesitantly.

"I know I need to leave, but I finally have a legit reason to stay," he said, leaning down to kiss me. I kissed him back and he eventually stopped and started to pull away. I looked up into his eyes and for a brief second I saw my future in them. I put my hand on the side of his face, and poured my heart into my kiss. Somewhere in the middle of the kiss something changed and I led Ross back into the house. At the bottom of the stairs, he swept me up and carried me to bed. He hesitated before he put me down on the bed looking at me for reassurance.

"Are you sure?" he asked, gently leaning over me. I nodded in response, pulling my shirt over my head and dropping it on the floor next to the bed. He leaned back, and I pulled his shirt over his head, dropping it on the floor next to mine. Carefully and gently, we explored all that was left to explore between us before finally making love. Afterward, I curled up next to Ross, who had joined me under the covers and listened to his breathing deepen as he started to fall asleep.

"Ross?" I whispered. I waited for a response but didn't hear anything.

"I love you too," I whispered again before falling asleep.

CHAPTER 33

....

Ross and I settled into a familiar pattern. I would get up with Ross for breakfast, and he would leave for work while I would go for a run. After work, we would eat dinner on the back porch and spend most of our evening on the sofa where I would write in my journal and he would play the guitar and write music. On many evenings, we joined our friends on the beach, hanging out, listening to music, and more specifically, listening to Ross play the guitar and learning the latest town gossip from Mandy. It was a comfort and security that I hadn't felt in a long time. It made me relax. It was this routine that carried us through the end of the summer to Labor Day weekend.

"I can't believe everyone is coming to visit this weekend," I exclaimed one night at dinner.

"You can at least pretend to be excited your friends are coming," Ross said teasing me.

"Given the past year, this is the longest the three of us have gone without seeing each other," I said, ignoring his comment. "Are you nervous?"

He was fidgeting with his food. "I have played in front of thousands, met some pretty big names in the business, but strangely, yes," he said. "Spending a weekend with you and your two best friends terrifies me."

"You have nothing to worry about. They already love you and you have met Lanie before."

"Under extremely different circumstances," he commented as I continued to prattle on about our weekend plans.

After 15 minutes, he interrupted me. "Do you want me to stay at my uncle's this weekend?"

"Why?"

"I just don't want to get in the way of your time with your friends."

"Don't be ridiculous. They want to meet you and I want you to meet them."

"I understand that, but if it's weird about me spending the night …"

"No. Don't be silly. Your place this weekend is with me." I ruffled his hair as I walked past him on the way to the kitchen.

"Okay." He laughed.

....

Stella's plane flew into Raleigh and Lanie and Mary Elizabeth were going to pick her up before heading to the beach. I had spent the better part of the week cleaning and making the guest bedrooms as inviting as possible. It was a little after noon on Friday when they pulled into the driveway. I flew down the stairs and met them at the car before they could even get out.

Stella got to me first and embraced me in a long hug.

"Let me take a look," she said, pulling me back.

"Look at what?" I asked in confusion.

"No scars," she said, looking at my face. She was referring to my stitches and fractured jaw.

"Nope. No evidence it ever happened," I said, turning to Lanie for a hug to avoid further inquisition from Stella. The doctor had removed my stitches and cleared me on all my injuries several weeks earlier, which I had already told Stella several times.

"Jill, you look really good, happy," Mary Elizabeth said when I embraced her.

"Thank you. It's taken a while, but I'm getting there." I helped them with their luggage as I directed them to their rooms.

"Where's the boy toy?" Stella said, once we got inside.

"He has to work to the end of the day," I answered, showing everyone the final improvements that had been done around the house. Stella nodded and reached into her bag to pull out two bottles of champagne. I giggled and showed her the two I was already chilling in the fridge.

"Perfection," she said as she opened one and poured everyone drinks. We settled in on the back porch with our drinks and snacks and chatted until I heard the front door open and close.

"Does he have a key?" Lanie whispered, and I nodded my head and leaned back to wave to Ross, who walked out onto the back porch and instantly kissed me on my forehead. He was dressed in long ripped jeans and construction boots with a semiwhite, tight shirt that showed his muscular figure. He greeted everyone before excusing himself to shower and change.

"Is he living here?" Stella whispered.

"I guess for the most part," I said, shrugging my shoulders. We had never had a formal conversation about it. It just happened. As we spent more time together, he started keeping some of his things at the house.

"I'm sorry if I'm being rude, and you know you don't have to worry about me, but, damn, Jill, he's fine," Mary Elizabeth said. I paused for a moment, looking at Mary Elizabeth before we all burst into giggles. It felt so nice to have everyone under one roof.

Ross joined us after he had showered. He was dressed in dark jeans and a, faded polo with the collar up. He passed when Stella offered him a glass of champagne and instead helped himself to a beer in the fridge. As soon as he sat down, Stella, Lanie and Mary Elizabeth launched into a battery of questions for him. I excused myself to start preparing dinner. At one point, I stepped outside to see if anyone needed refills and I stole a glance with Ross. He just shrugged his shoulders and took it all in stride. I called everyone in for dinner around seven and the conversation shifted away from Ross and onto general topics. It was well past midnight when we all said goodnight and I crawled into bed next to Ross.

"That wasn't too bad?" I asked as he leaned over and turned off the lights.

"No, it wasn't. They are all very nice," he said, pausing. "I kinda feel like I just met your parents."

"Not a bad analogy," I said, thinking it over. "Ross, is this moving too fast for you?"

"Is what moving too fast?"

"Us—this relationship. I mean, you're fairly young. Most people your age are still dating, going out every night, hooking up with random people. We have kinda settled into a domesticated relationship. We do practically live together." I could feel him tense up slightly but I couldn't read his face.

"Two thoughts," he finally said after a pause. "First, would you rather I shacked up with a stranger every night?"

"Well, no," I replied.

"Didn't think so. Second, I wouldn't trade what we have going on, domesticated or not, for anything." He leaned down and kissed the top of my head. "I mean, my age is just a number. So what if you were born in an era when they still used rotary phones and cassette tapes? I think it's cute."

I laughed and snuggled up closer to him as I fell asleep.

．．．．．．．．．．．．．．．．．．．．．．．

In the morning, Ross helped me make breakfast for everyone. We were enjoying our first cup of coffee, waiting for everyone else to get up, when his phone rang. He grabbed it and motioned he would be right back as he stepped out on the porch. Just then, Stella came around the corner.

"Good morning," I said.

"Coffee?" she asked, and I pointed to the counter.

"How did you sleep?"

"At first I couldn't sleep because there was no noise, but once I did, it was nice not to be woken up this morning by a honking taxi or garbage truck."

"That was the best night's sleep ever," Mary Elizabeth added as she and Lanie came around the corner, also directly heading for the coffee.

"Breakfast is on the table if you guys are ready to eat." I motioned to the pancakes and fruit sitting on the table.

"Where is Ross?" Lanie asked.

"He took a call out on the porch," I said and shrugged my shoulders when Stella asked who had called.

We settled in for breakfast and Ross joined us a couple of minutes later.

"Everything okay?" I asked as he sat down.

"Yea," he said, clearly distracted by the call.

I let it go and we enjoyed our breakfast and discussed our plans for the rest of the day. It was unanimously decided that we would spend the day on the beach and then head out for dinner. After breakfast, Lanie and Mary Elizabeth insisted on doing the dishes. We were standing around talking when Ross came up behind me.

"Can I talk to you for a moment," he whispered in my ear and touched my arm.

"Sure," I said, looking at him in confusion. I excused myself to curious glances and we headed upstairs to the bedroom. I had barely closed the door when Ross starting speaking.

"That call, it was J. King's manager, Jane," he said excitedly.

"What did she want?"

"Apparently, J. King fired his lead guitarist last night and wants me to join him for the rest of his tour." He rushed out the words.

"That is awesome," I said, caught up in the excitement. "When?"

"I would leave today." He paused to gauge my reaction.

"For how long?"

"Two back-to-back shows in L.A. as they finish up the first part of the tour. Then the show actually goes on hiatus for several weeks before wrapping up the last part, which will last five weeks," he said.

"What did you tell her?"

"I said I would call her back after I talked to you."

"Why? No. You call her back and say yes. This is your chance."

"So quick to get rid of me." He teased me but looked relieved.

"No, of course not! But this is huge. Who knows what this could do for you, open so many doors."

"I know, I know. I thought that too. And us?" he asked, looking suddenly tentative.

"What about us? I'm not going anywhere," I said firmly and he smiled, catching me up in a big hug. He grabbed his phone and called Jane back and then confirmed last minute details.

"Do you need a ride?" I asked.

"I can't ask you that. You have your friends here."

"No. I want to do this. Plus, they are just going to drink and sit on the beach. Wilmington is a short distance from here, so I will be back before they miss me." He reluctantly agreed and said he had to run home and pack a bag and asked if I could pick him up in 20 minutes. I told everyone that I had to drop Ross off at the airport for something that had come up suddenly. I would be back shortly and explain everything when I returned.

"Do you have everything?" I asked Ross as we pulled up to the airport.

"I guess. It's just two days, Jill. I will be back on Monday," he said trying to reassure me.

"Stop worrying about me. My friends are here. I'm going to be just fine."

"What flight are you taking?" I asked as I came around the side of the Jeep.

"I'm not. I'm actually supposed to take a private jet. Someone related to the tour has one nearby and I will get to L.A. just in time for the show tonight."

"Will you have enough time to prepare?" I asked, suddenly nervous for him.

"They were going to have copies of the set list and music on the plane for me to rehearse." "Convenient. Well, good luck—break a leg!" I said, not sure what the correct sentiment should be and Ross chuckled.

"That works," he said, embracing me. "I will miss you." He said, and kissed me.

"I will miss you too," I whispered.

He grabbed his bag and started to walk away.

"Wait, Ross!"

"Yea?" He turned to look at me.

"I love you," I said after a moment.

"I know," he said with a smile and strode through the doors of the airport.

CHAPTER 34

....

Back at the house, I joined Stella and Lanie on the beach to soak up the rays. Lanie let me know Mary Elizabeth had gone in to take a nap before dinner.

"So ..." Stella started, not five minutes after I had sat down.

"So?" I asked back.

"Airport?" Stella asked again.

"Remember that story I told you several weeks ago about going to the amusement park and getting tickets to J. King's concert?" I asked and they both nodded. "Well, his manager called Ross this morning and basically hired him as the guitarist for the rest of this show. He has two shows in L.A. before Monday and then they have a couple days off and he will be on the road for a couple more weeks." I tried to sound casual.

"That's a great opportunity for him," Lanie said, leaning back in her chair and pulling her sunglasses down.

"What does that mean for you?" Stella asked, flipping over from her stomach to her back.

"I don't know, nor do I know if it matters. He needs to focus on his career right now. He doesn't belong on Oak Island."

"Jill, that's nice, but you will have to deal with it if it goes further," Stella mumbled from her towel.

"I guess I will deal with it then."

"You could travel with the band," Stella suggested.

"I'm not interested in being a groupie."

"I'm just saying you aren't working. You have the means to travel, so you could make it work," she mumbled.

"I suppose. Right now let's just focus on our girls' weekend and enjoy the last true weekend of summer," I said, effectively ending the subject.

We stayed out on the beach for another hour before heading into the house and cleaning up before dinner. My guests were getting a bit stir-crazy so we decided to walk the couple of blocks to Rusty's to have dinner there instead of staying in.

We had settled in at one of the picnic tables when I heard my name called. I looked up to find Mandy, April, Mark and several others waving to me from the order counter.

"Friends of yours?" Stella mumbled as they approached.

"Friends of Ross and therefore now friends of mine."

"Where is Ross?" Mandy asked as they approached the table.

"Um ..." I didn't know how to respond.

"He's out on tour with J. King," Stella said, squaring up Mandy and the others.

"He's what?" Mandy exclaimed, looking at me for confirmation.

"J. King called him this morning to fill in for two shows in L.A.." I didn't want to spark any wild rumors while Ross was out of town.

"Oh, that is so cool," Mandy said while the rest of the group stood around somewhat awkwardly.

I quickly made introductions between the two groups before Mandy and company decided to sit at another table.

"They are ..." Stella started to say as they walked away.

"Be nice," I warned Stella.

"What? They are very hipsterish," she added, taking a bite of her lobster roll.

"They really are nice. April did Ross and me several favors right after the incident with Harry," I said, pointing out which one April was, again.

With the mention of Harry, Stella asked Lanie if she had any updated information on him. From the conversation, I gathered that Lanie knew the psychiatrist who was evaluating Harry and therefore had more information than she should have had. All this information was new to me, and I did my best to listen, but my mind kept drifting to that afternoon. I still had incomplete memories of that incident. We got up to leave, and I waved to April, Mandy and Mark as we left. Mark called out that they would be on the beach that night if we wanted to join them. I politely declined the offer. The thought of Lanie and Stella on the beach around the bonfire, drinking beer, made me laugh to myself because it was so far out of their normal comfort zone. I did convince Stella and Lanie to get ice cream before we headed back to the house, insisting it would be the best they'd ever had.

Back at the house, Stella opened another bottle of champagne and Lanie got out the cards. For the rest of the evening we sat around playing cards and gossiping about friends or their coworkers, most of whom I had never met. We called it quits after midnight and I curled up in my empty bed, falling asleep quickly.

....

"Jill!" I heard my name being called over and over again. Someone was shaking me..

"What?" I asked, confused to find both Stella and Lanie standing over my bed.

"You were having a bad dream of some kind," Lanie said, looking concerned.

"I was? I don't remember dreaming," I said, trying to remember if I had been dreaming.

"You were literally screaming," Stella said.

"I'm sorry. I really don't remember," I confessed.

"It's okay ... Move over," Stella said, sliding into bed with me.

"You good?" Lanie asked, looking at us.

"Yea," Stella said as Lanie left to go back to bed.

"Have you been having other dreams?" Stella tried to ask casually before turning out the light.

"I don't remember if I do. Surely Ross would have said something if I was," I said before falling back to sleep.

. . . .

It was a little past six in the morning when my phone began to ring. I searched my room and found the phone on the dresser. Trying not to wake Stella, who was now sprawled out in my bed, I crept downstairs before answering it.

"Hey Ross," I said, whispering into the phone.

"Hey ... Why are you whispering?"

"Everyone is still sleeping."

"Oh, right. It is six in the morning there," he said, making me laugh.

I teased him back. "Well, it's three in the morning there and you clearly forgot about the time change, so I don't know what is worse: you calling me at three or six"

He laughed. "Sorry."

"How was the show?"

"It was amazing. The energy of the crowd was unbelievable and J. King let me sing my song again tonight. He said that he would actually like me to put together several songs and he will let me have a little time during the opening act if I liked." He spoke quickly, with excitement in his voice.

"That is awesome."

"Hey, did you tell anyone about me coming out to L.A.?"

"Oh … well, I didn't, but Stella did." I told him about the run-in at Rusty's the night before.

"That explains so much. My phone blew up during the concert. I got out and had all these missed calls and text messages from everyone. I didn't understand what was going on."

"Yea. Stella couldn't help herself. Sorry."

"No. It's cool."

"Hey Ross?" I asked when there was a lull in the conversation.

"Yes?"

"Do I have nightmares when you spend the night?" I could hear him draw in his breath on the other end.

"Why?"

"Well, I apparently had one last night, and I woke the whole house with my screaming. Stella and Lanie grilled me about it, but I don't remember any of it."

"You used to have nightmares all the time, but you haven't had one for a while."

"Really? You never told me?" I said more loudly than I had probably meant to.

"At first I would try and wake you, but I could never get you completely conscious. So I just started singing softly to you when it happened and you would stop. You never brought it up and neither did I. I wondered if you even knew you were having them. I didn't want to worry you anymore with everything that has happened."

"I had no idea, and I don't even know what they are about."

We chatted for a bit more and then I let him go so he could get to bed and rest up before the next show.

I prepared breakfast but waited until everyone was up before I cooked up the eggs and bacon. Breakfast conversation focused on my elusive nightmares and the endless possible causes. I was much less interested in the conversation than Lanie, Stella and Mary Elizabeth were. Lanie and Mary Elizabeth kept throwing out medical terms and the possibility of my having any one of a number of medical conditions. Finally, by the end of breakfast, I got up and left, doubting that anyone had noticed. I went upstairs to shower and when I came down, they were all seated on the sofa, chatting about what we should do that day.

"Where did you go?" Lanie asked when I came downstairs.

"I just went to get ready." I smiled sweetly.

We decided to spend the rest of the day in the town of Southport, shopping and exploring. After spending more time in town than we had originally planned, we grabbed dinner at one of the restaurants down by the water. It had recently been featured in a movie and Stella was superexcited to eat there. Back home, we opened the last two bottles of champagne and sat out on the porch drinking and talking well into the night. When it was time for bed, Stella asked if she should sleep in my room again. I told her it wasn't necessary and I crawled into bed. Unable to sleep, I texted Ross.

To: Ross Powers
Hope tonight is as epic as last night was.

Not expecting a response for several hours, I grabbed my journal and started to write. It wasn't till I heard my phone chime that I looked at the clock and saw it was six-thirty in the morning and I had been writing all night.

From: Ross Powers
It was awesome but nothing is epic without you.
—R

It was followed by another text.

From Ross Powers
I will see you in a couple hours
—R

I smiled and decided to go for a run before everyone else got up. My head was swimming with thoughts of my relationship with Ross, Ross's career, my odd reoccurring dreams, Jay and general life ambitions. I had been sitting at home without work for nearly a year. I knew I had to figure out something, but I wasn't sure what opportunities were available to me especially there on Oak Island. By the time I had finished my run, I had solved none of my problems, but strangely, my head felt clearer.

Back at the house everyone was already up when I walked into the kitchen. Lanie was making breakfast, and I quickly excused myself for a shower before it was time to eat. Breakfast was quiet as Stella and Mary Elizabeth nursed a slight hangover. Lanie informed everyone they had to leave in an hour in order to get Stella to the airport on time. I told them I would clean up the breakfast dishes while they packed.

"Bye, Mary Elizabeth. Thank you so much for coming," I said as we hugged.

"You have a beautiful home and Ross isn't so bad either," she whispered to me before she got in the car.

"Are you going to be okay?" Lanie asked me with a worried look.

"I'm better today than I was yesterday and the day before that," I told her earnestly.

She nodded in agreement and got into the car.

"New York in a couple weeks?" Stella asked.

"Sure, whenever you need me. I'm not doing much these days." I smiled at Stella.

She nodded and gave me a quick hug before heading to the car.

"Thanks for a great weekend," Lanie called out of the window as they backed out the driveway.

I waved and watched them drive out of sight before I returned to the house. I finished cleaning up the dishes and picked up around the house until I couldn't keep my eyes open anymore. I grabbed the blanket from the back of the sofa and lay down for a nap.

I was standing in the dark and I could hear voices all around me. Panic set in and I was suddenly running through a maze, twisting and turning. Every turn lead to a dead end. My mom appeared, telling me it was okay and that I just needed to let go, but I kept running. My dad was at the next turn, staring at me and trying to say something, but I couldn't hear him. I felt as if something was closing in, causing me to run faster.

Up ahead I saw Harry and he was beat up and bloodied with a wild look in his eye. He whispered to me in a hollow voice. "I'm gone too. You have to let me go. You have to let us all go." He kept repeating it over and over as I screamed at him to stop. He finally disappeared and I could see up ahead a small clearing that I tried to run to.

I thought I saw Ross ahead and I tried calling to him, but he didn't hear me. When I looked again, I saw Stella and Lanie huddled together, whispering something. I yelled at them as I had at Ross and nothing happened. They couldn't hear me and walked away. The more I moved forward, the harder it became. When I turned around, I saw Jay holding onto my arm, keeping me back. "What are you doing?" I asked him, trying to reach out and touch him.

He stared blankly at me. "Join us."

When I looked down, my mom, dad, Harry and Jay were all pulling at my legs, pulling me into a dark abyss, and I started to scream.

"Jill!" I heard Ross call my name as I struggled to break free. "Jill, are you awake?" He shook me slightly.

I opened my eyes and looked into his panicked face. "I remember," I whispered, leaping off the sofa into his arms.

CHAPTER 35

....

Ross convinced me that I needed to call Lanie and tell her the entire story about all the nightmares as well as my newly developed fear of the dark. I agreed and finally phoned her shortly after dinnertime, replaying my nightmares and panic over the dark. At first she was upset I hadn't been honest with her over the weekend. I defended myself, telling her I didn't think that the two things were related. She calmed down and then expressed some concern over the uncertainty of everything. While she didn't feel comfortable officially diagnosing me, she referred to my nightmares and fear as night terrors, which could induce my panic attacks and cause my new fear of the dark. Lanie said that, normally, treatment included medication and therapy. However, she also said that some current methods included detailed journaling of all events to help the brain process everything, especially in my situation in which so much had happened in a short period of time. I agreed to try the journaling method as medication. Therapy wasn't appealing to me.

By the time I had gotten off the phone, Ross had finished making dinner and was waiting for me at the kitchen table. I told him about my conversation with Lanie and he nodded occasionally, asking very few questions.

"Are you okay? You're very quiet for someone who just got back from tour," I asked after a few moments.

"I was thinking that maybe I shouldn't go back out on tour."

"Why? Didn't you enjoy it?"

"No. I really enjoyed it. But I just don't think you should be alone."

"Not you too! ... Ross ..." I reached over and took his hand. "The last year has been hard on me. I'm not even going to try and pretend I handled it gracefully because I didn't. But going through all that drama doesn't come without its own problems. Surely you can relate to that." I looked at him and he nodded in agreement. "But this is something I need to sort through and this is my battle to fight on my own. Yes, you can support me, but you cannot and will not jeopardize your career because of it. You have this amazing opportunity and you're going to see it through," I said as fiercely as I could.

"You're amazing," he said and leaned over to give me a kiss.

"I know."

....

We quickly fell into a comfortable routine, similar to the one we had before Ross had left for L.A.. Instead of going to work, he now sat and wrote music all day long, preparing for the tour. I tried to stay out of his way as much as I could, but I was drawn to the music. I would sit on the sofa and listen to him play and write in my own journal. In the evenings, we would walk along the beach or join his friends there.

"Jill?" Ross asked on the night before he was scheduled to leave.

"Yes?" I said, looking up from my journal to where he sat on the sofa with his guitar in his lap. He was wearing jeans and a long-sleeved shirt and his hair was messed up from constantly running his hand through it in frustration.

"Come with me."

"Sure. Where are we going?"

"No. Come on tour with me."

"I don't think I can just go on tour with you."

"Why not? What is keeping you here? You're not tied down to a job or family. Come with me," he pleaded slightly.

"Why?"

"Why? Isn't is obvious?" he asked.

I got up from my spot and sat down beside him on the sofa.

"I love you."

"And I love you."

"I know you love me and I will visit you on tour. I actually can't wait to be sitting in the front row cheering you on."

"But—"

"But I don't want to just follow you on tour. I don't want to be a groupie. You need to do your own thing, develop yourself as a musician and person without me around." I hoped I wasn't hurting his feelings.

"I get that, but I worry about you here all alone. What if your nightmares get worse? What if Harry gets out and comes looking for you? What if …" He was rambling.

I teased him. "I'm glad you haven't been overthinking this."

"Jill, I'm serious."

"I know and life doesn't have any guarantees. What if I go on tour and you miss out on some opportunity because I'm always around. What if I smother you? What if we break up?"

"That's not possible."

"Everything is possible. You once told me not too long ago we should always have hope and I do. I hope your career takes off. I hope that you never feel pain, loss or heartache ever again and mostly I hope this: us ... I hope this might be forever," I said shyly, looking at him. "But if I have learned anything over this last year it's that you have to live your own life too so that if something we hoped for doesn't work out, you still have two legs to stand on, you still have your own path."

"Profound as always," he said with a smile and kissed me on the cheek. "A simple no would have worked too," he said in mock irritation after a couple of minutes. I threw a pillow at him.

I spent the rest of the night listening to him playing songs as he tried to create his own set list for the show the following day in Toronto.

....

"I have a slight feeling of déjà vu," I said, looking at Ross as we stood in front of the departure door at the airport.

"So, I will see you in a week?"

"Yes, I will be there for both shows in New York. I know Stella and Lanie are going to join me one night, but it might just be me for the other one." I shrugged.

"You are all I ever need," he said, hugging me.

"I love you," I said into his chest.

"I know ... and I love you too," he said, kissing me.

....

When I got home from the airport, it had become a warm October day, a stark contrast to what this day was like one year earlier. It was a day I would never forget. I didn't tell Ross before he left for the airport out of fear he would insist on staying with me. For what? He didn't lose anything on this day a year ago. I lost everything. Needing to clear my head, I set out for a jog on the beach and, as always, with each step, I was able to work through my stress. As I neared the end of my run, I could see the house in the distance. I looked up at the sky. Purples, pinks and oranges streaked across the horizon and an overwhelming feeling of serenity came over me, stopping me in my tracks. I closed my eyes as the soft breeze off the ocean whirled around me. I could hear the voices of the past: Jay, Harry, Mom and Dad. I took a deep breath and exhaled, letting each one of them go. There was no more guilt, remorse or heavy burden of responsibility. I finally felt free of the past that had tormented me. I opened my eyes and looked at the sky one more time and I felt that someone was looking down on me, letting me know it was okay. I was okay and I believed it.

....

"Are you okay?" was the first thing Lanie asked when I picked up the phone later that afternoon.

"I'm fine. Why?"

"Well, I know what today is."

"For the first time in a long time I can honestly tell you that I'm okay. I promise."

"Okay. If you need me, I'm here."

"Thanks, Lanie ... for everything."

....

"Jill, you should have told me," Ross said when I answered his call.

"Shouldn't you be getting ready to go onstage?" I asked, looking at the clock.

"Lanie called and told me what today meant to you," he said, concern in his voice as I silently cursed my friend.

"Ross, I'm okay. This day changed my life not yours."

"You can't just keep these things from me."

"I wasn't trying to keep anything from you. You want the truth? One year ago today was the worst day of my entire life. I lost my best friend and the man I loved, the man I promised to love until death. It shattered me. I wasn't able to cope and I carried that with me for a year. But I am a stronger person today than I was then, and I'm finding a way to move on."

"How?" he asked quietly.

"Hope … you … Stella … Lanie—you all give me hope, hope to keep going and to finally let go of all those ghosts in my life." I thought of the beach and how peaceful it felt to let go. I heard someone call his name in the background.

"I have to go, but—"

"Go! Have a great show. I'm not going anywhere," I said and we ended our call.

....

I cautiously walked through the house, turning out every light along my way. I double-checked all the doors twice and then headed up to the bedroom. Getting ready for bed, I hummed a song Ross had been singing the day before and it brought a smile to my face. I got into bed just as my phone chimed.

From: Ross Powers
I can't change the past but I can promise this next year will be better.
It always gets better over time.
—R

To Ross Powers
A lot can happen in one year. All we can have is hope.
—J

I turned the light out in the bedroom and rolled onto my side as the glow of the room faded. There were no noises echoing in the house, no ghosts to haunt my dreams, and for the first time in a long time, I fell into a dreamless sleep, finally feeling safe and sound.

- END -

Visit the author's website
www.tskrupa.com to learn about future novels

CPSIA information can be obtained at www.ICGtesting.com
Printed in the USA
BVOW03s1945221213

339671BV00004B/10/P